Kick-Off

Moti Nandy (1931–2010) was one of the few writers in the world to have created an entire body of fiction centered around sports. A Sahitya Akademi award winner and former sports editor at the *Anandabazaar Patrika*, he wrote more than twenty-five novels in Bengali for adults, and as many for children and young adults. Nearly all his novels are set in Kolkata, where he lived, and capture the struggle and success of the underdog in sports, ranging from football to cricket, tennis to swimming, athletics to boxing.

Arunava Sinha translates classic, modern and contemporary Bengali fiction and non-fiction into English. Over thirty of his translations have been published and he has won the Crossword Translation award twice: for Sankar's *Chowringhee* (2007) and Anita Agnihotri's *Seventeen* (2011). He has also won the Muse India award for his translation of Buddhadeva Bose's *When the Time Is Right* (2012) and was shortlisted for the Independent Foreign Fiction prize (2009) for his translation of *Chowringhee*. Besides India, his translations have been published in the UK and US in English and in several European and Asian countries through further translation.

Kick-Off

STORIES FROM THE FIELD

Moti Nandy

Translated from the original Bengali
by Arunava Sinha

hachette INDIA

Striker and Stopper first published in English in 2010 by Hachette India
This revised and expanded edition first published in English
in 2017 by Hachette India
(Registered name: Hachette Book Publishing India Pvt. Ltd)
An Hachette UK company
www.hachetteindia.com

SRD

*Page 248 is an extension of the copyright page

***To the East Bengal Football Club* – AS**

ISBN 978-93-5195-215-2

Hachette Book Publishing India Pvt. Ltd
4th & 5th Floors, Corporate Centre,
Plot No. 94, Sector 44, Gurugram – 122003, India

Typeset in Minion Pro 10/12.5 by
InoSoft Systems, Noida

Printed and bound in India
by Manipal Technologies Limited, Manipal

FSC www.fsc.org MIX Paper from responsible sources FSC™ C043100

Contents

A Note from the Translator

'Striker' and 'Stopper' may have been among Moti Nandy's most popular novellas and stories featuring football, but Nandy wrote many more championing the sport that has been an obsession and passion with Calcuttans for generations now. All Nandy's short stories about football have been brought together in this volume.

A few caveats about the stories in this collection: In the 1980s, Nandy wrote two stories with almost identical beginnings, but very different endings. The initial scenes, characters and dialogue of 'The Pearl' and 'Reddy' are similar, but the storylines diverge considerably later on. Both the stories are presented here.

There's no football in the story 'Abinash's Forty-eight-and-a-half', but what comes through strongly is the tenacity of a footballer, and the tragedy of a sportsperson of integrity. To my mind, it's a 'football story' without an actual football, and so it finds a place in this collection.

There are abbreviations in the narrative that I haven't elaborated on to enable smooth reading. BNR is Bengal Nagpur Railway and KOSB is King's Own Scottish Borderers – the first a Calcutta team, and the second a British team that used to play occasionally in India.

The kind of football strategies and club dynamics depicted in these stories are no longer seen in Indian football, where the game has changed greatly – though not as much as in the rest of the world. But the spirit of the sport remains unchanged.

Striker

1

I had a dream last night.

Winding past three crossroads, a white car glided to a halt at the spot where our lane meets the main road. No one in our neighbourhood had ever seen such a large car and people instantly crowded around it, although they were afraid to come too close. A middle-aged foreigner got out, his complexion as dark as night, his suit as white as his car. He had salt-and-pepper hair and a cigar hanging from his mouth, and was wearing dark sunglasses.

Waving his hands about, the foreigner said something to the crowd in Portuguese. Our neighbours, who knew no other language besides Bengali, with a smattering of English, Hindi and Oriya thrown in, simply looked at one another in confusion. The tone of his voice suggested that he was trying to ask something.

Stepping out from the crowd, Nutu-da asked in Hindi, 'What do you want?' Then, having managed to translate the words in his head, he repeated the question in English.

The foreigner responded in unaccented Bengali, 'Does someone named Prasoon Bhattacharya live here?'

Though taken aback at hearing the foreigner speak in Bengali, everyone was reassured and a buzz of curiosity instantly filled the air. Prasoon? Prasoon! Prasoon!! What does this man want with Prasoon? Why is this man here?

'You mean Anil Bhattacharya's eldest son Prasoon?'

'Yes, I'd like to meet him,' the foreigner told Nutu-da, not looking so anxious any more. Nutu-da was a fellow tenant in our house and worked as a compositor at a press. Since his wife's death two years ago, his daughter Nilima had been the only other member of his family. A simple, straightforward man who had only one major flaw – he couldn't help offering unsolicited advice. He was also a committed fundraiser. Whenever the opportunity arose, he would go around collecting money for the latest cause – be it a small local event or a larger community celebration. People of all ages referred to him as Nutu-da. Nilima was roughly my age. A tenth-grade student, she slaved away day and night at home and elsewhere. She was also a great friend of mine.

'And what business do you have with Prasoon?' Nutu-da asked the foreigner sceptically.

The man's cigar had gone out. Relighting it with his lighter, he said, 'I've come from Brazil. I'm sure you've heard of the Santos Football Club. I'm the manager there. And if Prasoon agrees to join us, we want him.'

'What do you mean, want him?' Nutu-da said.

The foreigner responded quickly. 'Of course, my club will pay him. And we'll even pay his airfare to come home once a year.'

'How much will you pay?'

'I will discuss that with his father,' the foreigner answered guardedly. 'We've done our homework and know that he's not legally an adult yet. He's just seventeen years and four months old.'

Nutu-da escorted the foreigner to our house, closely followed by a procession of local people. To get to the house, you had to pass through an unpaved lane just thirty inches wide. Nutu-da and our family occupied one and a half rooms each on the ground floor of the house, while the landlord, Bishwanath Datta, occupied the first floor. He had four daughters, two of whom had been married off.

Bishu-babu, who was about to go out, was flabbergasted at the sight of the entire neighbourhood trailing a foreigner into our lane. Retreating quickly, he sent his second daughter, Shonamukhi, out to deal with the situation. Bishu-babu was terrified of the police.

Seated on a low stool, my father was reading the morning paper. My mother was in the kitchen with my brother and sister – Pintu, my brother, is the middle child, and Putul, the youngest. No sooner had he entered the house than Nutu-da started yelling for my father. Baba's was a taciturn personality – most days, we hardly exchanged a single word. I generally tended to avoid him.

'Anil-babu, the manager of Santosh Club is here.' Nutu-da was panting with excitement. 'Pelé plays for them.'

'Pelé who?' Baba asked sternly. 'Where does he live?'

Nutu-da was taken aback. Smiling gently, the foreigner stepped up to speak. 'Santos is a Brazilian club. Our city is a famous port from which coffee is shipped all over the world. Our club is among the best in the world, and Pelé is the world's greatest footballer. There hasn't been another talent like him ever.'

Running his eyes over the crowd gathered behind the foreigner, Baba said, 'I don't follow football. Tell me what you want.'

'We want your son Prasoon to play for our club.'

'Talk to him. I have nothing to say about this.' Baba disappeared into his room quickly, followed by the foreigner and Nutu-da. Meanwhile, emboldened by the knowledge that the visitor wasn't a policeman, Bishu-babu came up to our door too.

'Since Prasoon isn't an adult yet, he cannot sign the contract. As his guardian, you have to do it,' explained the foreigner.

'No, I will not sign on anything connected to football. I do not wish to earn my son's curses by leading him into damnation.'

'Anil-babu was a footballer too,' Nutu-da whispered to the foreigner. 'He was a fearsome left-in for Calcutta's top club, Juger Jatri. But he gave up the game after his left knee was injured during the Rovers Cup in Bombay.'

'Who said I gave up the game?' Baba suddenly shouted. 'I was forced to give up! My injury was never treated. I couldn't afford it, and the club didn't offer a paisa. I still have to walk around with a torn cartilage. The club forced me to play with the injury. It was the IFA Shield final, against East Bengal. With three minutes to go, the match still goal-less, there I was, six yards from the goal, with Taj Mohammed on the ground, Byomkesh Bose rushing towards me, Ghatak not able to make up his mind whether to give me the charge or not, the stands roaring in unison for a goal – and from that distance I shot wide.'

Looking embarrassed at his sudden outburst of passion, Baba lowered his head and limped off to the bed, dragging his left foot behind him. Smiling wanly, he said, 'I'd told them I wouldn't be able to play. They gave me an injection and forced me to play, promising me a job if I did. I did try; I tried very hard, to score that goal.' His agitation had made him almost unintelligible as he continued, 'They spat all over me, accusing me of having tanked the game for a bribe. My forehead split under their blows.' Distractedly, he rubbed the scar that lay exactly in the centre of his forehead.

'Footballers meet the same fate all over the world,' the foreigner said sympathetically.

'Why should they?' Baba's eyes blazed, reflecting his anger and hatred. 'When I was rolling on the pitch in agony, they all said I was pretending. They didn't stop to consider that the man they were vilifying had once scored at ease from twenty-five to thirty yards out. I had been the top scorer in the Calcutta League for two years! They humiliated me cruelly, so cruelly, not knowing how much I had dreamed of wearing the shield-winners' medal, and of scoring the winning goal for my club…'

Baba stopped.

'We'll pay well. The first season we'll pay the equivalent of two thousand rupees every month. That's the standard for our second team. If his performance can get him into the first team and he plays well, he'll make at least two lakhs a year between his salary, bonus and endorsements.'

'What?' said Bishu-babu, walking into the room. Nutu-da stared at the foreigner, bereft of speech. The crowd murmured.

'Imagine Prasoon having it in him! You can't tell from looking at him, can you?'

Baba used to work as a timekeeper at the Aruna Glass Factory, which had been closed due to a lockout for over three years. Still, he had never once defaulted on our house rent of thirty-five rupees in all that time. His self-respect was so strong that it was intolerable for him to even imagine being insulted by the landlord. Ma said he now worked at a chemist's, leaving home every afternoon and returning late – well after I'd fallen asleep.

'You should talk to Prasoon directly. I haven't been to watch a game for the past twenty years. I don't even look at the sports page of newspapers any more, so I'm not going to say yes or no on this subject.'

'Anil-babu!' Nutu-da pleaded in a low voice. 'Prasoon will earn up to a lakh. You could live like a king!'

'Unbelievable. Imagine earning so much just for kicking a ball! You should accept the deal,' said Bishu-babu.

'Footballers have their pride, Bishu-babu. Prasoon plays football because he wants to, not because I've asked him to. I have never watched him play. I don't want to hear anything more about football. I've said all I have to say.'

Although the foreigner, as well as Nutu-da and Bishu-babu, tried to persuade Baba, he just shook his head obdurately. Eventually, the Brazilian gave him his visiting card, saying, 'Please think it over and let me know. Since Pelé plans to retire soon, we want to prepare Prasoon immediately so that he can replace him later.'

The foreigner left, and so did the crowd. Alone in the room, the card still in his hand, Baba walked up to the window, shred the card into little strips and flung them outside. As they floated around like flowers in the wind, Ma dashed out of the kitchen to catch them, Nilima running behind her. Still chasing the strips, Nilima passed by my window and whispered, 'Wake up, Prasoon. It's five o'clock!'

2

Waking with a start, I saw Nilima standing outside the window, saying, 'You asked me to wake you up, didn't you?'

Since we didn't have a clock at home, I'd asked Nilima to wake me at 5 a.m. She had morning school and usually got up at dawn to draw the water, light the stove and cook for her father before going to class. Nemai, Anwar and I were scheduled to appear for a trial with Shobhabajar Sporting at their grounds today. Harsho-da had told the club coach Bipin Sinha that we'd be going.

I stayed in bed for a while, reflecting on the dream and feeling rather embarrassed. I wondered why I'd had such a bizarre, unreal dream. But then, I reminded myself, unreal, unbelievable things were meant to happen in dreams. Imagine a Portuguese-speaking Brazilian talking in Bangla! It couldn't happen anywhere else but in a dream. And yet, I'd also heard that dreams were never entirely unfounded – that they were reflections of things we have thought about or wishes we have harboured.

Did that mean I wanted to be Pelé, then? Wasn't that arrogant of me! 'P…e…l…é.' I said the name softly, slowly, over and over again. I'd heard about him many times from Harsho-da, who was a voracious reader and football lover, despite never having played the game. He used to live in our neighbourhood and was someone I had known since childhood. He was the first to tell me, 'You have the potential, Prasoon. If you concentrate on your game you can be a great player.' But even I hadn't been aware of my secret yearning to be a Pelé. I had a powerful right-foot shot, yet was nowhere as good with my left. I couldn't trap the ball perfectly either, and shut my eyes when heading. People said I was speedy and had excellent dribbling skills, but that I lacked the stamina for a seventy-minute game. Nor did I know when and how to find free space and wait for the ball.

Despite having many other weaknesses to add to that list, here I was, dreaming of becoming Pelé's successor! I was a complete ass, and angry with myself for it. What if Nemai got to know about this dream? He would have a great laugh at my expense. Two lakh rupees a year! You had to be a complete lunatic to even dream of so much money.

Just the day before, none of us had eaten more than six rotis at lunch, and four at dinner. Although my insides were being gnawed away by hunger all evening, I'd divided one of my rotis in half for Putul and Pintu and told Ma to put a couple of them away for me to eat in the morning. I was worried about going for the trial on an empty stomach, lest I got cramps. Of course, Ma knew about the trial. So did Nilima.

My room was rather damp, with the lack of light making the afternoon resemble evening. The plaster was peeling off half the wall. There were termites in the overhead beams. Both the shutters of the only window in the room were broken, letting in water whenever it rained. You couldn't possibly call this eight-foot-long and five-foot-wide space a room. I occupied it by myself. There was no space for even a stool, although there was a shelf on the wall, with a few of my schoolbooks on it, and a rope strung across the bed, from which hung two pairs of trousers and two shirts.

Ma came in. I doubt whether there's another mother like mine in the whole world. Even in our household of deprivation, where hunger, heat, humiliation and hopelessness drove us insane, she never lost her smile. Not a person of many words, when she spoke it was in a low, sweet voice that seemed to wipe out every trace of pain from the planet.

Entering, she said, 'Are you up, Khoka? Leaving already?'

'Yes. Is Baba up too?'

'No, he seems unwell. Probably has a fever. I've put aside some rotis for you.'

Ma gave me four rotis. I had always felt she loved me more than the others, and was sure she hadn't eaten the previous night to ensure that there were enough rotis for me in the morning. I would have made a fuss about it any other day but not that morning. We had to be at the ground by seven, and Nemai and Anwar would be waiting for me at the bus stop.

Before leaving, I stopped on a whim to touch Ma's feet in respect. I was merely going for a trial with a first division club, not to actually play for one. But if Bipin Sinha liked what he saw, we'd get a chance to play on one of the hallowed football grounds of the Calcutta Maidan! The world of football had long been a fairy-tale palace for me. And today I was walking up to the door of the dream I had been nurturing for years. If I managed to get in, I was determined to climb the stairs and reach the very top. I had to. I would work as hard as was necessary.

Ma put her arms around me and kissed my forehead, saying, 'Do your best, Khoka.'

3

As I walked briskly towards the bus stop, kitbag in hand, Ma's words buzzed around in my head. I wouldn't simply give it my best, I'd give up my whole life! She had spent all her life in a state of deprivation, and I was determined to ensure happiness for her now. I knew Shobhabajar Sporting would not pay me anything, for they could not afford to. I would have to go to Mohun Bagan, East Bengal or Juger Jatri for that. Shobhabajar was only the first step, and I would have to get myself noticed in a year or two. I wanted my game to gain me entry into a top club, and then to win me the Indian jersey. I needed both money and fame, but the latter first.

Nemai and Anwar were waiting for me. Glancing at his watch as I arrived, Anwar said, 'We'll be there by six-thirty.'

That all three of us had fallen victim to anticipation as well as to anxiety was obvious from the fact that none of us could speak a word. Normally, Nemai was the most voluble of us all. Indeed, he was without equal for playing jokes on people or mimicking them.

He lived about a mile away from us in a locality named Shanti Pally. All the houses in that area were built on community land appropriated by refugees from what became East Pakistan at the time of Independence. His father was dead, and his brother ran a textiles shop in Hatibagan. Nemai hadn't been to school since failing his exams in class five.

Strikingly fair, six feet tall and weighing sixty-five kilos, Anwar was the affluent one among us. His father owned a hotel as well as a couple of densely populated slums. The calm and composed Anwar had a style of play that matched his behaviour and clothes – neat and clean. About three years older than Nemai and I, he was now in the first year of a bachelor of commerce course at college. When he was with us, neither of us had to spend a paisa. Needless to add, we didn't go a yard without him.

None of us said a word till the bus reached Shyambazar. I knew that I probably should have spent a few minutes with Baba before I left that morning, but somewhere within me there burned a strange anger towards him. He had never tried to discuss football with me, never asked how things were going, nor even watched any of my games. I knew his apathy concealed a deep loathing for football. Ma would sometimes say, 'Why not ask your father for some tips?' but would then add quickly, 'Never mind.' Once I overheard Baba telling her, 'Football consumed me. It'll do the same to Khoka. Stop him.'

Switching buses at Shyambazar, we got off at the Esplanade at exactly a quarter past six. At the Shobhabajar tent we found twelve young men busy dressing for training. 'Bipin-da will be here at seven,' one of them informed us. 'We're going to run down Red Road, cross the tram lines and run around the Brigade Parade Ground. Bipin-da will be waiting for us when we get back.'

We didn't know what we were supposed to be doing. Then Anwar came up with a suggestion. 'What's the use of waiting?' he said. 'Let's run with them too. Bipin-da will be impressed.'

We joined them. But instead of running to the Brigade Parade Ground as planned, the players suddenly changed direction after five minutes and headed towards the Esplanade. Entering the Maidan Hawkers' Market, they splashed water from a tube well on their bodies and clothes. Seeing our puzzled faces, they laughed.

'What are you looking at?' the oldest of the players asked us. 'Splash yourselves. Bipin-da won't be satisfied unless you're soaking with perspiration. He'll make you run again. Now we're going to pant all the way back to the tent.'

'Don't you dare reveal any of this to Bipin-da. If you let the cat out of the bag...' said a burly fellow among them, glaring at us menacingly.

4

We finally got a chance to show what we could do. Nemai and I were on one side of the ground and Anwar was about sixty or sixty-five yards away on the other. His shots were very powerful – apparently, he had once broken a goalkeeper's wrist. And I believe Shailen Manna had a booming shot as well. Instead of power, however, I tried to demonstrate skill – outswingers, chips, volleys and a couple of attempted but unsuccessful bicycle shots. I had tried to copy them from photographs of Pelé, only to realize later on that you couldn't perfect techniques like that without some natural gymnastic ability and a coach to guide you.

Anwar kept up his long-range shots, which Nemai kept having to fetch from the other side of the pitch, whining all the while. 'Am I his servant? All he can do is shoot!'

'You and I will be dropped, Prasoon,' Nemai warned. 'Anwar has no real skills...why don't you tell Bipin-da to let us show some trapping, heading or dribbling?'

Bipin-da was busy getting the other players to practise long shots over and over again. Going up to him, I asked, 'Bipin-da, could we do some skill practice now?'

'Skill!' Bipin-da looked at me as if he had heard the word for the first time. 'Whatever for?'

Scratching my head, I said, 'I meant…we need some skills for our matches, don't we?'

'Skills at Shobhabajar Sporting?' Bipin-da looked as aghast as if he had seen people enter a temple with their shoes on. 'We got seven points from twenty-eight matches last year, five the year before. We were only saved because there was no relegation or promotion in the division. Skills are needed for teams that compete for the championship – the Mohun Bagans, East Bengals or Juger Jatris. What does a team like ours need them for?'

'Then what about these long-range shots?' Without being rude, I tried to challenge his startling approach to coaching.

'This is strategy, our strategy,' answered Bipin-da with a big smile. 'We have to play every match under pressure. When nine of them are in your penalty box, what are you going to do?'

'Clear the ball.'

'Excellent! I see you have brains. But how will you clear the ball?'

'Kick it far away.'

'Veeeery good. That's what our long-range shooting practice is for. This is the one skill that's the most useful for us. Later, I'll teach you a couple of tackles as well. But for now, concentrate on shooting. What's the name of that fellow who came with you?' He pointed at Anwar. 'Good player, fits in well as stopper,' he remarked upon learning Anwar's name.

I then realized that Anwar had made it. I was genuinely happy for him since my position was striker, which meant that we weren't competing for the same place on the team.

I recounted my conversation with Bipin-da to Nemai. 'I'm not worried,' he said. 'I'll get in as soon as he sees my technique for making them trip. You'd better think about yourself though.'

I was disappointed, not having expected such a disheartening introduction to first division football. Bipin-da had shattered all my dreams of learning and perfecting the finer points of football, of getting recognition and fame, of climbing to the top. Leaving the pitch, I sat down on one side. No one noticed. They were now practising heading, using four balls. One of them kept up a barrage of corner kicks, which ten or twelve of the rest rose to head out of the penalty box. The whole process was interspersed with jokes, laughter and invective. During one such mêlée, one of the players had an elbow shoved into his face and ran off the pitch, his nose bleeding. A little later, the goalkeeper was forced to miss an approaching ball when someone pulled his shorts down so low that saving his modesty became more important than saving a goal.

Holding a handkerchief to his bleeding nose, the player who'd been elbowed came and stood next to me. He was as thin as a reed and seemed about six or seven years older. 'What position do you play in?' he asked as soon as our eyes met.

'Striker,' I replied.

'Where did you play earlier?'

'Local club. It's my first time on the Maidan.'

Suddenly, I saw Anwar crouching down in pain and clutching his abdomen. Someone had kicked him. He pulled himself back to his feet immediately though, glaring at the burly fellow player who had kneed him. 'What's his name?' I asked, pointing at the culprit.

'Palash Tikadar. Dangerous chap. Slapped the referee last year, broke an opponent's leg, took a bribe and scored an own goal. Even stole four pairs of trousers from the tent once. We avoid him like the plague.'

'Was it Palash who hit you on the nose?'

'No, that was Robi. He's a decent sort. Not his fault – he was only acting on Bipin-da's instructions.'

I noticed that Tikadar seemed to be avoiding Anwar, moving away every time Anwar came near him. Nemai remained at a distance from the crowd.

'How many years have you been playing for Shobhabajar?' I asked out of curiosity.

'About five.'

'No plans to change clubs?'

His face fell. Pressing his blood-soaked handkerchief to his eyes for what seemed an eternity, he said, 'Bipin-da has promised me a job in a shop somewhere.' Then, bunching up the handkerchief in his hand, he said, 'Back to action.'

The heading practice was over. They'd probably form teams now for a game.

I started taking off my boots.

As on our way to the club that morning, we didn't talk much on the way back either. Nemai only asked me, 'Why'd you leave? You can't have moods at clubs like these, you know.' Then a few minutes later, he added, 'That Tikadar is in trouble – he's rubbed Anwar up the wrong way.'

Back home, Ma asked, 'How did it go?' Not in the best of moods, I could only manage a desultory response. 'There was a little practice and lots of running to build stamina. That's how it'll be initially.'

I was very relieved that Nilima didn't ask me any questions. I had extolled the merits of first division football to her to such an extent that the three Maidan football grounds had become the holiest of holy shrines to her. And if I were to shatter that illusion the very first day, I would probably fall in her esteem.

5

I went over to Harsho-da's that evening. Listening to my account of the day's events, he said, 'Just do as Bipin Sinha wants, and listen to what he has to say. You haven't joined his club to learn football from him, have you? For that, you will have to catch the eye of a top club – a Mohun Bagan, an East Bengal or a Juger Jatri. But you still need to make a start somewhere, don't you? Who else but Shobhabajar will give a chance to an unknown junior like you? Even a middle-level club like Sporting Union or a George Telegraph won't entertain you.'

'But, even more than getting a chance to play, I want to learn.'

'Match play is important for learning too,' he insisted. 'If you make a name for yourself this year, we'll try a bigger club like Aryan or Bhratri Sangha next year. Since you're still young, you'll find it easier in a big club if you can get a couple of years' small club experience before that.'

You couldn't argue with Harsho-da because he always had logic on his side to shut you up. I wanted to ask him why I needed to waste a couple of years with a small club when I could be playing for Mohun Bagan straight away. Mohun Bagan was my favourite team, and I had cut out dozens of photos of their striker Chuni Goswami from the newspapers and pasted them in my old school notebooks. The Mohun Bagan club tent was no less than the Taj Mahal for me.

That East Bengal fanatic Nemai had once told me that his dream was to score a hat-trick against Mohun Bagan. And I'd harboured a slight feeling of hatred for him ever since – frequently leading me to lose my temper with him. I always regretted it afterwards though, for Nemai would simply turn his face away in silence whenever I had one of my outbursts, and would tell me afterwards, 'You're too impatient, you get angry far too quickly.'

I knew I lacked the temperament and patience, unlike Anwar, who played with a cool head, moving like a cat despite his size, and making clean tackles with the ferocity of a tiger. Anyone who fouled him usually got a look that ensured that it never happened again. Nemai, on the other hand, accumulated a series of small fouls, usually without the referee's knowledge. If, for example, the stopper on the other side was proving to be a tough customer and refusing to let us past him, Nemai would always be the first to get on his case. In five minutes, he'd be chasing Nemai instead of the ball, his face swollen, leaving me to cash in on the gaping hole in their defence – which I usually did.

Nemai could provide incredible through-balls, his slight frame weaving past four or five defenders like a slippery eel. He always knew where I'd be waiting, sending the ball to my feet like a pet dog and leaving me with only one task – to either tap it or blast it into the net. Many people said I'd never be able to score without Nemai, which made me both uncomfortable and angry. I didn't want to feel dependent on anyone for my goals, as though no credit was due to me. Deep down I really hated Nemai. But he didn't know that. He loved me.

I wasn't able to make it beyond the first sixteen at Shobhabajar Sporting. Anwar and Nemai played seven games on the trot in the first division – all of which we lost. East Bengal scored five; Eastern Railway, four; Kalighat, two; Mohammedan Sporting, four; Aryan, five; Sporting Union, two; BNR, three. We hadn't scored a single goal all season.

Anwar had played all seven matches in their entirety, growing to be a favourite of Bipin-da's. The twenty-five goals that Shobhabajar had conceded in seven matches would probably have been fifty had Anwar not played. He had already acquired a reputation as a promising player. Nemai had played two matches from start to finish, and the rest in part.

I felt bad for him. Dodging past two or three defenders and pushing the ball into the goalmouth area, as was his wont, Nemai would be forced to watch helplessly as it was collected by the opposing team's defenders or goalkeeper. He would look around in frustration, knowing that the only player who knew his style was sitting on the bench. I knew I could have scored from ninety per cent of the openings he created and felt like weeping in anger. Every time he looked at me in helplessness, I averted my face.

I knew he felt the same way as I did, and that he was dying of guilt because he was getting to play while I wasn't. Eventually, he stopped trying when he realized that all his efforts were going to waste. I trembled with rage when a winger or a striker abused him for mis-passing.

Anwar and I had told him to try and score himself. Against East Bengal, he had thrice slid between defenders Shanto Mitra and Nayeem to go one-on-one against their goalkeeper Thangaraj, but still hadn't been able to score. Twice he shot wide, and once directly to the keeper. 'I lost my bearings,' he told me afterwards. 'Such a huge man charging at me – I was so scared that I shot too quickly.'

'Don't make excuses,' I answered angrily. 'With the kind of position you were in, not even Yasin would have been able to stop those goals. You didn't score because you're a supporter of East Bengal. If I had had Mohun Bagan at my mercy like that I'd have put their goalkeeper Balai Dey into the net too.'

'And then you'd have atoned for two days by fasting,' Nemai said with a big smile. A little later he said softly, 'When they took us to the tent for water, P. Sinha asked about me – my name, how long I've been playing, where I live, things like that. Why do you suppose that is?'

'To sack Parimal Dey next year and replace him with you.'

Chastened, Nemai lapsed into silence. Then suddenly he flared up and exclaimed, 'I'd score a hat-trick against Mohun Bagan if that happened!'

I finally made it to the team list the evening before the match with Rajasthan. For three days, the skies had been overcast and it had actually rained on two. The final list had two group headings written on it. There were five names written under the first heading: If Rain. And another five under the second: If No Rain. Mine was among the second lot. Someone explained that the list indicated who would play if it rained, who would play if it didn't, and who would play in either case. My name was next to Tikadar's. If it didn't rain, I'd play. If it did, he would.

I couldn't sleep that night, and kept glancing at the sky every minute or so. The stars were invisible, the skies the colour of a muddy river. As I agonized over whether it would rain the next afternoon, and whether I'd get to play my first game in the first division, I was suddenly overcome by terror. For some reason, I was certain I'd miss a sitter the next day. It had happened to me before.

6

A club named Paikpara Agragami had once hired us to play a local tournament for them in a suburb named Chatra. As I was leaving the field after scoring four goals in the semi-final, a man came up to me and said, 'You're a good player, my boy, but your left foot doesn't work at all.'

I later heard that he was known as Lefty Montey: the stopper of the team we'd be playing in the final. He used to be a well-known forward at Aryan about twenty years earlier, but now turned up as a defender sometimes. Nobody knew his real name. The other defenders had represented the junior India team at the Asian Youth championships in Bangkok or Seoul just a couple of months earlier. While watching their semi-final game, I remember asking the man next to me, 'What's the name of the right-back?'

'Sudhir Karmakar. Going to be a star, the way he's playing.'

I had fretted all night long about the stopper and the two wing-backs who played for the opponents, Tribeni Jubo Sangha. I couldn't sleep at all the night before the final. Lefty Montey's words wouldn't stop buzzing around in my head: your left foot doesn't work at all. And I kept seeing Sudhir Karmakar's tackles as well. On the morning of the final, Lefty Montey visited our room. The Tribeni team were in the next room. Niley-da, our captain, welcomed him enthusiastically. 'Hope you're playing today, Montey-da.'

'Not sure. Feeling a bit lethargic. Won't play unless I can get myself fit with a swim in the Ganga. Nothing better than a swim to make you fighting fit.'

Being only fourteen, I yearned to be fighting fit too.

'What my experience tells me, Niley, is that you shouldn't train on the day of a match. Just a swim in the morning and rest in the afternoon – get some deep sleep. By the time the game begins, your body is raring to go and your brain is in fine fettle as well. The forward line simply must go for a swim. And if you can get an oil massage to loosen your muscles beforehand, that's even better. Take Goshtho Pal, Samad, PK and Chuni – they all swam on match days. Do you know why India lost at the Rome Olympics?'

We looked at one another. Lighting a cigarette, Montey-da slouched down on the floor. Our right-winger, who played for Eastern Railway and was something of a reader, said, 'The Hungary team had Alberto, after all.'

'So?'

'Tichy too.'

'So what?'

We were devastated at not knowing the answer. Taking a deep drag on his cigarette and knocking the ash on to the floor, Montey-da said, 'There wasn't even a water tank where the Indian team could have a swim. None of them could get fighting fit for the match. Chuni and PK spent all morning looking for a lake or even a pond to swim in – but to no avail.'

'Does Chuni go for a swim on match days?' I asked.

'Of course! Ask him how he's developed that dodge, those skills, that brain of his. It's all thanks to Mother Ganga. You have no idea of the benefits of a swim where there's a current. How do you suppose Arun Ghosh became such a good player? He lives in Shibpur, a stone's throw from the Ganga.'

Taking a last drag on his cigarette, Montey-da said, 'I'd better look for some body oil.'

Nemai wasn't there. Paikpara Agragami had hired only Anwar and me. 'Should we go to the river?' I asked Anwar. 'The river!' He did a double take. 'I don't even go near a tank because I can't swim!'

The Eastern Railway winger and the Sporting Union midfielder who were playing for us left the room in search of body oil. By the time we got into the river, having first loosened up our muscles by spending half an hour massaging half a litre of oil into our bodies, Montey-da had also arrived with a small bowl of oil of his own. We began swimming at a comfortable pace.

'How can you paddle around in the shallows like girls? Do you call yourselves footballers – or Ludo players?'

Stung to the quick, we set off for the middle of the river – only to return exhausted after half an hour. Rubbing oil into his arms, Montey-da said, 'Now *that's* swimming! All right, time to rest – just float on your backs.'

We complied, letting the water support our tired bodies. But when we chanced to look towards the bank ten minutes later, we got the shock of our lives. Without realizing it, we had been carried along for what seemed like miles by the ebbing tide. Swimming back against the current, we just about managed to reach the riverbank and stretched ourselves out in exhaustion.

Just about to dive in for his own swim, Montey-da said to us sternly, 'Now lunch, followed by sleep. Don't forget, the final's in a few hours.' Covering his ears with his hands, he emerged from the river after a couple of quick dips.

I was ravenous. And after wolfing down the meal of mutton and rice, I went to sleep immediately. When they woke me up, the rest of the team was already dressed and ready to leave. I was aching all over, my head felt like a ton of bricks, my eyes still heavy, my stomach bloated. All I wanted to do was sob.

I couldn't chase the through-balls that came my way. Jumping for a header was a complete impossibility. I couldn't even raise my foot to shoot. With just ten feet between me and the goal, and no one in the middle, I found myself robbed of the ball by Sudhir Karmakar. A wave of catcalls and abuse echoed around the ground, most of them aimed at me. The spectators were vastly amused at the way the oldest man on the field, Montey-da, was hoodwinking younger players like us. The Paikpara officials were the only ones who didn't find it funny. At half-time, the midfielder and I were both substituted.

I couldn't look anyone in the face, I was so embarrassed, and was envious of Anwar for not knowing how to swim. He had played like a lion that day. In the end, Tribeni won 2-0. And it was Montey-da who scored the first goal from a penalty. Anwar later told me that when Montey-da placed the ball on the penalty spot and looked at the goalkeeper, the poor fellow discovered that Montey-da was cross-eyed and got completely flummoxed about which side to dive towards. He finally chose to go to the right, even as the ball was entering the net three feet to his left.

On the eve of the game against Rajasthan, the cloudy sky, as murky as the Ganga had been back then, reminded me of that final match. Remembering how I'd missed a sitter, I wanted to laugh. Not tomorrow. Oh God, don't let it rain tomorrow. I was to play provided it didn't rain. Don't take away my chances of playing a first division tie. I finally fell asleep just before dawn.

7

I woke to discover that it had rained heavily during the night. Yet the clouds had largely disappeared, and the sky was now dotted with patches of blue. I felt fit and refreshed. 'I'm playing today,' I told Ma.

She didn't pay much attention, since I played every day. 'My first-ever game in the first division,' I added.

Ma seemed distracted. 'Play well,' she said cursorily.

I'd expected her to glow with excitement but nothing of the sort happened. Irked, I changed the subject. 'Is there something to eat?' Ma turned pale. I understood – and became angry. But whom could I be angry with? Aruna Glass Factory – where the ongoing lockout had robbed Baba of his job? He now had a job with a salary that couldn't put anything but a few rotis on our plates twice a day.

Having learnt to accept our poverty, Pintu had matured beyond his years. Instead of making demands or throwing tantrums over the lack of food, he would simply walk out of the house grimly. But when poor Putul couldn't help crying, Nilima would take her home and try to distract her. Since her mother's death two years ago, Nilima had become the homemaker, managing the family with the money that her father gave her every month.

The anger I felt eventually turned inwards. I could have contributed to the household as well, I realized. All I had done until now was take, without giving anything in return. Having dropped out of school when I failed in Class Ten – not only did I hate school, but was also smart enough to know I wouldn't amount to anything academically – all I enjoyed was football. And playing football was all I did. That helped no one – not my parents, not my brother, not my sister.

Unable to be of the slightest help to my family, I felt completely redundant at times. With just friends and football in my life, what right did I have to demand a square meal? Football had not yet given me the right to make demands of my family. The only place I would be able to earn money was on the football field. If I couldn't become a great footballer, the only thing I'd be good for was to enlarge the ranks of the unemployed.

Smarting with the pain of this realization, I got dressed and left home with the football in my hand. Our training ground was a small plot of land five minutes away, next to a factory in which iron pots and pans were cast. This was where I began my football life. I could hear Pintu having a furious argument with his friends. 'Forget it, Nayeem will have to go back to school before he can be as good a stopper as Jarnail Singh.'

As soon as he saw me, Pintu ran up. 'Can I come with you?'

'Sure.'

He took the ball from my hand. I had asked the club to let me have what had now become a rather pear-shaped football, stitched up with several patches. I used it to practise my skills whenever I could – day or night. Sometimes Pintu and his friends joined in as well.

Once, I had planted bamboo stakes in a line four yards apart to practise dribbling between them. Upon seeing what I had done, Harsho-da had remarked, 'When he was asked to train this way, Garrincha said, "Since the opponent will tackle me rather than standing like a wooden post, I need to practise my dribbling against people who can actually move."'

That made sense to me. And ever since then, I had tried to get Pintu and his friends to join me when I practised. But none of them had come that day. When questioned about this, Pintu hesitated before replying, 'No need.'

'What's the matter? Have you quarrelled?'

After a pause, he replied, 'Is it true they haven't let you play a single game? Apparently Anwar-da and Nemai-da have been playing every game.'

Words suddenly escaped me. 'I have a knee injury. Someone named Tikadar tapped my knee so badly that I still can't shoot at full strength.'

I shrank within myself as I saw Pintu's face brighten in relief. I had no idea why I lied in order to maintain my position as his hero. Perhaps out of fear. A formidable striker was poised to unleash a bruising attack on the defence of my self-respect. I had to commit a terrible foul to stop him.

Normally, I used the three-storey-high factory wall as my goal to practise shots. Using a red brick to trace a rectangle eight yards wide and eight feet high on the wall, I would then divide it into six smaller rectangles with the numbers 1 to 6 written on them. Pintu – or someone else – would call out a number, whereupon I would try to kick the ball so that it hit the target rectangle. As the ball bounced back, they would call out another number, and I would try to hit it again – either by shooting or by heading the ball without stopping it. Ten minutes of this practice winded me, although I always resumed after a few minutes. It had been Harsho-da's idea. Some days all I did was take a hundred penalty shots. Other days, I practised chipping, volleying and heading, or dribbling against five or six of Pintu's friends.

It was just Pintu today. He kept calling out the numbers, and I kept shooting into the wall-goal, running out to retrieve the ball from the road each time in case it rolled away. After a while I noticed Nilima watching me train. On her way back from school, she was dressed in a white sari with a blue border, holding her books against her breast. In a sari she looked older than her age. Although her school was a couple of miles away, she walked every day to save the twenty-paise bus fare.

I ran to retrieve the ball from the road and Nilima smiled as our eyes locked. 'Back from school?' I asked. She nodded. Her face was drawn, the perspiration making a few stray hairs stick to her forehead. She wiped the sweat off her neck and shoulders with the end of her sari.

'My school starts in the afternoon.' I laughed.

'And these are your studies?' Nilima's beautiful teeth gleamed.

'I'm a very bad student, may not pass.' I feigned hopelessness.

'If you work hard you're bound to pass.'

Nilima's tone, eyes and posture no longer betrayed any amusement. Instead, a certain determination glided lightly over her face, like a bird on outstretched wings. I kicked the ball that I had been holding in my hand up in the air. 'Three,' Pintu called out.

I amazed myself with what I did next. Lying flat on the ground, I back-volleyed the ball – a shot that I'd never taken this way before. Astoundingly, the ball slammed into the centre of the rectangle marked with the number 3 and rebounded. Pintu chased it, waving his arms in the air and shouting in excitement. Nilima's large eyes grew even wider, whereas I was no longer sure whether I was Prasoon Bhattacharya or not.

'Once more!' Pintu said, throwing the ball to me.

I knew very well that it had been beginner's luck. Not even the Almighty could predict whether a second attempt would send the ball soaring over the factory roof or into the road.

'I have a knee injury which hasn't healed yet,' I told Nilima. 'Another knock and…'

'No need, don't try any more,' she said in alarm.

'Once more.'

'Not before it's healed completely,' she insisted, raising her hand to stop me. I breathed a sigh of relief. A few petty fouls to stop the striker were all part of the game.

'I'm starving.' I put my hand on my stomach and screwed up my face in misery. I knew Nilima always carried a small plastic purse with money.

'Hungry as soon as you start studying!' Nilima pretended to scold me whilst fishing out her purse from her blouse. Unclasping it, she said, 'I can't spare much, thirty paise at most.'

'Just thirty for a back volley like that!'

'Thirty-five, then.'

'No, no, please make it fifty. I'm starving!'

I was not pretending any more. One look at my face and Nilima promptly handed me fifty paise.

'I owe you.'

'What does it add up to now?' she asked sombrely.

'Keep track – you'll get it all back in one go.'

Nilima left. I had borrowed at least fifty or sixty rupees this way from her over the past year, telling her every time to note down the loan and that I would pay it all back. Indeed I would. All my efforts would not go to waste, I wouldn't let them.

With the money in my hand, my hunger became more intense. Giving the ball to Pintu, I said, 'Go home.'

'It's not safe to train any more. The injury could get aggravated,' he told me, trying to offer sage advice. I stifled an urge to laugh as he left, bouncing the ball.

About fifteen minutes later, whilst drinking a glass of water at Bodu's store after having finished my meal, I remembered that Pintu hadn't eaten either that day. My stomach churned as the rest of my body turned to stone.

8

Palash Tikadar and I exchanged glances and resumed scanning the sky. It was blue-grey in the north and the east, but there were thick dark clouds in the north-west, and no breeze. We stood there in the stifling heat, unable to guess whether it would rain or not. The fate of my debut was written in the sky.

All of a sudden, a gust of cool wind sprang up and the cloud became larger, getting closer – one end was already above the Mohammedan ground. Beaming with joy, Tikadar went off to put on his boots. Still staring at the sky, I discovered that the cloud was now moving off to the west, with the wind blowing in that direction as well, and breathed a sigh of relief.

When he emerged in his boots, Tikadar was extremely irritated by the fast-clearing sky. Ten minutes later, however, a small cloud suddenly passed over, drenching the ground in a swift shower before disappearing. I stood forlorn in one corner of the tent, boots in hand. Nemai, who had been putting on his boots at the time, came up to me and asked, 'Playing today?' I left the tent without answering.

About five minutes later, Bipin-da bustled up, looking for me.

'What a mess, throwing up five minutes before the game! Where's Prasoon? Ah, here you are. See the state Nemai has got himself into? Go on and get ready quickly.'

Nemai was lying on a bench, his eyes covered with his arm. Apparently he had started throwing up suddenly. I asked Anwar what had happened as we left the tent.

'If you drink half a bottle of iodine, you're bound to throw up,' Anwar answered, without showing the slightest bit of concern.

It was a tremendous shock. All I said was, 'Nemai is capable of anything.' Then, leaning over Nemai, I whispered, 'Count them. Three goals.'

'Against Mohun Bagan, right?' Nemai asked without moving the hand that covered his eyes.

'No…' I paused. 'Today,' I said.

I didn't get a hat-trick in my first game. Within five minutes, I was forced to drop back to our defending zone to tackle the Rajasthan midfielders. Two of their attackers, Sukalyan Ghosh Dastidar and Subhash Bhowmick, kept passing Anwar on either side, and all ten of us were in our penalty box.

We should have been five goals down in fifteen minutes. Of the three cannonballs let loose by Sukalyan's right foot, one hit the post; another, Anwar's shoulder; and the third, by some miracle, was tipped over the bar by our goalkeeper. Subhash wasted the other two opportunities that he got. Then, in the eighteenth minute, a stray ball somehow made its way to the centre line. Trapping the ball, I saw only one player between me and their goal – the stopper-back Fen.

I began my run with the ball diagonally, towards the right corner flag. Fen ran with me, covering the left side, even as their left-back was retreating. Unsure of being able to dribble past the experienced Fen in a one-to-one situation, I decided to beat him on speed instead. Stopping suddenly, I tapped the ball about fifteen yards to the left, leaving Fen behind to my right with a furious sprint that took me into their box. As I entered, their goalkeeper Arun gave me the charge at top speed, along with two other defenders who had dropped back.

I was watching Arun. He had drawn himself back, taut as a bow before the arrow is released, poised like a cat about to pounce. As I leant to the left, he floated towards me, arms outstretched. Instantly, I tapped the ball to the right and, with a perfect low punch of the right foot, sent it flying into the net just as the left-back shoulder-charged me viciously into the turf.

My first goal!

I lay prone on the grass, in shock from the incredible thing that had just happened, staring at the brown ball nestling innocently against the net. My entire world was that ball now. I wanted to hold it to my breast forever.

Two of my teammates – the right-winger and the right-in – helped me to my feet. Anwar was running towards me, his arms raised. I felt dizzy. He was babbling as he kissed me on my cheek. I looked over at the members' gallery, where less than fifty people were standing. How few witnesses there were to my first goal! The entire Shobhabajar team was embracing me and patting me on the back. Someone yelled jocularly from the stands, 'Enough now, get on with the game. It's not like you've scored the IFA Shield-winning goal!' I was very embarrassed.

Subhash equalized within two minutes, heading in a cross from the right-winger. He scored again a minute later, with an identical header. At half-time Bipin-da gave me excited instructions. 'Don't you dare fall back. Never mind if they score. And Ratan, just send the ball upfield whenever you can.'

Ratan was the player who had split his nose during training the first day, and to whom Bipin-da had promised a job. Ratan threw a glance at me and then flung his exhausted body down on the turf and shut his eyes.

An aluminium glass and a bucket of water had been laid out. Each player took a drink of water from the bucket and passed the glass to the next in line. As I waited for my turn, Tikadar said, 'So we're getting a treat today.'

'What for?' I asked in irritation.

'For the first goal for Shobhabajar this season.'

Smiling faintly, I reached out for the glass. 'Don't you think you need to compensate me for having taken my place?' asked Tikadar.

It felt good to hear him say that. 'Another time, not today,' I replied.

I glanced up at the stands before re-entering the field for the second half. Nemai now sat hunched up in one corner of the top row. We had left him lying in the tent. He held up three fingers.

During the second half, Rajasthan attempted to set themselves up for a hat-trick, but failed after Subhash made them waste a couple of perfect chances. When Sukalyan did finally manage to score a goal, I noticed that he looked strangely glum. He hadn't expected his shot, taken from fifteen yards away, to enter the net unchallenged. Enraged, Subhash slammed his right fist into his left palm and went back snorting. Then, two minutes later, he knocked Anwar to the ground with a violent shoulder-charge.

It was Ratan's behaviour, however, that surprised me the most. Never mind Bipin-da's instructions, he seemed to have completely forgotten the rest of this teammates as well. Each time he got the ball, he would charge off on his own, turning a deaf ear to my pleas for a pass. His reedy chest was pumping like a pair of bellows. His eyes bursting out of their sockets, his face red and sweat pouring down his body, he kept chasing the ball and running off with it by himself – only to have it taken off him every time. He ran madly all over the field as if he were possessed, but to no avail. And I wasn't the only one who was getting increasingly impatient and irritated by his foolish behaviour. All this time, Bipin-da kept shouting from the sidelines, 'Ratan, leave the ball alone, let Prasoon get it!'

But instead of simply leaving the ball alone, Ratan left the field. Walking towards the sidelines, he suddenly tripped over his own feet and found himself unable to get up again. Two or three people helped him and lay him down beyond the sidelines, with Tikadar coming on to take his place. Rajasthan earned a penalty almost immediately afterwards. As their left-out was about to cross the ball from our goal line, having got past two of our defenders, Tikadar kicked him in the stomach. Subhash then scored from the penalty kick that followed.

Being 4-1 ahead, Rajasthan began to let up on the pressure. I got the ball twice but couldn't put it to use. The first time, I volleyed a cross from the right-winger over the crossbar. The second, I ran into Fen after dodging past two of their players. With no one around to play a wall-pass with, I tried a shot from the edge of the box, only to have it tipped over the bar by their goalkeeper Arun.

I remembered Nemai. Had he been there, I would have pushed the ball to him and moved into a spot at a forty-five degree angle to the right post. Nemai would have unleashed the perfect pass a yard in front of me. And then all I'd have had to do would have been to feint to the left and jab the ball into the net at lightning speed with the right foot.

A fist fight nearly broke out between Anwar and Tikadar after the final whistle. Anwar felt that Tikadar had needlessly let the other team score a goal with his foul. And truth was, the left-winger's cross needn't automatically have led to a goal as the ball could have been cleared. The fact remained, however, that Tikadar had directly ensured a goal for Rajasthan by conceding that penalty.

Tikadar responded to Anwar's criticism with a few choice invectives that promptly led to him being knocked to the ground by a furious Anwar. His eyes blazing with anger, Tikadar glared at Anwar for a few moments. Then, through clenched teeth, he said, 'All right, my turn will come too,' and left the ground.

By that time, Nemai had come down from the stands to join us. Bipin-da patted me on the back, saying, 'Well played, Prasoon.' Ratan looked at me with a strange mixture of apprehension and melancholy. When we were leaving after our ration of two slices of toast and a boiled egg, Ratan signalled to me that he wanted a chat.

'Like yours, my family's a poor one too,' he told me dully. 'Since they don't pay us here, I'm sure you'll go to some other club next year. I know you will. Why should someone as talented as you stay here and rot?'

I was silent. Putting his hand on my shoulder, Ratan said, 'Bipin-da has promised me a job.'

'I know,' I said.

'If you ask for a job, he'll try for one for you first. I knew it when I saw you play today.' Ratan sounded miserable. Removing his hand from my shoulder, he then grabbed my hand. 'I need the job, Prasoon. My family's in desperate shape – I need the job much more than you do. Promise me you won't ask for anything here. Promise me you won't stay here another year.'

Not able to look him in the eye, I turned away and said, 'I don't mean to stay on here. I want to be a better player. I want to join a big club.'

Ratan breathed a sigh of relief. Squeezing my hand, he said, 'Where do you want to play? I know people everywhere. East Bengal? Mohun Bagan? Aryan? Juger Jatri?'

'Mohun Bagan.'

'Right away? No, you should spend another year somewhere else. You're still a junior player. If you join a big club now, you won't get a game. Wasting a year now can do so much harm. Can't you learn from my experience? I was lured into a big club too once. They benched me for a year. But I still couldn't give up on the dream and stayed on another year, hoping against hope. I got just half a game that year. Then I moved to Wari, and now Shobhabajar. I had the same dream as you – to be a great player.'

Ratan's words trailed into silence, mingling with the darkness descending on the Maidan. Depressed, I walked on, my eyes fixed on the ground. Ratan spoke intensely. 'Today I was playing out of fear. You scared me. My only thought was that I had lost my place in the team to you. Please don't be offended.' He squeezed my hand. I nodded.

Then, lowering his voice to a whisper, he said, 'You must score, score lots of goals, and join a big club. And you must look after yourself. You will have to increase your weight and work harder. For that, you will have to be selfish. You cannot afford to think of your family and skip a meal – on the contrary, you have to grab the food off their plates. The poor have to be cruel if they want to succeed – if they want to avoid ending up like me. How could anyone become a good footballer with a physique like mine?'

Turning away from me abruptly, Ratan went into the tent. Anwar and Nemai, who had been waiting for me impatiently, asked what we'd been talking about. Depressed by the conversation, I answered, 'I'll tell you later. Nothing serious.' Changing the subject, I added, 'No hat-trick, Nemai.'

'You know what? I wish I could have played for Rajasthan today. Would have got Subhash his hat-trick,' said Nemai with a poker face. 'It's amazing how he bursts through the defence.'

That comment wound Anwar up. 'Amazing? My foot! All of them are one-foot players. What do they have besides speed and their shooting? Watch Habib when you get the chance. He's the amazing one – the game-maker who plays up and down the pitch, and covers so much space. Have you seen the way he jumps into the fray when his team's in trouble?'

Nemai didn't argue. But before we got into the bus I told them, 'Enough. We have to shift to another club next year.'

9

Bipin-da somehow found out that all three of us were planning to leave Shobhabajar Sporting. Drawing us aside, he said, 'I'll get all of you into the junior Bengal team if you stay on until next year.'

We exchanged glances without saying a word, a sense of discomfort taking root within us, for we all knew that Bipin-da was capable of keeping his word. Parimal Bhattacharya, the club secretary, was part of a clique within the IFA that controlled all the committees. It had conspired to put a halt to all promotion and relegation. The clubs stood to gain as they would no longer be obliged to spend large sums of money on good players capable of helping them climb to a higher division or preventing them from being relegated to a lower one. If a player wanted money, they could simply show him the door. They thought along these lines. We can pick any eleven people off the street and play them. We don't care even if we lose every game.

To tell the truth, three rank outsiders like us would never have got a chance to play for a first division club had this not been the case. There were at least two or three Shobhabajar players who got into the junior Bengal team every year. And last year, there were even two of them in the junior India team.

'You don't believe me?' Bipin-da asked.

'No, it's not that, but…' Nemai became our spokesman.

'But what? Money? Jobs?'

'It's not that. Everyone wants to play for a big club, after all.'

'You mean there are clubs bigger than junior Bengal? Bigger than junior India? Once you've got that stamp, the big clubs will chase you all the way home to sign you up.'

I was tempted to tell him that dozens of players with such

stamps could be found on the Maidan, but that only a handful were real players. But there was no point – not only would it not serve any purpose, but it might also cause bitterness. So I said, 'Bipin-da, we want to learn the game, learn from great players. Can't you understand Nemai's, or Anwar's or my situation, game after game? Nobody here can put up a real fight, provide some opposition, or even pass properly. They have no stamina, no skill and no intelligence. I get no inspiration here. You cannot play football by yourself, can you?'

I saw Nemai and Anwar nodding in support as my voice rose in indignation.

Bipin-da's face suddenly became thunderous. 'Parimal-da will be angry if you leave. Do you think you will go places if you antagonize him? Every club fears him. He can stop you from playing for India no matter how good your performance is. Now, will you still refuse to play for his club, despite my request?'

We looked at one another again.

Bipin-da understood our dilemma only too well. 'Stay on another year. Promotion and relegation will probably be resumed next year. You know the state we're in here. With only a handful of members, we have to survive on the IFA's donation to last the season. It's never enough, which is why we have to beg. Still, I promise you some pocket money next year. Stay on. Don't forget it was Shobhabajar that gave you your break in the first division. Don't you think we want the three of you to be great, to be famous? We can boast about you then.'

Bipin-da looked pathetic, his voice ardent and tearful. What he told us was troubling. Although we'd only seen Parimal Bhattacharya from a distance, we'd heard a lot about him. And we knew that he was capable of doing anything to protect his own interests and power. Indeed, putting an end to a player's career was little more than a minute's work for him, as Bipin-da's subtle threat reminded us.

Suddenly Nemai said, 'All right, let us think it over.'

Bipin-da looked at the three of us in turn and nodded.

I went off to pay Harsho-da a visit. I found him on his terrace, sitting on his haunches, attending to his flowers. He didn't say a word for a long time as he listened to me, but simply continued turning the earth in the flowerpots with a rod. Then, carefully snapping off a dead twig from a rose plant, he asked me softly, 'What do *you* want?'

'I can't make up my mind. Nemai and Anwar are in the same dilemma. They're swaying between "Let's stay back, it's only for a year" and "Rubbish, why should we waste a year".'

'Prasoon, the gauntlet has been thrown down at your feet. And it's you alone who has to decide whether to pick it up or not.'

Stiffening at Harsho-da's cold, stern tone, I stared at the dead rose twig for a while. Following my gaze, Harsho-da smiled. 'That twig is dead, but do you see how alive the plant is? The other branches are budding. That's the way it always is. We grow by shedding our dead branches and leaves. We make the new branches flower. And all that requires nurturing – fertilizer, water, sunshine. The plant absorbs the life force from its roots. If the root is not cared for, it wastes away and the plant will no longer grow. A man's root is his character. If you want to take favours – slipping through the back door to climb the stairs of success – your root will certainly rot. This plant has stayed alive by fighting. I merely gave it some help. When a man cannot get help, he must help himself. But if his character has already rotted away, he cannot do that – he is defeated, demolished. Challenges come in many forms. A man has to tackle all of them.'

As I listened, I felt the blood course through my veins with a roar, while in my breast, a wave cascaded with an indistinct sound from a distance. And it was as if someone was asking me from the crest of that wave, 'Striker, look at their defence. It is invincible. But you can break it, can't you?'

'I can,' I said aloud for my own benefit, lowering my head.

Looking at me in surprise, Harsho-da threw away the dead twig and said, 'Do you remember me telling you Hemingway's story –

The Old Man and the Sea? It says there that a man can be defeated, but not…' Then, breaking off all of a sudden, he exclaimed, 'Why didn't you finish school, Prasoon? You could have read it in English for yourself! Some things are lost in the telling.'

'I do remember it, Harsho-da. A man can be defeated but not destroyed, isn't that right?'

Not waiting to hear his answer, I got up and left.

10

I wandered through the streets all by myself for about an hour. I ran into several people I knew, but looked through them all as though they were mere shapes floating by. Ignoring everyone who called out, I walked on like a ghost, Harsho-da's words running endlessly through my mind. 'You must now decide whether to pick up the gauntlet that's been thrown down at your feet.'

'Now you can't even recognize me, Prasoon?' I stopped in my tracks and looked up. Nilima was standing before me with a frown on her face, hands on her hips and amazement writ large in her eyes. 'If this is what you do when your name's in the papers, how'll you behave when they print your picture as well?'

'What rubbish. Plenty of people get their names in the papers every day,' I stammered in embarrassment. 'I'm just a Shobhabajar player, we don't get our names in the papers. Honestly, I didn't see you. Where are you coming from? Are you going home now?' Like a player clearing the ball into the stands when under pressure, I tried to ease my discomfort by asking her questions at random.

Nilima was really surprised now. 'Have you forgotten my routine? What's the matter with you? You didn't bother to stop when I waved to you. And now you're talking like we are meeting each other for the first time. For heaven's sake, what's going on?'

'I was thinking about a dilemma I've got myself into. Just met Harsho-da. Shall we walk a bit?'

We walked along slowly, neither of us talking. When she was serious, Nilima looked more like a middle-aged woman than a young girl. The last two years spent running the household after her mother's death had undeniably taken away some of her youth. It was a complicated balancing act to run the household on her father's insignificant salary and her own earnings from giving lessons. Then there were her own studies to think about as well.

Harsho-da's words seemed to burn holes in my skin. 'You cannot do anything more if your morals have rotted.' 'A man's character is his root.' 'Challenges come in many forms.' What was going on? What was I supposed to do with all these homilies? What did all this have to do with football or inter-club transfers or playing for India? And if all I needed for my game was skill, speed, dribbling, stamina and wiles, where did character and morals come into the picture? I was seized by an intolerable helplessness. For once, I could neither size up my opponent nor identify his strategy.

In the hope of lifting my mood, I started a conversation with Nilima. 'Where did you go?' I asked her.

'To a publisher's. I'm learning how to read proofs. Baba set it up for me.'

'Are you getting lots of money?'

Nilima swished her pigtail from the back of her head to the front. Then, wrapping it around her finger, she answered, 'Lots. A lakh or two.'

'You're joking!'

'Not at all. A hard-earned rupee, made honestly, is worth a lakh to me.'

'I'm not earning anything yet – can't contribute a paisa at home.' I tried to smile. Nilima smiled too.

'I've heard you can earn thousands playing football. Yours is a kind of job too – just like in an office or factory, school or college. Don't footballers have to learn too, just like everyone else?'

'Of course. I really want to learn.' I paused and continued, 'You know, I'm not able to learn anything at the club I am in now. They're asking me to stay for another year, promising me money and a place on the junior Bengal team, maybe even the junior India team. I can't figure out what I should do. Shobhabajar's Parimal Bhattacharya has so much influence in national football that no player can make it if they get on his wrong side.'

Nilima remained silent, as if pondering over what I'd said. I continued, 'Harsho-da said this is a challenge.'

'What else did he say?'

Hesitating, I answered, 'That the tree grows on the strength of its roots. And that the root is your character – if it rots, you will die.'

Standing in the middle of the road, Nilima spun around to face me. 'Those who cannot accept and overcome a challenge don't deserve the greatness they desire. Only those who do not cheat on their education become great. And cowards cannot achieve greatness. Are you a coward, Prasoon? Are you unwilling to work hard?'

'No. But you need luck on your side too. After all, even Brazil has lost despite having Pelé and Garrincha on the team.'

'I have no idea who Pelé or Garrincha are, or how well they play. But the other side could have had good players too. It's true that your father had the misfortune of being humiliated into giving up the game with a leg injury, but the same fate may not lie in store for you. Besides, should you not avenge your father's humiliation? Should you not force the people who had once spit on him to swallow their own insults? How do you expect to do that without achieving greatness? You can keep the right people happy to make your way into the Indian team, but you cannot become a great player that way.'

I gazed into her wide eyes. A weight was being lifted off my chest, leaving me light and carefree again. Baba – my father – was an honourable but humiliated footballer. He had given so much of himself to football, to thousands of football lovers and to his club Juger Jatri, without receiving anything in return. And now he was trying to support his family, like a beast of burden toiling under the whip all day. Baba, my father, was a lonely, humiliated footballer. I was his self-centred son.

'You love my father, don't you, Nilima? You know, after Nemai and Anwar, Ma and you are my closest friends.'

Nilima reddened and looked away immediately. 'That's enough. I don't have a paisa to lend you.'

'Don't tell me your purse can't even make it to the snack shop.'

11

I had been pulling my hair out in anticipation of the game against Mohun Bagan. By match day, I had already informed Anwar and Nemai that I would be switching clubs the following year. Yet, despite their various attempts to make me see reason, I refused to go back on my decision, shaking my head each time we spoke of it. I told them that all I wanted was to be a great player, and that I was prepared to take whatever risks might be necessary to achieve that goal. They were silent at that.

The match against Mohun Bagan was the first major match of my football career. Players of insignificant teams like ours got an opportunity only twice or thrice a year to play before huge crowds. And this also meant getting oneself noticed and written about in the newspapers. George Telegraph had lost to us 0-2 in the previous game, with both goals being scored by me.

On the Friday before the Mohun Bagan match, I went to the club tent and looked at the noticeboard where the players' list had been put up. My eye immediately sought out No. 10 and I was dumbfounded by what I saw. S. Datta! Why Sadhan Datta? The gangling Sadhan, who brought up grass and earth when taking a shot and freely delivered the ball to anyone who tried to tackle him. Where was my name? I asked myself, slowly turning to stone as my eyes ran down the full list. I saw that both Nemai and Anwar were on it.

I went to Bipin-da, who told me grimly, 'They're honouring my request. They aren't betraying me.'

The ground beneath my feet started to quake. The blow had come. A voice within me said, 'Prasoon, you're on the pitch now. The opponent has scored first. Be ready, striker – you not only have to equalize, you also have to score the winning goal. You *have* to.'

We lost 0-6 the next day. I watched the game from the stands. Nemai and Anwar avoided me after the match, stricken expressions on their faces.

I didn't go to the Shobhabajar tent any more.

Harsho-da got me a job at a petrol pump which was owned by a friend of his on VIP Road. It brimmed over with equipment for servicing cars: air compressors, pneumatic grease, mobile pumps, hydraulic lifts, water compressors, grease and water guns, and lots more. I was appointed mate in the servicing department at a daily wage of two and a half rupees.

My shift started at eight in the morning. The car being serviced was first raised on an H-shaped lift and my job was to stand under the vehicle, scrape off the dried earth from the mudguard and chassis, and then wash it down with the water gun. Madhu Saha, the head mechanic, inspected my work from a distance. I worked apprehensively, a blue cap on my head and a strip of cloth covering my nose. Occasionally he would shout out, pointing at some area of the car with his finger, 'There, the mud's still there, under the differential…use your eyes, boy, use your eyes, look at the tyre rod joint.'

To all intents and purposes, my customary morning training was now over – a fact which greatly unsettled me. I tried to get up at dawn for a five-mile run and half an hour of ball control practice before heading off to work. Yet not only did such limited practice not help, it also led to tiredness at work, forcing me to suffer even more of Madhu Saha's tirades. And when work finished at five, I simply didn't feel like training any more.

I was very worried. There was no doubt in my mind that my

game would go to the dogs if I continued in that job. It occurred to me, however, that filling tanks with petrol or diesel would be far less taxing than the work I was presently doing. I wondered whether I might be able to switch to that role instead, and work nights as well. That way, I'd get a lot more time to myself during the day. I'd heard you could even sleep during night shifts. If anyone wanted petrol, they'd simply wake you up with their loud demands.

I disclosed my problem to Harsho-da, who agreed to help me. A couple of days later the owner of the pump sent for me.

'I believe you play football.'

'Yes, sir,' I said apprehensively.

'I believe it's becoming difficult to play with the job.'

'Not to play, but to train. I don't get to play matches right now.'

'Why?'

I told him the whole story. Muttering 'I see, I see', he tapped his forehead with a pen, seemingly lost in thought. Then he said, 'All right, if it's night duty you want, that's what you'll get.'

I was relieved.

By that time, the IFA Shield had already begun and Shobhabajar was up against Burnpur United in the first round. Although I had a player's card, I decided to buy my own ticket as I didn't want to run into Nemai or Anwar. The galleries could seat twelve thousand people, yet there was only one other person watching the game from the stands with me. And even then I was extremely surprised by the fact that a spectator was ready to pay for a ticket to watch a game like this one.

The whole situation was still a bit of a mystery to me. The names Prasoon, Nemai and Anwar had previously been synonymous with the Three Musketeers – we had even been known by that title at many tournaments we had played in. In the past, we had spent all our time together – at the game or away from it. I couldn't remember a single day in the last six or seven years when we hadn't seen one another.

But now I had drifted away from them. One moment I would

yearn to meet them, then the very next I would conclude that since they had taken the decision to stay on by themselves, without involving me, they simply didn't want to be around me any more. Our differences had created a rift between us, with their road to football success taking a different direction from mine. And at times it seemed as if they were right – why look a gift horse in the mouth? But I wanted to craft my own ladder to the top. That was the difference – I was prepared to work much harder than they were.

Nemai or Anwar hadn't tried to meet me either. They probably felt guilty. After all, they hadn't protested when Shobhabajar dropped me. Then it struck me that they had perhaps been wise not to try and meet me. What if I asked them why they hadn't stood up for me? Or why they had chosen to play in the match that day anyway. What kind of answer could they give to such questions?

Although I still missed my friends, my job helped me put them out of my mind during the day. After four hours of training on the road and on the ground, I now slept in the afternoons, and went to a nearby club in the evenings to work out. There were hardly any cars after midnight at the petrol pump, allowing me plenty of sleep.

12

Burnpur won 3-1. Nemai played a fantastic game. Knowing they'd be wasted, he no longer sent his famous through passes, preferring to try and score himself. Although tailed by two defenders, he managed to work himself free a few times before scoring Shobhabajar's only goal. But how can one or two good players possibly shore up a rickety outfit? Immediately after conceding the goal, Burnpur struck back at Shobhabajar, seizing it by the scruff of its neck. Even Anwar was forced to commit three fouls. By half-time Burnpur was ahead 2-1.

A little later, a miskick from Burnpur's left-half brought the ball into the stands, from where it bounced off the seats into the space below. So I had to go fetch it. Just as I was about to kick the ball back into the ground, I saw Nemai approaching. I waited with the ball in my hand, watching him halt in his tracks the moment he saw who it was. Throwing the ball to him, I said, 'Go for it.' A flash of agony appeared on his face, transforming itself into a wan smile. After that he lost his touch or appeared to be uninterested in retaining it. I left before the final whistle.

The lockout at Aruna Glass showed no signs of ending. By now, people had become so familiar with the sight of me returning from my daily five-mile run dressed in my shorts, T-shirt and running shoes that they no longer batted an eyelid when they saw me. Silently entering the house at an hour when Baba gave lessons to Pintu and Putul, I would go into my cubbyhole, polish off the rotis left under a cover for me and then leave again with my football, pausing on the way at the kitchen to give Ma a rupee. I got a great thrill out of being able to pass on some of my earnings to her.

I used the remaining one and a half rupees to buy high-calorie food for myself. I'd stopped going to the movies. My shirt and trousers had now lasted me nearly one and a half years, thanks to frequent use of the needle and thread. I desperately needed a pair of boots, however. Had I accepted the requests to play as a hired hand in local tournaments, I could have got myself not just boots but also clothes. But I didn't. Every morning, as I headed for the nearby ground, football in hand, young boys and girls would be heading for school, books in hand. This would always remind me of what Nilima had said: I was going to school too – the ground being my classroom; the ball, my books.

One morning I spotted Baba walking past distractedly, his eyes fixed on the ground. A few local boys and I were practising heading on the ground next to the factory. One of them said, 'Prasoon-da, your father used to play for Juger Jatri, didn't he?'

'Yes, how did you know?'

'My uncle was saying he was a fabulous player. Was an equally good shooter with both feet, apparently.'

'I never saw Baba play. He gave up the game a year after my birth.'

I noticed some of the boys exchange looks and covert smiles with each other, although I didn't realize why at first.

'Your father played against East Bengal in the IFA Shield final, didn't he?' one of them asked.

'That was his last game,' added another.

'My uncle said that if he hadn't missed that sitter, East Bengal would have lost. Even a blind man could have scored.'

'Oh, indeed,' I said coolly, controlling my anger. 'Has your uncle ever played football in his life?'

The boy hesitated.

'Probably not.'

'How do you know?' he asked belligerently.

'Had he played, he would not have claimed that a blind man can score.'

'Yes, he can in some cases, unless he's been bribed.'

'Meaning?' I was shaking with rage now, a liquid fire running through my brain, obscuring my vision.

'It's obvious. Everyone knows what happened.' As he curled his lips into a sneer, everyone else laughed.

The next thing I knew, I was walking away. The fellow who I had been talking to was now writhing on the ground, clutching his stomach. I remember seeing blood trickle from his split lips, but not whether I had kicked or punched him. I walked on furiously.

Returning home an hour later, I saw a crowd assembled in our narrow lane. A bald man in his fifties, with affluence written all over his face, stood at our door, his fist raised, and shouting, 'I'll say it a hundred times over – you were bribed, you were bribed, you were bribed! I was in the stands that day, I saw it all.' He choked. 'That… that chance.' Wiping his eyes on the sleeve of his silk shirt, he muttered brokenly, 'We still haven't ever won the IFA Shield.'

I quickly retreated, and ended up pacing around the streets for some time. But as soon as I returned, Ma ran up in full view of everyone and began to slap me, grabbing my hair.

'Why? Why did you beat up someone else? They came and humiliated your father in his own home. You...because of you.'

Ma started panting. My tender, tiny, soft-spoken, ever-smiling mother. Her slaps hurt me, while tears streamed down her eyes. Pintu and Putul stood to one side, grave expressions darkening their little faces. The door to Baba's room was shut. The landlord's daughters were watching everything from the first-floor balcony. All the nearby windows were lined with curious faces. When Nilima came and tried to take Ma's hand, she shouted even louder, 'You're a disgrace. It's a sin even to look at a son because of whom his father is maligned.'

Leaving Nilima holding on to Ma, I ran inside and kicked open the doors to Baba's room. Lying on his back, shading his eyes with his arm, he gave me a single look upon hearing me enter.

'Did you take a bribe, Baba?' I asked agitatedly.

He didn't answer, although I saw a muscle move on his face.

'I need to know.'

'I see no need to answer you. If you are ashamed, do not reveal the name of your father.'

'I don't believe what they say.'

Baba remained silent. He didn't look at me. At that moment, his prone body seemed to me like a branch broken off a tree – dry, lifeless.

'My request is that you do not get into arguments with anyone over me. That you do not beat them up. You cannot instil your belief in thousands of other people by beating up each one of them. Better to let me be as I am.'

Finally he removed his arm from his eyes to look at me. The brown scar in the middle of his smooth forehead gleamed, dazzling my eyes. I left the room.

The next morning, as I was about to leave after putting the usual one rupee down on the threshold of the kitchen where Ma sat fanning the flames in our ancient earthen stove, she called me over. Putting her hand on my shoulder, she raised her face to me as a little girl would and said, 'My hand really hurt yesterday.'

'Naturally.' I laughed. 'You shouldn't have hit me so hard.'

'Will you play like a champion? Promise me you will.'

I gazed at Ma's lovely face. I didn't feel like saying a word. Putting my arms round her, I buried my face in her bosom and said, 'I will.'

Putting her hand on my head, she whispered, 'Can you be as great as your father?'

Suddenly I felt a tremor within me. With Ma's touch on my head and the scent of her body in my nostrils, I felt as though I was dribbling with the black-and-white ball on a bed of silken green grass. Feinting to the right, weaving to the left and rising in the air, I was now a fawn, now a cheetah, now a falcon. This must be the joy of the beautiful game, I told myself – to be a great player and make the field your mother's bosom. Isn't that what you want?

'Yes, that's what I want too,' I answered Ma in a trance.

13

Another year rolled by. I was a year older. I was now five feet ten and a half inches tall, although I was relatively light, weighing only sixty-five kilos. Nilima had taken her final exams at school and I was earning three and a half rupees a day on the night shift. The Aruna Glass Factory was still shut, which now came to fourteen consecutive months of closure.

Baba still went out every afternoon, as usual. He had become even thinner and even more taciturn. While our nightly quota of rotis remained unchanged, Ma had not cooked any meat, fish or eggs in over a year. Pintu and Putul desperately tried to bury themselves in their textbooks on the days when the scent of mutton wafted over from our landlord's kitchen.

Harsho-da had told me several times that the only way to replenish the energy being burned by all my exertion was to eat well. Footballers need a lot of protein – if you cannot get meat, milk and eggs, you'll be in deep trouble. I was afraid. What if my body gave way? But where could I find the money for meat?

I saw the names of the players selected for the junior Bengal team for the B.C. Roy trophy in the newspaper. One day, someone woke me up just before dawn, demanding ten litres of petrol and explaining that they had to catch an early morning flight. I sprang awake upon looking into the car. Nemai and Anwar were seated in the back, while Bipin-da was sitting next to the driver. They were amazed. 'So, Prasoon, is this what you're up to now? Wonderful! Can you speed it up, they need to make the Delhi flight.'

Smiling, I poured petrol into the tank, my eye on the meter. 'You didn't trust me, but see, Nemai and Anwar are going for the Junior Nationals. You would have too. You had so much potential,' Bipin-da shouted out of the car window and made regretful noises with his tongue. When I brought him the change, he whispered, 'Join us next year. We'll give you fifteen hundred, more than we give them. Don't waste yourself like this. Next year teams will get relegated and promoted again.'

I smiled again. The two of them sat there like zombies, Anwar looking out of the window but Nemai staring at me. I felt really envious after their car left. I would also have been in that car, heading for the airport, had I stayed on with Shobhabajar. Then Parimal Bhattacharya would have ensured a place for me in the junior India team, after which it would be off to Bangkok, Seoul or Tokyo. If only I'd stayed on just one more year.

I was angry with myself, wondering if I'd simply been stupid and shot myself in the foot by acting the way I had. As I sat there transfixed, pondering my situation, a voice suddenly whispered in my breast, 'What harm have you done, Prasoon? There will be plenty of time to make amends. Go on, get going for practice. Work harder, even harder. You haven't done anything stupid. Never forget that it's your game alone that will bring you glory, and not the Bengal or even the India jersey.'

As I ran along VIP Road, a plane flew low overhead, going westwards. Gritting my teeth, I sprinted on like a man possessed.

14

'Ratan has told me about you.'

The salt-and-pepper-haired, sixty-five-year-old Dashu Guha shook his head from side to side, surveying me from top to toe. Suddenly he rose from his chair and punched me hard on the chest. I kept standing, not letting my face reveal that it had hurt. He then stood behind me, leaving me wondering what he would do next. Suddenly I felt a giant shove – but managed to retain my balance.

A smile appeared on Dashu-da's face. 'Striker?'

I nodded. 'Kamal, Kamal,' he called loudly. The short, fair Kamal Pandit came running. 'Make him do twenty-five rounds,' Dashu-da told him.

Kamal-da was the trainer for Shonali Sangha. He had played for India as a defender about ten years ago and was rumoured to have incredible stamina.

'Brought your shorts?'

'No.'

Kamal-da went and got me a pair. A game of hockey was in progress, with a few scattered spectators on the sidelines. I noticed a few young men in football boots, bare-bodied, singing outside the tent. It looked as if they were waiting for the hockey game to finish so they could start training. They looked at me curiously. I recognized Runu, the goalkeeper, whom I'd seen a couple of times with Ratan at the Shobhabajar tent, although I didn't really know him.

Kamal-da got me started on a run around the ground, beginning at a pace just slightly faster than a brisk walk. After five rounds, I found Kamal-da running ahead of me and increasing his pace. I had no problem keeping up and stuck to him like a leech. After seventeen rounds I saw that the hockey game had ended and that the others were now on the ground with footballs. On the twentieth round, I overtook Kamal-da and pulled away. Dashu-da, who had been getting the players to practise passing and inter-passing, was now looking at us. I wasn't anywhere near out of breath. The gap with Kamal-da kept increasing. I broke into a sprint on the last round, leaving Kamal-da one and a half rounds behind. Dashu-da beckoned to me.

'What did you say your name was?'

'Prasoon.'

'Why didn't you get your boots?'

I'd heard that Dashu-da only said that to people who were good enough to make it to the first team. I scratched my head in pleasure. Kamal-da had arrived by now and wrapped his arms around me in joy. 'My first loss, Dashu-da,' he said, panting.

'The boy's got stamina,' said Dashu-da and resumed his supervision of the training. Stepping outside the playing area, I watched the others. One of them sent high crosses into the penalty box from the right, while the other three tried to head or volley it into the net. For the most part they missed the goalmouth, sending the ball over the crossbar.

Walking over to Dashu-da, I asked, 'May I try?'

Dashu-da nodded. I ran in.

Two of us ran forward together, while a third player crossed the ball from the touchline on the right. The cross, which wasn't a good one, was going to fall behind us. I turned, my back facing the goal, and received the ball on the full, using my instep to stroke it upwards and then trying an overhead bicycle kick. Turning my head, I saw the ball bounce into the goal off the underside of the crossbar and the goalkeeper staring at me in amazement. It was the same shot I'd once demonstrated to Nilima. But while I'd been lucky that time, now I could send eight out of ten such shots into the net.

As Dashu-da and Kamal-da whispered between themselves, the other players looked at me admiringly. 'Do it again,' one of them said.

I couldn't. Receiving the ball on my chest, I bounced it to my thigh and floated it upwards. But because it drifted to my left, I took a half-turn instead of a bicycle kick and volleyed the ball into the net, evading the goalkeeper's outstretched arms as he dived for it

Dashu-da then beckoned to me again. He started asking questions – about my family, what my father did for a living, what I did for a living, about my studies…and lots more.

'Give up the job,' said Dashu-da. Then, upon seeing my surprise, he added, 'We'll give you the same amount every month, but we can't afford any more.'

I agreed immediately. Among the lesser teams, Shonali Sangha had something of a reputation for playing to a plan, using modern techniques. The boys were serious here, training with dedication under Dashu-da's watchful eyes, with Kamal-da helping them hone their skills. Shonali imposed a regimen of strict discipline on its players, which they had to follow not just on the ground but also at home. Dashu-da frequently dropped in unannounced at his players' homes to keep tabs on what they were eating or when they were going to bed – what their lifestyles were like.

'Transfers start next week. Kamal will take you to the IFA office to sign up. And you can join the training starting tomorrow.'

On the way back in the crowded bus to Shyambazar, I remembered that I had said 'no' when Dashu-da asked whether anyone in my family had ever played football.

15

I ran into Bipin-da at the IFA office. Nearly a thousand people were milling around on Sooterkin Street, on the stretch between Chittaranjan Avenue and the *Anandabazar Patrika* office. Bipin-da was among those waiting. He signalled that he wanted to talk to me, which made me a little uncomfortable.

'I heard you're planning to sign for Shonali.'

'What brings you here?' I asked, avoiding his question.

'Nemai and Anwar are staying on with us. They're coming at two to sign.' Then, glancing at his watch, he said, 'So you aren't considering my offer. How much are they giving you?'

'Not a paisa.'

Letting out a surprised 'Oh', Bipin-da's expression became grim. Since I was supposed to be meeting Kamal-da near the *Anandabazar* gate at two, I started walking off in that direction. A group of people were discussing something animatedly, with names like Nayeem, Arun Ghosh, Ashim Moulik, Papanna, Habib, Dhiren De, Jyotish Guha and Shailen Manna floating around. Suddenly they ran towards the IFA office, calling out Nayeem's name, returning a few minutes later muttering about rumours. I started fantasizing about how they'd wait the same way for me one day, running towards the IFA office if they heard I'd come to switch to a different club. It was hilarious.

As I was climbing up the IFA office stairs with Kamal-da, I saw Nemai and Anwar coming downstairs behind Bipin-da. I shrank against the wall, letting them pass. Nemai was dressed in a trendy pair of off-white trousers, very tight and worn well below the waist. He was wearing shoes with pointed toes, and had changed his hairstyle, with his hair now covering half his forehead. Anwar was dressed in a blue nylon sports shirt that suited his complexion very well.

'How are you?' I asked.

They almost stumbled. Neither had expected me to talk to them.

Nemai spoke first. 'You've lost weight, Prasoon.'

I smiled.

'We'll see you later, need to go now,' Anwar said softly. I nodded.

As soon as I returned home the next evening, Ma came up to me looking very excited and said, 'Come in here, I want to show you something.' As I ran in behind her, I noticed that she had five hundred-rupee notes in her hand.

'From where did you get those?' I asked in surprise. Ma simply showed me a handwritten letter in response. It said, 'Wait for me at exactly 2 p.m. tomorrow at the IFA office, where we met yesterday. Yours, Bipin-da.'

I held out my hand to take the money from Ma.

'This has to be returned immediately. It's a bribe.'

The notes slipped from her hand, almost as though she had dropped them. All she said, in a weak voice, was, 'Bribe.'

When I reached Bipin-da's home it was ten at night. 'At this hour? What's the matter?' he asked in surprise.

Putting the currency notes down on the table, I turned to leave and said, 'Your money was with me for a few hours. I owe you the interest for that. I'll pay it back the day we play Shobhabajar.' On my way out, I heard him say, 'Oh really?'

16

Our third game in the Calcutta League was against Shobhabajar.

In the first two matches Shonali had drawn 2-2 with Aryan and defeated Wari 3-0. I had scored all five goals, including the first hat-trick in the tournament. *Jugantar* wrote, 'P. Bhattacharya, Shonali Sangha's new recruit in the forward line, proved himself an exceptional opportunist by scoring three goals and earning the distinction of being the first player to secure a hat-trick this season.' Pintu had kept the clipping. He had been coaxing me to take him to watch a game. I hadn't, in case I played badly. He was my biggest fan. But that day I took him along, for I was confident of playing well.

Anwar waved from a distance, and I waved back. We were warming up before the game when Anwar jogged up to me and said, 'Great going, but you won't be able to score today.'

'I saw Nemai and you have been selected for the junior India camp.'

Anwar merely smiled at that and left. Nemai didn't come anywhere near me. Running my way to collect a stray ball, Ratan said, 'Be careful today.'

'Why?'

'Trust me.'

I tried to make sense of what he had said but couldn't. There were three minutes to go to half-time when I finally understood what he had meant. As our right-out crossed the ball inside the Shobhabajar box, I ran to meet it, with Tikadar running alongside me. The ball had bounced two yards away. What should I do? A volley would take it miles over the crossbar. The only way out was a diving header. As the goalkeeper charged out, I felt Anwar's boots thudding to my left and decided to fling myself forward.

No sooner had my head made contact with the ball than I felt a sharp pain as though someone had plunged a knife into my ribs. Tikadar had kicked me. I felt as if I was about to pass out, unable to breathe with the pain. Through it all, I heard a long whistle from the referee.

I was brought out and made to lie down by the touchline. They had taken off my jersey to rub my chest with ice. The first thing I saw on opening my eyes was Pintu's tearful face. Trying to reassure him with a raised hand, I felt a stab of pain in my ribs. All I could do was smile. Dashu-da and Kamal-da were leaning over me. It was half-time.

'Did I score?' I spoke slowly.

'You did,' Kamal-da said.

'Anyone take my place yet?'

'Sushanto will.'

'Stop him,' I sat up hurriedly. 'I'm fine, I can play.'

'You don't have to play, Prasoon.'

Turning to see who had spoken, I saw Anwar's ruddy face in front of me. 'Another blow and you'll be out for the entire season.'

I instantly flew into a rage. 'That's what you people are trying to ensure. Cowards!'

At that, Anwar stormed off without another word, his eyes blazing.

'Think you can make it? I have no objection if you can,' said Dashu-da.

'But Dashu-da…' Kamal-da's words trailed away as Dashu-da signalled to him to keep quiet. 'Anwar-da picked you up single-handedly and brought you out,' whispered Pintu. 'How strong he is!'

Back on the ground, I could hardly move from the pain. The ball was in our defending zone. Although Nemai kept dribbling past our players and sending passes, the Shobhabajar forwards kept wasting them. Eventually Nemai equalized himself, as I knew he would – for the Shonali defence was not capable of stopping him. With eight of our players crowding our box, he sent three defenders the wrong way with a single shimmy down the middle, following it up with a weave to the left and then to the right, and ended with a tiny chip that left our off-balance goalkeeper gaping helplessly as the ball went in.

Trying a couple of runs, I realized I couldn't do it. Despite Tikadar sticking to me like a shadow, I attempted to reach the top of their box by playing wall-passes with the right-half. Dribbling past the right stopper-back who tried a tackle on me, I found myself face-to-face with their left-half. I pushed the ball to the left, where our left-out had timed his run well, and ran into the invitingly unguarded space behind Anwar. Our left-out then passed the ball to our left-back, who in turn looked around for someone to pass to. Then, seeing me wave, he sent me the ball just as four Shobhabajar players came running towards me.

I was unable to trap the approaching ball, however, and watched with frustration as it deflected off my feet into Anwar's path. I knew that Anwar was bound to kick it into the gallery seeing that he had little other option. But I tried to reclaim it anyway, whereupon Anwar suddenly hesitated. All of a sudden, I found myself and Tikadar rushing towards the ball at the same time.

'Aaah!'

There was a muted cry of pain and I looked down to see both Anwar and Tikadar rolling on the ground. With the goal just six yards away, I swiftly collected the ball that had run loose and finished the job with a small tap of the foot. Turning around to find Tikadar still writhing in agony and clutching his stomach, I looked enquiringly at Anwar.

'What on earth?'

'What business is it of yours?'

Bipin-da ran screaming on to the pitch. 'I'll suspend you! Hitting your own teammate, you swine. You think I don't understand you were trying to do your friend a favour?'

I moved away in embarrassment. Ratan nodded at me, as though he knew something like this was going to happen. Shobhabajar lost its way after Tikadar was carted out. And with our right-out scoring two goals in succession, Dashu-da soon waved me off the field.

That night, the pain in my chest began. I called Ma. I guessed Pintu must have told her the story. Why else would the first thing she said to me have been 'Why did you have to score so *dangerously*? Why do things that make them kick you in the chest?'

Hearing her use the English word 'dangerously' made me laugh. She must have been echoing Pintu. 'The only way to score is dangerously,' I said. Grumbling, she went to fetch hot oil. Later, rubbing the oil into my chest, I heard her mutter, 'Football is going to kill me.'

17

The pain was worse the next morning. But the only thing I was scared of was my hard work during the year going to waste. Dashu-da would drop me from the team if he found out that I had been badly injured. And I hadn't even played any of the big teams yet. We had a match against Kidderpore in two days. If I stayed away from training that day and the next, someone was bound to come looking for me and discover the truth.

Thinking it over, I decided to tell Dashu-da or Kamal-da that I'd had to go out of town for my aunt's wedding. But whom could I send word through? Pintu, the only one available, wasn't yet grown-up enough to go as far as Dashu-da's home in Kalighat or Kamal-da's in Garia. I didn't know Dashu-da's phone number – or even his real name. Harsho-da might know, however. So I dispatched Pintu to Harsho-da's home, warning him not to reveal anything about my injury, or else I'd never again take him to watch a game.

Pintu did get hold of the phone number. But then came the problem of whom to get to make the phone call. Calling Nilima, I explained the whole thing to her. She nodded and went out immediately with the number, returning after half an hour. My heart leapt to my throat at the sound of her returning and I glanced towards the door.

Nemai and Anwar were also standing there with grim expressions on their faces.

Pressing my chest lightly with his thick fingers, Anwar nodded at Nemai on seeing my face twist in agony. Nemai nodded too, after which the two of them whispered briefly before Nemai went out, saying to Anwar as he left, 'Can you help him on with a shirt? We need to take him to a doctor.'

I just stared at him without a word. Propping me up in bed without paying the slightest attention to my protests, Anwar asked, 'Can you walk?' I nodded. In the meantime, Nemai had got hold of a taxi. The two of them helped me into the taxi and we headed off towards Shyambazar.

I didn't have a fracture. Without an X-ray, however, there was no way to tell whether there was a crack. The doctor bandaged my chest very tightly, warning me to stay in bed and not move around. We took a taxi back home, none of us talking. When I saw Nilima I asked her angrily, 'Who asked you to go and call them?'

'I made the phone call. Said you're going to be away for two weeks.' Nilima gestured to me to stay in bed and went out.

The X-ray report revealed nothing.

I stayed in bed through five games – against Kidderpore, Eastern Railway, Mohammedan Sporting, Kalighat and Rajasthan – out of which we lost three and drew two. I couldn't stay in bed any longer, so the morning after the game with Rajasthan I tried to run and exercise a little – there was no problem. So I went to the club tent in the afternoon, the day before the game against Sporting Union. Scolding me mildly for staying away so long, Dashu-da said the team list was ready and that I was on it. The player who had replaced me hadn't made any headway at all.

I played the game carefully, without taking any risks – practically without running. We won 3-0. I scored two goals with shots off well-directed passes from the edge of the box. The next match was with BNR. I was excited at the thought of testing my skills against the famous Arun Ghosh. But I was very disappointed and felt almost deprived when I heard he wouldn't be playing against us.

I stunned everyone by scoring twice within nine minutes against BNR. They had probably imagined that a lowly placed team like Shonali would play a defensive game. But instead, we went after them from the beginning. Five minutes into the game, I volleyed the ball into the net from a punch made by their goalkeeper to a cross from our right-out. The second goal was almost identical. Although BNR managed to settle down after that and corner us, they still couldn't score, with our goalkeeper Robi making four spectacular saves.

The next match was against Juger Jatri, the team which was heading the League, not having dropped a single point. Mohun Bagan had lost to Eastern Railway, while East Bengal had drawn its game against Rajasthan.

Although I had played only five matches so far, the buzz on the Maidan and in club tents was all about me. Apparently people were even discussing which of the big clubs I'd head for next season, and at what price. With eleven goals in five games, I was the top scorer in the Calcutta League so far that season, followed by Ashim Moulik with ten from ten and Ashok Chatterjee with eight from eleven.

18

Nilima had passed her final school examinations, although in the second division. Even before I was up that morning, there was a hubbub all over the house. Our landlord Bishu Datta was shouting, 'Treat, treat, Nutu-babu!'

'Of course, of course. What would you like?'

'Rabri. From Burrabazar.'

Emerging from my room, I saw Nilima touching my mother's feet in respect and then entering my parents' room, where Baba was. 'Do you have any money?' Ma asked me. 'I want to buy her a sari. How hard she's worked!'

'Doesn't Baba have any?'

'Just about enough for this month's expenses.'

'I have about twelve rupees. Is that enough for a sari?'

'Never mind, later then,' Ma said after some thought.

'How much older than me is Prasoon?' asked Nilima, emerging from the room. 'More than six months?'

'About that much.' Ma smiled.

Nilima then bent to touch my feet as well in the traditional display of respect – an act which embarrassed me fearfully, making my head spin as though I had missed a goal from a distance of four yards before a stadium full of people. Passing exams clearly made you take leave of your senses. I escaped, stammering, just as I heard Nilima say, 'I'd have won a scholarship if I had studied as hard as Prasoon practises.'

I peeped out later to see Nilima heading for the bathroom, bucket in hand, and called to her.

'And so to college?'

'Yes, I need to get hold of the money though. Nearly a hundred rupees.'

I shrank back, wondering if she was going to ask me to repay the money I had borrowed from her. 'I want to buy you a gift,' I said hurriedly. 'I wish I had enough money.'

As Nilima was about to respond, Pintu entered.

'Someone's calling for you, Dada. Says it's urgent.'

I found a fair man in his forties with light eyes and a colourful bush shirt waiting for me outside. As soon as he saw me he said, in a very familiar manner, 'I need to talk to you, Prasoon – can we go for a spin?'

'Whatever it is, you can tell me right here. I'm a little busy, can't go anywhere.'

Pointing to a Fiat, the man said, 'Why don't we go for a drive? I'll tell you in the car. I need to tell you something in private.'

I couldn't stand the way he spoke, and the prospect of talking to him privately was even less appealing. 'You can talk to me in private right here, no one can hear.'

Looking around him, he cleared his throat and then whispered, 'Don't play in tomorrow's game.'

'Not play against Jatri!' I practically screamed. 'What do you mean!'

'I know how much you earn from Shonali – a hundred a month. I keep track, I keep track of every club.' He suddenly pulled out a hundred-rupee note from his pocket and, grabbing my hand, thrust it into my fist. 'Of course you'll play if you want to. It's just that after twenty or twenty-five years, we finally have a chance to win a major trophy in Calcutta. Please don't get in the way of that tomorrow.'

I was still in a state of shock. 'Me come in the way?'

'You're the one we're scared of, Prasoon. All the big clubs fear you – Mohun Bagan, East Bengal, Mohammedan, all of them. Just don't score tomorrow, please.'

Slowly recovering from my stupor, I put the hundred-rupee note back in his pocket and said, 'Not now. Why don't you come home with me and give it to my father?'

'What does your father do for a living?' he asked, hesitating.

'He's jobless. The factory he used to work in has been shut down after a lockout.'

'So these are difficult times for you,' he said, pleased, touching his pocket. 'You should help your family out.'

Without another word, I took him directly to Baba's room, where Nilima was explaining the difficulties of getting admission to a college. Without any preamble I said, 'Baba, we're playing Juger Jatri tomorrow. This gentleman is offering me a hundred rupees not to play, or not to score even if I play.'

I spoke so abruptly that not only Baba and Nilima but also the man with light eyes stiffened. Finally Baba asked softly, 'Who're you playing against?'

'Juger Jatri.' I thought I saw Baba's eyes flash. My gaze was involuntarily drawn to his forehead.

Looking downwards, Baba replied, 'I don't know. I'm not going to say anything. You can decide for yourself whether to accept the bribe or not.'

Baba raised his eyes to look at me. I felt a tremor in my breast. Nilima was trying to say something. I hesitated. And then I heard a voice within me saying, 'Prasoon, look at your father's humiliation written on his forehead. It's you who must put the mark of victory there – yes, you.'

'I *shall* defeat Jatri tomorrow,' I said through clenched teeth, and then shouted at the top of my voice, 'Get out!'

Surprised but not scared, the man left with a smile, saying, 'Maybe you will score, but can you stop us from scoring? Don't forget that football is a game with eleven players.'

Sitting in my cubbyhole with my back against the wall and head between my knees, I felt someone coming towards me. Raising my head, I saw Nilima looking down at me. 'Did Baba say anything more?' I asked her eagerly.

'No. But I did see him wipe away a tear much later.'

'Didn't I do the right thing, Nilima?'

Nilima spoke softly, gently. 'You've given us such a wonderful gift, Prasoon. Oh, how wonderful it is. I'm sure you'll play brilliantly tomorrow. And win.'

19

The next day I was reminded of the harsh truth that football is a game with eleven players.

And I learnt another lesson too – never claim that you'll win. We lost 2-3 to Jatri. I hadn't imagined there would be so big a crowd. Most of them were Mohun Bagan and East Bengal fans who had become Shonali fans for the day because they wanted Jatri to lose. They were all hoping for a miracle from me.

But Jatri was no Shobhabajar. They had an extremely tight and well-organized defence. Their left-half Amiyo and right stopper-back Dulal had played for India in the Merdeka tournament the previous year. On one of his good days, their goalkeeper Shyam wouldn't even let a fly into his goal, although no one could predict when these good days would be – not even Shyam himself.

Bishnu, the right-in, had been selected for the junior India camp that year. His ball control was extremely good, although not as good as Nemai's. Yet he was much more hard-working than Nemai and could play deep into his own half as well as the opponent's. He was not a very intelligent player on the whole, however. Abraham, the left-out, was easily the fastest winger in Calcutta. Ninety per cent of the shots that he took with his left foot from the corner of the penalty box went into the net. The diminutive Shivaraman, the left-in, was a very cunning forward who skulked around inside the penalty box. It was impossible to fathom just when he would steal a goal. He never gave his opponents any opportunity to realize he was no longer as young as he used to be.

We had vowed to play like desperados. During the first fifteen minutes, both sides played a cautious midfield game. Then Bishnu suddenly made a sortie with the ball towards our goal, chased by our right-half. He moved towards the left-hand corner flag, while Abraham cut inside. Bishnu gave a back-pass to Amiyo, who passed onwards to Abraham, who in turn look a weak, low shot from twenty yards. Robi, the Shonali goalkeeper, dived for the ball but couldn't reach it. It seemed to me that Robi had intentionally dived late. I remembered what Light Eyes had told me. 'Maybe you will score, but can you stop us from scoring?'

I was shocked. So they *had* found people at Shonali for sale at a hundred rupees. But I didn't know just how many of our players they'd managed to buy. And now I suspected everyone. When the right-out sent a ball out of play whilst trying to trap it, I was suspicious. If he'd been able to control it he was bound to have passed it to me, because I was in an excellent position. Then when Abraham tried to dribble past our right-back and failed, the right-back took so long looking for someone to pass the ball to that Abraham snatched it back – and I was even more suspicious. Every time someone from Shonali made a mistake, my suspicions grew stronger.

Two minutes before half-time, Jatri scored their second goal. Starting a fabulous move from the right, Abraham ended it on the left. The ball entered the goal like a cannonball, just near the junction of the crossbar and the upright, giving Robi no chance whatsoever. At half-time, I shared my suspicions with Dashu-da, telling him of the previous day's events. Dashu-da went up to Robi to talk to him. Robi looked stunned. As Robi started to argue with him, waving his hands frantically in the air, Dashu-da signalled to Ajit, the reserve goalkeeper, to warm up. Robi turned pale.

I scored within half a minute into the second half. Picking up the ball on the centre line, I dribbled past three players and took the shot from sixteen yards away. Shyam hadn't ever imagined that a ball that seemed as if it would miss the goal by at least three yards could curve wickedly at the last moment and go in. A huge roar of applause shook the East Bengal ground, making it the loudest ever reception to a goal I'd scored. Three minutes later, our right-out raced upfield and sent a cross. With Shyam delaying his charge by a couple of seconds, I waited for the ball to bounce and swiftly half-volleyed it into the net.

A thunderclap seemed to shake the stands and lightning strike the ground. At least five teammates were trying to climb on to my shoulders, making it impossible to breathe. The only cry that could be heard from the galleries after this was, 'Give the ball to Prasoon.'

As Jatri started attacking with renewed fervour, we dropped back one by one to stem the tide. The pressure kept mounting. The inexperienced Ajit was playing the game of his life. I noticed two Jatri players tailing me all the time. After sixty-five minutes, Jatri could be denied no more. Bishnu's header from Amiyo's chip rebounded off the crossbar. But in trying to clear the ball, the right-back only managed to miskick it into Bishnu's path again, allowing Bishnu to score easily.

We lost. Despite the murmurs of 'Well played, Prasoon' and 'Bravo, Prasoon' as we left the ground, I was not feeling triumphant. My arrogant claim to my father of beating Jatri had come to naught. Someone patted my back lightly and said, 'You really scared us, you know.' I turned and saw Light Eyes disappear into the crowd.

I had wanted to say a few things to Robi back at the tent but didn't get the chance to do so. He sat in one corner for a while, apparently lost in thought, and then left the tent silently. Since Pintu was with me, I left soon as well. In the bus on the way back, Pintu said, 'Nemai-da was sitting in front of me. When this other fellow in the stands abused you, Nemai-da slapped him.'

'Was Anwar there?'

'Yes. He kept saying, "If you'd been there, Nemai, Prasoon would have got two or three more goals."'

'What did Nemai say?'

'Nothing.'

Back home, I switched off the lights and went to bed. Pintu had told everyone the score. Ma came in and went out again. I fell asleep without dinner.

20

Eventually Jatri didn't become the League champions, as a court injunction prevented the IFA Shield from being completed.

But the most significant event for me occurred at the start of the following year. Mohun Bagan, East Bengal and Juger Jatri all wanted to sign me up. My heart was with Mohun Bagan, but I had heard they were also signing on Habib and Sukalyan, while East Bengal had picked up Subhash. Even as I was absorbed in the dilemma of whether to join any of them or not, with doubts over whether I'd even get a game given the presence of all these great players, Jatri suddenly offered me six thousand rupees.

The discussion took place at Jatri secretary Anadi Biswas's home. Also present was Light Eyes, who, I learnt later, was universally referred to as Daku-da. A member of the selection committee, he spent about Rs 10,000 of his own on club expenses/hiring every year and thus commanded even more respect than the club secretary. Apparently, it was he who had specifically asked for me.

'Since you're Anil Bhattacharya's son, Jatri naturally has a special claim on you,' the secretary said and glanced over at Daku-da, who merely nodded in reply. 'It's only natural that the son should play for the same club as the father. Besides…' the secretary paused, looked again at Daku-da, cleared his throat and continued, 'Jatri wasn't fair to your father. I know that – though I was just an ordinary member back then. I watched that particular final – how well your father played, I can still see it now. And yet, imagine him having to suffer such calumny. We must atone for that, I must do it personally.' He choked with emotion. I was swayed by the praise for my father, which proved that not everyone believed the slur on his name.

'We're planning to build a young team this year. Most of our team are getting on now, which is why we want to replace them with youngsters like you. We won't hire players from other states this time. We want you to snatch the team slots from these geriatrics. Once you've passed your school final exams, we'll get you a bank job as well. You can stay at the chummery – great food, a comfortable life and top performance on the field. At this age, there are so many possibilities lying ahead of you.' I was overwhelmed by the sincerity in his voice.

'No one except us will offer you six thousand right now,' said Daku-da, examining his nails. 'This isn't a bribe though.'

I was embarrassed. 'I just want to earn honestly.'

'Of course, that's the spirit!' The secretary slapped the table and rose. Glancing at his watch, Daku-da added, 'So there it is, Prasoon. Think it over – you have a month to make up your mind.'

I went directly to Dashu-da's home. Once he had heard the whole story, he said, 'You should go to Jatri. I'm not going to ask you to stay on in Shonali. Football is everything for you. You should sign for a big club now. But be careful, for you'll find as much politics there as money. And that Daku is not a nice man – he's harmed a lot of young players, ruining their careers.'

'What harm can he do to me? If my game can speak for itself, who can stop me? Whatever progress I've made is on the strength of my game. That's what will take me further,' I said confidently.

'I do hope it does.' Dashu-da smiled.

I signed for Jatri, getting two thousand rupees from Daku-da the same day. The rest would be paid in four instalments over the year. Two days later, I read in the papers that Anwar and Nemai had signed for Jatri too, and was thrilled.

I had told Dashu-da that no one would be able to come in my way as long as my game spoke for itself. But how was I going to prove myself if I didn't even get a chance to play? I spent Jatri's first five games on the bench. I didn't get a game apparently because of my inexperience. It seemed that I wasn't even good enough to play against average teams like Bally Protibha or Kalighat. Jatri's committee members fretted over these games as much as they did over the big ones. They didn't dare to field newer, relatively inexperienced players, because it was the committee who would be blamed if the match ended in a draw and caused a loss of points. It was safer to continue with senior players who could assume all responsibility in the event of an adverse result.

Anwar didn't get a chance to play in the first two games either. But after a good game against Bally, he found a permanent place on the team. Nemai played half of that game and half of the next one against Kidderpore. Having picked up a knee injury ten minutes into the game against Kalighat, Sivaraman was substituted with Nemai, who went on to score two goals and simply could not be dropped after that.

One day I asked the coach, Priyo-da, impatiently, 'Did you sign me up just to bench me?'

'My hands are tied,' the non-confrontational Priyo-da replied after looking around furtively. 'The team is finalized by the selection committee, which basically means Daku-da. He doesn't pay any attention to us. You'd better ask him.'

I cornered Daku-da the very same day. There was a small clique of players that he favoured, two of whom, Bishnu and Abraham, were chatting with him on the lawn outside the tent. 'Daku-da, why did you sign me on if you won't give me a game?' I asked him directly.

'You'll get a game when the team needs you,' he answered, looking at his nails.

'And when will that be?'

'I don't know. You may not even be needed this season.'

'Then why did you spend so much money on me? My skills are rusting,' I said miserably.

'A club like Jatri won't go bankrupt simply because it has to pay a couple of players like you and keep them on the bench. Since you're playing for money, why worry so long as you get paid?' He looked away in irritation.

Then Bishnu turned to me and said, 'Later, Prasoon, we're busy now.'

I walked away glumly. Nemai was laughing and joking with a couple of players inside the tent – young men from clearly affluent families. They went out with Nemai quite often in the evenings. Nemai looked at me briefly and then resumed his conversation. Anwar wasn't there that day. Leaving the club, I walked down to the riverside.

Staring into the water, I remembered the festivities that had taken place the day I had arrived home with the two thousand rupees from Jatri. Pintu, Putul and Nilima had all crowded around me. And even Bishu Datta had come downstairs. But Baba hadn't been in.

'My God, if only I'd known you could earn so much from football, I'd have flogged a ball when I was young,' Bishu Datta had told me.

'Not everyone can get there, Mr Datta,' Nutu-da had replied, speaking in a tone aimed at belittling Bishu Datta. 'This is a gift from God. We should organize a reception for Prasoon.'

'But we deserve a treat first. How about it, Prasoon?'

Ma had immediately handed over some money to Bishu Datta and he had gone shopping. Everyone was invited. 'Now I can pay back all my debts,' I had told Nilima proudly 'Now I'm in college too – the college of football.'

Baba usually came back home late. So I had stayed awake that night. Surely Ma would tell him, I said to myself, wondering how he would react and whether he would be pleased – or whether he would look the other way, as usual. When Baba eventually returned home, I heard Ma talking to him in the other room. Then the lights went out. The next morning, I asked Ma whether or not she had told him. 'He was astonished,' she had answered. 'He said, "I didn't earn that much even after seven years of playing football."'

21

The first time I met Anwar and Nemai at Jatri was the day before practice began. Sitting stiffly next to the two of them, I listened to Priyo-da deliver a smallish lecture on football and realized that I hardly knew any of the other twenty or so players gathered in the dressing room. Next to Priyo-da sat Daku-da, who also said a few words on the glorious tradition of Juger Jatri and our responsibility to uphold it.

'Football is a very simple game, unless you choose to complicate it,' Priyo-da told us as a preface to his speech. 'Despite being such a great club and a team with so much tradition behind us, we've never managed to win either the Calcutta League or the IFA Shield. We did manage to get to the Shield final once, but…' And at that moment, Daku-da paused to look at me – as did everyone else in the room.

From the expressions on their faces, one would think that they were looking at a strange beast. Some were sneering, whilst others were laughing quietly. I broke out in a sweat, my eyes downcast. It appeared that Daku-da had deliberately put me on the spot – as though he was taking revenge for something. Suddenly Nemai said, 'One team or the other has to lose in the final. We'll get Jatri into the final again, and we'll win the Shield too.' Nemai looked around at everyone, but Anwar was the only one who responded, saying, 'Of course we will.'

Nemai lived in the chummery at Beleghata with four other Jatri players. Anwar and I lived there too, until the Calcutta League began. Every day after morning training finished, I would return home annoyed and disappointed at not having played a single game yet. And in no circumstances did I even speak to the other players at the chummery.

In particular, I avoided Nemai and Anwar. We'd talk if we happened to meet – but even then we would only engage in small talk. The old intimacy was gone forever. I could see that they wanted us to be the Three Musketeers again, but I wouldn't let that happen. Ever since Daku-da had raised the issue of the IFA Shield final, I had withdrawn into a shell.

Nobody discussed football at home. When I left home in the afternoon on match days, the only person I thought of was Pintu. But he was in school at that hour. And even when he was home, he didn't fuss about coming to watch the game. He understood my situation. Nilima and Ma didn't say anything either. They treated me the same way people do when someone in the family has failed an exam despite studying very hard. The only person who had said anything was Bishu Datta, who had called out to me one day from the balcony: 'How come we don't see your name in the papers any more, Prasoon?'

Sitting by the river now, I didn't know when I had started crying. I slowly let out the sighs that had accumulated in my breast, letting them mingle with the cooling breeze on the river. A voice whispered in my ear, 'Don't give up. Don't lose hope. Be ready. Strike when the time is right.' I shook my head. I wouldn't be able to do it. I took the last bus home from the bus stop next to Eden Gardens.

Jatri was up 5-0 against Howrah Union, with about ten minutes to go to the final whistle, when Daku-da beckoned to Priyo-da, who then came up to me and said, 'Warm up, Prasoon.'

I was amazed. Was my luck about to turn at last? Priyo-da substituted me for right-out Salil Kar. I trembled as I touched the ground with my fingertips and brought them to my forehead. Running up to me, Nemai said, 'I'll make sure you get the ball. Just make sure you score!'

Within half a minute Nemai dispatched the ball to me, midway down Howrah's half. Although I ran for it, I couldn't get to it. There was a titter in the stands. I felt uncomfortable. Everything seemed different. I couldn't gauge the distance between myself and the other players. It all seemed so unclear – when I should start my run, where the free space was or even where the ball would come from.

Things that had been crystal clear to me after years of studying suddenly slipped out of my mind. It was exactly as though I hadn't been in touch with my books for a while. Overcome with anxiety – after all, the final whistle was only minutes away, which left very little time to achieve anything – I shouted for the ball, wondering if I'd be able to dodge past three or four of them.

A roll of laughter rose from the stands as I fell flat on my face after getting past one of the defenders. Not only could I no longer sense the ball at my feet as I used to, I couldn't even figure out whether the ball was still with me. I no longer had any idea how to take those half-turns, or how to feint or dodge.

As Nemai moved towards the corner flag on the right, I entered the penalty box. Dribbling past the left-back, he pushed the ball towards me, saying, 'Give it back,' as he ran forward with the stopper shadowing him. As I mis-passed directly to the stopper instead of him, the galleries roared their disapproval. Looking sadly at me, Nemai said, 'Don't get rattled. Be steady.'

Since we were leading by five goals, my stupidity and incompetence caused a good deal of sniggering amongst the spectators. With nothing left in the game, their cruelty was showing. Piling on one mistake after another, I felt as if I was drowning. Bishnu laughed, hands on hips, while Amiyo said, 'Hey, pass the ball to Prasoon.' The crowds convulsed with laughter. Even a couple of Howrah Union defenders couldn't contain their smiles upon seeing me shoot Nemai's defence-splitting pass like a bullet four yards wide of the post. I sank to the ground, covering my face with my hands. The final whistle blew. Feeling someone pat me on the back, I looked up to see Nemai walking away.

I didn't visit the Jatri tent any more during the Calcutta League. They sent people for me. Sivaraman had accumulated fluid in his knees and was going to be out of action for the rest of the season. Under tremendous pressure, Nemai and Bishnu hadn't been able to rest for a single game. When one of them was unfit, Dipak-da, who had started playing thirteen years ago but could no longer manage a whole game, had been forced to take their place. Among the newcomers, I saw Soumen and Balai mentioned in the papers

Jatri finished fourth in the League, the high point being the draw with Mohun Bagan. Nemai had scored first, with Pranab Ganguly equalizing for Mohun Bagan from the penalty spot. With no Jatri supporters among reporters, the newspapers offered no clue about Nemai's performance. I was sure Nemai must have been pleased as Punch to have scored against Mohun Bagan.

I was practising with Pintu in my makeshift school by the factory when Nemai and Anwar appeared. I stared at them in surprise. Dressed in colourful shirts, they had grown their hair and their sideburns, and were sporting expensive sandals and foreign watches.

'How come we don't see you at the tent any more?' asked Nemai.

'You know very well why not.' I smiled faintly.

'These things happen. You'll get your skills back as soon as you come back to the ground and start practising,' Anwar said. 'Why are you ruining your game, knocking around with kids in this tiny space?'

I could have argued with them but didn't bother. 'I'll come,' I said. 'Is training on?'

'Of course it is. The Shield games are about to begin. We need you – we don't have any other forwards. Bishnu played the last few games with an injury – another blow and he'll be out for the count.' Nemai was looking at his watch as he spoke.

'Think Daku-da will let me play a game?'

'You have to make a start somewhere. Then we'll see. It won't do you any good to stay away from the Maidan. Will you come tomorrow morning?'

My heart began to beat even harder. Just hearing the words Maidan, Shield, football got the adrenaline going. But even as my secret desire to play in the IFA Shield reared its head, so did the echo of the mocking laughter from the Jatri stands. 'I'm scared,' I blurted out.

They were astonished. 'Scared? Of what? Of the public? All it needs is one goal for them to start cheering for you again,' said Anwar.

'I'll make sure you get your goals,' added Nemai. Then, looking at his watch again, he said, 'We're getting late, Anwar. Raju and the rest are waiting for us. Tomorrow, Prasoon?'

When they left, I thought about how the Anwar and Nemai I used to know wouldn't have spoken to me so formally, nor abandoned me to go off with other friends. Thinking about what they had said, I concluded that they were right – I was going nowhere playing with kids on this tiny pitch. I had to get to the full-sized grounds of the Maidan, to the thousands of people who came to watch, to the excitement and anticipation in the air. I had to absorb it all into my mind and into my body.

I decided to resume training with Jatri.

22

As soon as Jatri entered the final I realized only too well how many friends and relatives I had. A ticket, a ticket, just one ticket. 'Prasoon, you were so young then, how you've grown…', 'Prasoon, remember what you said?', 'Prasoon-da, I won't give up, there will be a hunger strike at your door, I won't let you go to the stadium…'

I was being deafened. I sidestepped them with smiles: 'I'll see.', 'I'll try.'

Juger Jatri was in the IFA Shield final after twenty years, after beating Mohammedan Sporting 1-0 in the semi-final. The scorer, unbelievable but true: Prasoon Bhattacharya.

Bishnu and I played one half each in Jatri's first match in the tournament, against Cuttack Combined. In the second round Bishnu was limping. Priyo-da replaced him with me. We won 3-0, with one of the goals being mine. As soon as Nemai's header from Amiyo's long throw landed at my feet, I half-volleyed it into the net from twelve yards out. The goalkeeper didn't even move. In the third round we beat Vasco from Goa 2-0. I couldn't score; the goals came from Salil and Abraham.

In the other half of the draw Rangoon United had entered the quarter-final. They beat Jalandhar Leaders 2-1 to enter the semi-final. This was the first football match I watched in Eden Gardens. The Rangoon centre-forward and right-half impressed me. Those were the only names I could remember: Mongba and Lee Sun.

Mongba was quite old, at least thirty-five. Rangoon were restless after conceding a goal, their game becoming temporarily undisciplined. Mongba held on to the ball, dodging past opponents calmly and distributing passes. The way he used his control over the ball to slow down the game till the team had regrouped earned my respect.

Lee Sun was a veteran too, retreating all the way to his own penalty box and then going upfield with the ball. Quickly pushing the ball to a teammate, Lee San sped up like a bullet to collect the return-pass, two defenders going the wrong way. He could shoot perfectly with both feet, and rose higher than the field when it came to heading the ball. I was told both of them had been left out of the Burmese team this year.

We went into the semi-final beating Aryan and Sikh Regimental Centre. I couldn't score in either game. Mohammedan Sporting drew twice before beating East Bengal 1-0 to line up a semi-final match against us. The other semi-final would be played between Mohun Bagan and Rangoon United.

We were put up at the club president's house in Park Circus the night before the match. A huge hall on the second floor had been set aside for us. Abraham, Shyam, Amiyo and some others played cards late into the night. Standing in the veranda in the morning, I thought I spotted Tikadar from Shobhabajar entering through the gate. A little later Priyo-da drew two of the senior players aside with a grim expression.

After lunch Shyam whispered to me in a corner, 'There's some terrible news, Prasoon – apparently Anwar has been bought off.'

I was stunned. Unimaginable and a complete lie. 'I don't believe it,' I said.

'It's not a question of whether it's true or not. But when there's a rumour about someone just before a game they have to be dropped. The trouble is, the match is against Mohammedan Sporting and Anwar is a Muslim. It's easy for everyone to believe it.'

'Where did the news come from?'

'There were two anonymous phone calls in the morning, and besides, Tikadar came to tell us that he had seen Anwar come out of Grand Hotel the day before yesterday with two Mohammedan officials.'

'That's a lie!' I screamed. 'Anwar and I left the tent together the day before yesterday and went home. This is Tikadar's doing, he's trying to take revenge.'

Rushing into the room, I saw Daku-da and Priyo-da standing grimly. The rest were astonished, some silent and taken aback, one or two people speaking softly. Anwar was sitting in a corner, leaning against the wall.

'It's best for Anwar not to play today,' said Daku-da. 'It's hard to play when your mind is not at peace.'

'Of course he will play.' There was something in my voice that jolted everyone. 'Why should we bow to lies and rumours?'

'If Jatri loses today, and if the goal is because of Anwar's mistake, do you realize what will happen to him and to us?' asked Daku-da. I had never seen him so worried.

I looked at Nemai. He had been listening in silence. He said, 'Jatri won't lose if Anwar plays.'

Clearing his throat, Shyam said, 'Anwar will play today. Else let someone else keep goal.'

'Anwar must play,' said Abraham.

Hearing a thud, we turned to see Anwar had slumped to the floor, unconscious.

Anwar played that afternoon. I may have scored the goal, but that was the first time I learnt how one man can battle an entire team. We left the field with Anwar on our shoulders. In the entire match,

Shyam had to touch the ball just twice. I saw Anwar four times in the Mohammedan penalty box, when he came up to try to score.

Mohun Bagan lost 0-2 to Rangoon United the next day.

23

I couldn't sleep that night. There were less than forty hours to go before the IFA Shield final. We were supposed to meet at the president's house the next morning, before being taken to Eden Gardens to play the final. I kept tossing and turning in bed, kept awake by a combination of restlessness and excitement, as well as fear and hope that ran like a current all through my body and made my head throb. Suddenly someone entered my room. Even in the dark, I knew it was Ma.

Sitting down by my side, she cradled my head and said, 'Can't sleep.'

I knew it wasn't a question – she was informing me. 'Mmm,' I said and rested my head on her lap.

'I know. This is how it is. I know only too well what a final match is.'

'Didn't Baba say anything? What did he say about me playing the final for Jatri?'

'He's tossing and turning in his bed, just like you.'

As Ma lightly ran her hand all over my body, sleep slowly started to descend on me. My body was giving in, languor creeping all over me. A scent of grass and wet earth rose from my mother, suffusing the room. I felt as though I was in the game already. Drowsily I said, 'I'll send you tickets tomorrow, you must come for the game.'

I began to weave and roll as I went forward with the black-and-white ball in my mind. I leapt, I ran suddenly, I fell and then rose again. In Ma's breast I could hear the sound of huge waves crashing, as though a torrent of floodwater was rushing through a breach in a dam.

'Your father's going to be playing too, son. Through you he will get back what he lost. You'll win, for sure you'll win.'

Ma's voice faded away gradually, only to be replaced by a giant roar. I felt as if it was going to sweep me away. Where would I flee, where would I find some shelter? I cried out for help, 'Striker, striker!'

The roar became even louder and enveloped me.

So many people – at least sixty or seventy thousand. All of them roared in unison as soon as my shot kissed the Rangoon cross-post and went out of play. I'd taken the shot from thirty-five yards out. All of a sudden.

Priyo-da was waving his arms like a lunatic from the sidelines, signalling to me to fall back. He had told me hundreds of times that morning, 'Gopal is going to stick like a shadow to their number ten. You need to fall back and cover his space. Lee Sun is the dangerous one – if we can block him, their attack will lose its edge.'

Lee Sun was weaving to the left and to the right, taking Gopal along with him. Gaping holes were appearing in our defence. I simply couldn't fathom which of them to try and plug. In the process of robbing their offence of its edge, our own had become blunt as well. Every time I moved up, Priyo-da waved me back. Eventually I told Nemai, 'They're bound to score if we go on like this. We need to get the ball into their box. If we don't pile on the pressure, there's no way we can take theirs.'

Just as I was saying this, they scored. Rangoon's left-winger sent a cross from the corner flag. Gopal was kept busy by Lee Sun. Their left-back, who had moved up into the open space, took a shot while the ball was still rolling, and it thundered in, brushing the left post. All of Eden Gardens fell quiet. You could only hear some scattered applause. The game was barely twenty minutes old.

Placing the ball on the kick-off spot, Nemai said, 'Move up. Don't even look at Priyo-da any more.'

Fifteen minutes later, the ball was passed from Nemai to Abraham, and then back to Nemai, who dodged past two of their players and reverse-passed to me. I smelt a goal. All of Eden Gardens was on its feet, chanting ferociously, 'G...o...a...l, g...o...a...l!' The goal was in my sights. I could see a small gap between their stopper and their wing-back. I hesitated – what if the ball didn't go through? Better to get a little closer. And that was my mistake. At the precise moment I tapped the ball to begin my run, Mongba's perfect sliding tackle brought me down on the pitch. The stopper snatched the ball away.

When I got back to my feet, screams of disappointment were streaming down from the gallery. As I walked back, my head bowed, someone shouted, 'Remember who his father was?' I looked up.

Anwar was playing an incredible game, as was Amiyo. It was one of those days when our goalkeeper Shyam was like a man possessed. He had saved three sure-fire goals and got the Jatri defence all charged up. He was virtually plucking out the crosses from the heads of the forwards on the eighteen-yard line, and even charging out of the penalty box several times to clear the ball. After we conceded the goal, Nemai and Salil both abandoned me and retreated midway down Jatri's own half.

Standing midway in the Rangoon half all by myself, I was suddenly beset by the fear that the spectators would jump on to the pitch and assault me. I have no idea why, but I immediately retreated a few steps in terror. And it was at that very moment that Anwar lobbed the ball to the precise spot in the Rangoon half where I had been standing all that time. There was no one there except Rangoon's stopper, who was running to his left to reach the ball. 'Get the ball, Prasoon!' Anwar screamed.

Something in his voice convinced me I'd succeed and I began a desperate, gut-wrenching sprint. When the stopper realized I'd get to the ball before he did, he made a last-ditch attempt to fling himself at my feet. Leaping into the air to clear him, I realized that there was no one between me and the goalkeeper, who was wondering whether to leave his goal and give me the charge.

As I began the long run towards the goal with the ball at my feet, I could hear footsteps behind me. The roar from the stands kept rising in volume as the goal came closer and closer. I entered their box. The goalkeeper had decided to charge out. The roar had become positively deafening now. I came to a halt, the ball at my feet. I knew someone was close behind me.

Swaying to my right, I lifted my left foot. In response, the goalkeeper leaned to his left. Then, in a fraction of a second, I swayed back to the right and chipped the ball ever so lightly over his head with my right foot. Thoroughly wrong-footed, the poor fellow could only turn his head and gaze helplessly at the ball soaring into the net.

Suddenly, the other ten Jatri players were on me, smothering me, and it was as if the roars of the crowd were bringing the skies down on our heads. Even when I got back to the centre line, I still wasn't sure of what I'd done. Had I really scored? The referee had blown his whistle for half-time before that wondrous spell was broken.

24

'What a goal! I was scared you were going to miss this one too.' Priyo-da was panting with excitement.

'Someone once missed one just like that,' I heard a voice say behind me. I didn't turn around to look. I knew that a pair of pale eyes were boring into my back. Many people still hadn't forgotten. Someone had switched on the transistor in the dressing room and I could hear commentator Pushpen Sarkar speaking. 'It may be too early to say whether they will win the trophy, but the exquisite skill with which the young Juger Jatri striker Prasoon Bhattacharya equalized for his team will shine brightly in our memories. As many of you know, this very same Prasoon's father Anil Bhattacharya played for Juger Jatri in the IFA Shield final twenty years ago. A new record has been made today, of father and son both having played in the IFA Shield final. Maybe Anil Bhattacharya is seated in the gallery today, watching his son...'

Baba! Could he really be watching the game? I'd sent four tickets the previous day – three for the people at home and one for Harshoda. But I couldn't believe that Baba might actually be there. Even so, I looked searchingly at the gallery as we went back on to the pitch for the second half. Thousands of hands were waving at me, but I couldn't identify a single face among them – only a million shimmering dots as seen through a translucent glass and seeming to create a network of lines. Was Baba sitting somewhere up there?

Rangoon United kicked up a storm during the second half. But after five minutes of rattling us to the bone, they suddenly ran out of steam. Jatri immediately moved up to colonize their half. Nemai and Abraham controlled the ball beautifully, keeping it on the ground and moving as if there were sparks flying off their feet. But although Nemai ravaged their half-line, he simply couldn't find a chink in their impregnable defence. I hunted desperately for an opening to penetrate, somewhere I could take a shot at the goal from.

The final whistle was drawing near and we still hadn't scored. The roars of the impatient crowds ebbed and rose. Suddenly, Rangoon's right-back fouled Nemai a couple of yards beyond their eighteen-yard line and we got a free kick. Placing the ball on the spot, Nemai raised two fingers. He was telling me where he'd send the ball – we had perfected these signals during practice.

They put up a five-man wall. Nemai and Bishnu were ready to take the shot. Abraham suddenly dashed off to the left, with one of their players following him immediately. I moved to the right and looked at the penalty spot that Nemai was observing. There was enough space behind the wall for the goalkeeper's view not to be obstructed. As soon as the referee blew his whistle, Nemai and Bishnu both moved towards the ball, Nemai a little behind Bishnu. On the surface you couldn't tell who'd take the shot, but as everyone knew, it was a much-used tactic: Bishnu would jump over the ball to distract the defence and Nemai would take the shot.

Playing his part, Bishnu leapt over the ball and ran to the left, but instead of taking a shot, Nemai essayed a perfect chip over the wall, aiming for the penalty spot. Now everything depended on the timing of my run and getting to the right spot at the right time. It was now time to test what I'd practised with Pintu, day after day, in my home school. Like a motorbike suddenly picking up speed, I accelerated with great force, darting in like an arrow unleashed from its bow.

It was too late. Before I had even taken five paces, it was obvious that if I half-volleyed the ball it would sail over the cross-post. Suddenly a voice within my breast said, 'Striker, you must strike now, strike with all your might.' Commanding all the energy at my disposal, I lunged from four yards out, not removing my eyes from the ball for one second. Feeling it touch the right-hand side of my forehead, I struck at it like a sledgehammer with my head – before falling flat on my face.

It became strangely quiet all round – almost silent. My nostrils were filled with the scent of grass and moist earth. I raised my eyes and saw the most amazing of sights – the Rangoon United goalkeeper retrieving my black-and-white world from his goal.

And then, slowly, a giant roar rose, shaking me from head to toe and consuming my entire frame.

'There's a woman looking for you,' Lakshman the gardener informed me.

The festivities were in full swing outside the Jatri tent. The sky over the Calcutta Maidan was lit up with the lights and resonating with the sounds of crackers and fireworks. Going out without my shirt, I discovered Nilima and Pintu. I had expected to see Ma.

'Oh, it's you. You came for the game? Still here? Where's Ma?' I let loose a string of questions. It was really wonderful to see people from home.

'Your mother's been at the temple since morning. And your father said, "Let's wait a little, maybe there'll be fireworks now, so..."'

'Baba? Where is he?' I choked.

'Outside. Told us to come and meet you.'

About to run out, I paused and looked beyond the railings through the flowering plants. A cracker had just been lit. It promptly flared up like an inverted chandelier. And in that light, amongst hundreds of other people, I saw a scar glittering on the forehead of one of them. With brilliance, with pride.

Spotting me in the glow of the fireworks, a crowd rushed towards me, chanting, 'Prasoon, Prasoon!'

The Pearl

Chandan Mitra had not imagined the car would let him down this way.

They had travelled smoothly to Kharagpur after leaving Digha at dawn. Chandan had seen Bratati and one-year-old Bablu off on the train to Jamshedpur. Bratati was going to spend a fortnight with her elder sister. They had spent a couple of days in Digha in a house owned by one of Chandan's fans.

It was an old Standard Herald, which Chandan had bought for six thousand rupees four months ago. He hadn't got round to learning how to drive yet, although he meant to. So he'd hired a driver. The three hundred rupees he was paying the man pinched him, but he had a strange fear of having an accident if he drove.

Most of the things that an astrologer had forecast after reading his horoscope four years ago had come true. Foreign travel, fame, financial success, marriage, a job – practically all of them. He'd been to Bangkok and Tehran to play in the Asian Games, and toured Hong Kong, Seoul, Nairobi, Singapore, Kabul, Colombo and Rangoon with the Indian team. He had been to Kuala Lumpur twice for the Merdeka tournament. Chandan didn't quite grasp what fame and glory meant. All he was aware of was people staring at him, women whispering, cars stopping to offer him rides, invitations to the homes of strangers and to the finals of football tournaments to give away trophies and make speeches. He featured in newspaper headlines, with adjectives like 'fragrant' being added to his name (which meant sandalwood). Once he had heard someone say as he passed in a taxi, 'That's the son of God there.' His goal, the only one in the match, had made Juger Jatri the IFA Shield champion just a few days earlier. If all this implied fame and glory, then Chandan had fame and glory.

He'd certainly been successful financially. He had just about scraped through his school examinations, but his club had got him a job with a bank, where he currently earned almost eighteen hundred a month. The astrologer had asked him to wear an onyx and a topaz, which he did. That same year his fee had risen to between forty thousand and forty-five thousand. He was now the owner of a flat, and he had a chemist's shop although not in his own name, fifty thousand rupees given out as loans that earned interest, and this car.

The astrologer had predicted a beautiful wife, and Bratati was indeed pretty. A film-director fan of Chandan's had even chased her for some time to give her a role. Chandan wasn't in favour of her acting in the movies. Bratati loved him, and he, her. She wished he'd drive, as confident people did. But the astrologer had said that as there was a threat to his life after he turned thirty, it would be best if he wore a pearl. He had been twenty-seven then. Let me turn thirty first, he'd decided, and had not bought the pearl then. He still hadn't.

His first thought on getting the car had been about the threat. His skin had prickled in fear. The same Chandan Mitra who did not hesitate to take on the most violent of defenders in the penalty box was secretly afraid of an accident. Severed limbs, crushed ribs, a mangled torso – he felt miserable whenever this image of himself floated up in front of his eyes. He had instructed Tripit Singh, the driver, repeatedly before they drove to Digha – don't go over thirty miles an hour, don't race with other cars, don't overtake, make way for trucks and buses and lorries.

Saying all this had made him feel he really had aged. It was obvious that his playing days were ending. The club had spirited away Tanmay, Basab and Pradip ten days before the transfers began, but the officials had seen no need to make an effort to keep him out of reach of other clubs. His rate had dropped ten thousand in one shot.

Looking at the broken-down car on Bombay Road, Chandan told himself he was getting old. The club was bound to discard him in a year or two. His earnings would drop. Had he really needed to buy the car? Even ten years ago he had depended entirely on trams and buses. And before that, there were those days when he played local matches for money and often wondered where his next meal was coming from.

Tripit Singh had returned to Kharagpur with the faulty distributor box. Chandan had tried to flag down a truck headed for Kharagpur and it had swept past him without stopping. But then a private car behind it had stopped on its own. The man sitting in the back seat had opened the door and said, 'Come in.'

Chandan had felt a mild sense of pride. But there was no one besides Tripit to witness the incident. Even last year he'd been on the cover of two magazines. They were halfway through the Calcutta League, and his photograph had already appeared thrice in the newspapers. Several million people knew what he looked like. Cars stopped because of him, they were still stopping for him. Bengalis really loved their football.

Tripit had gone to Kharagpur in that car. Who knew when he'd be back. Probably not for another couple of hours. Chandan remained to keep an eye on his car. But he grew impatient after a while and decided to take a walk, locking the car doors.

The highway here was broad enough for six lorries. There was farmland on both sides – rice and jute. Searing heat had made way for rain two weeks ago. It had rained last night as well. A farmer was ploughing the field in the distance. Gazing at him for some time, Chandan felt the urge for a cup of tea.

Several narrow trails led off from Bombay Road into the villages. He walked up to the head of one such path. A handful of shops with thatched roofs, a walled factory next to them. Some single-storeyed buildings. The hint of a village behind the trees.

A blacksmith's shack, followed by one for cycle repairs, and then a tea shop. Two men were sitting outside it on a bamboo bench with suitcases and bags. Probably a bus stop. Chandan sat down next to them. The time on his watch was ten-thirty.

The shop was decrepit, and so was the woman running it. Chandan could tell that her sari had been red once upon a time, just as he could see that her complexion had once been fair. Perhaps her appearance had been both graceful and youthful once. Now her eyes held an irritated anger and her face was wan. A boy of about ten was breaking lumps of coal.

'Is tea available?' Chandan asked quite loudly.

'It is.'

There were bread and lozenges, besides biscuits and cake. Paan and cigarettes too. All of them cheap, looking like they had been languishing for a long time.

So this woman was the owner. How did such a shabbily maintained shop do any business? Maybe her husband worked somewhere. Looking around as these thoughts ran through his mind, Chandan found nothing in the natural beauty of Medinipur capable of captivating him, and returned his attention to the shop. His car was visible from this spot.

A framed photograph hung from one of the walls, which were made of bamboo. Glancing at it idly, Chandan tried to make out its subject. It was faded, and the glass covering it was grimy. Unable to see clearly and his curiosity piqued, he went up to the photograph.

The woman turned to look at him as she made his tea. The boy, nearly naked, was blinking at him. The men on the bench were on their feet; the bus was probably approaching.

Chandan discovered that behind the dirty glass lay a photograph of a football team. What he saw on rubbing the dust off with his fingertips was indeed a huge surprise – it was the 1947 team of the IFA, which had toured Burma and Singapore.

'Who put this photo here?' Chandan's question was directed at the woman.

'His father.' She jerked her head in the boy's direction. Her voice was as harsh as her expression.

The same photograph also hung on the wall of the Juger Jatri tent. Four of the club's players were in the team. Chandan knew their names.

'Is he very fond of football?'

There was no answer. Instead of the woman, the boy spoke. 'My father is in that photograph.'

'Pot or glass?' The woman was staring at him in annoyance.

'Pot.'

Intrigued, Chandan asked the boy, 'Which one's your father?'

He came forward and laid his finger on the face of one of the four seated figures.

Shivakrishnan.

Chandan gazed at the boy in astonishment and turned back to the photograph.

Yes, Shivakrishnan of Juger Jatri. The formidable left-in. The most popular player of his time. Landing up at Calcutta as a young boy from a village in Hyderabad, he'd played for Kalighat and Sporting Union and then for East Bengal for two years before joining Juger Jatri. Chandan was four when he retired. Shivakrishnan's name was certain to crop up whenever the old-timers spoke of the past.

Apparently he was a master of the through-pass. A calm, controlled player. Not particularly good at shooting or heading the ball. He had always played barefoot. The ball stuck to him like glue and he could dribble past three players effortlessly.

'There's no inside-forward like Shiva in Calcutta football today. How many players can dribble past their opponents now? Remember how he feinted past KOSB's Henderson six times in a row?'

Everyone would nod in unison. The way Shiva held the ball was apparently a sight to behold. 'He ruined himself with drugs. Ganja, bhang, charas, everything possible. There wasn't as much money in the game then as there is now. Still, he squandered whatever he earned, twenty or twenty-five or whatever it was. But his passes!'

Everyone would nod again. Chandan had heard these stories about Shiva over and over. At first he had marvelled at them but later they began to irritate him. For the old-timers, everything good lay in the past. Apparently players would lay down their lives for their clubs, without even thinking of money. They also dripped decency like molten butter back then. 'The Juger Jatri that you see now, all this money, all these trophies, all of this began back in that time. They were the first to earn success for the club, to get it into the semi-finals and finals of the Rovers Cup and the Durand Cup. They were the ones who made Jatri popular, an all-India force.'

Everyone would nod. Chandan acknowledged all this. He had often advised youngsters in his speeches – respect your elders, don't forget the past. He himself touched the feet of veteran footballers with great respect whenever he saw them. And then, when he saw people looking at him admiringly, he felt himself growing a little taller.

'Is Shivakrishnan your father?'

There was clear disbelief in Chandan's eyes. The boy looked shyly at the woman.

'Yes,' she said, offering him the small clay pot of tea.

Accepting it, Chandan said, 'And you are?'

'His wife.'

'He's the same Shivakrishnan who played for Juger Jatri…'

'No idea.'

'No idea!'

She frowned at Chandan's astonished echo.

'He played football, didn't he?'

'Perhaps. I don't know anything.'

'Where is he?'

'At home.'

'Is he doing something? I mean, is he busy? Can I meet him?'

'What can he be doing? I do all the work. He's in bed all the time.'

'Is something wrong with him?'

'Headaches, pain in the knee, asthma, cough and cold. Does he know you? Can you have him admitted to a hospital?'

'I can try.'

Fixing her eyes on Chandan for a few seconds, Shivakrishnan's wife told her son, 'I can't leave the shop. Take him to your father.'

As Chandan started to walk off she called out from behind him, 'Your payment?'

Paying up, he set off with the boy. The car breaking down seemed to be a blessing in disguise now. Everyone in Calcutta would be dumbfounded. He had tracked down Shivakrishnan and spoken to him. Everyone had assumed he was dead.

The first people to gather around him when he recounted the story of meeting a living Shivakrishnan would be journalists from newspapers and magazines.

A small hut stood a short distance away. Just the one room. Pausing at the door, Chandan looked inside. An opening in the wall served as the window. A man seemed to be resting on a low cot. There was no other furniture in the room. A couple of aluminium plates and an upside-down mug on the floor. A clay pot, a pitcher of water and a few bottles. A tin trunk beneath the cot, along with a pair of old slippers. Clothes hanging on the wall. Some tins and a small mirror in a niche in the wall.

The man, that is to say Shivakrishnan – who was well known as Shiva on the football fields of Calcutta and of India just twenty-seven years ago – was lying on his side, dressed in nothing but a tattered lungi.

He turned towards Chandan when his son tapped him on the back.

'I'm here from Calcutta. My car broke down and I stopped at the shop for a cup of tea. When I saw the photograph I thought I'd meet you. I've heard so much about you.'

Shiva sat up on the cot. There was virtually no resemblance to the figure in the photograph. His hollow cheeks were covered with a grey stubble, his arms were like reeds, each of his ribs could be counted. Only from the shape of his head could he be assumed to be Shivakrishnan. It was disproportionately large in comparison to his body, the forehead extraordinarily wide. Yet his heading skill was supposed to have been terrible.

'You must have heard stories about me – you can't have seen me play. How old are you?' His voice was weak. His Bangla pronunciation was flawless, by virtue of having spent forty years in the state.

'No, I didn't see you play. I wasn't born at the time of that photograph. Are you ill? Is it serious?'

'No, I'm not ill or anything. Footballers always have niggles. Half an hour with the ball on the field and I'll be fine.'

'Do you still play?' Chandan was astonished. At this age and in this state of health – what was he saying?

'Play? Where's the field? Where's the ball?' Shiva smiled. 'Look at my health, look at my age. The thing is, I think footballers can get better only if they play, only if they move around with the ball. Don't keep standing, sit down.'

The boy had taken a rubber ball out from beneath the cot and was dribbling it around. Hearing his mother scream for him from a distance, he ran off.

'My wife is Bengali, her home is hereabouts. She used to work in the same restaurant in Calcutta as me, that's when we met. She did a lot for me, still does.'

'The state you're in – there's a lot of help available for ex-footballers these days, pensions. Why don't you apply? The money would always be helpful.'

Shiva's eyes didn't seem to convey a sense of grievance. Yet it was usually the old men who felt that way.

'Why did I play football then? I could have earned money some other way. I made no money from football.'

Chandan felt some discomfiture. This was true, what *did* these people play for? Was it for applause? What else could it have been but that pittance?

'Do you play?'

Chandan was about to say, I'm considered a star at your club now. But something seemed to choke his voice. 'A bit of football,' was all he could say.

'I see.'

No illness, no financial difficulties, I'm fine – Chandan felt the aged ex-footballer's attitude was just out of pride.

'Do you watch football?

'I watched a game in Kharagpur five years ago. That was after a gap of sixteen years.'

Chandan had taken a hundred and fifty rupees to play in an exhibition match in Kharagpur five years ago. Was it the same game?

'What did you think of the players you watched?'

Silence.

'The game has changed a lot since your time.'

'But what about skill, what about football sense, what about shooting?'

It was Chandan's turn to be silent now.

'I kept thinking of Rashid, of Somanna, of Mewa, of Appa.'

Chandan stole a glance at his watch. Nearly two hours had passed since the car had broken down, Tripit should be returning soon. He would start looking for Chandan. There was a game with Port tomorrow. An easy affair, but he should still get home soon and rest. The past three days had been strenuous…

'But the goals they were missing…'

Suddenly Chandan had an urge to make this man suffer. He'd often encountered such contempt. It was nothing but envy.

'Do you know how much footballers earn these days?'

'No, I cannot read the papers, I haven't even been to school.'

'Forty, fifty, even sixty thousand.'

'I once got two hundred rupees for scoring against Mohun Bagan. Bakai-babu gave it to me because he was happy. I wouldn't have scored if it hadn't been for Kamal's pass. I gave him a hundred.'

'Many players have cars these days, some own houses, they've set up their own businesses, saved thousands of rupees.'

None of this seemed to register with him. He appeared to have gone back thirty-five or forty years in time to relive his goal. A smile had appeared on his face.

'My heading was supposed to be poor and yet I scored with a header. Lies were spread about me. I've scored many goals with headers.'

Getting off his cot, he handed the rubber ball to Chandan and then led him outside. 'Throw this at me, I'll show you how I scored. Throw it.'

Both disturbed and amused, Chandan tossed the ball lightly up in the air above Shivakrishnan's head. He was ready, standing slightly hunched, his fists balled.

The ball fell on his shoulder. He'd missed it. Fetching it, Chandan threw it up lightly again, even higher this time.

Shivakrishnan was waiting, his face raised. As the ball dropped he jerked his head to head it to his left. It bounced on his chin.

Taken aback, Shivakrishnan stared at the ball, his eyes lowered. 'Again.'

Chandan tossed the ball up three more times. Shivakrishnan missed each time.

'Never mind.'

'No, I can do it, throw it once more.'

'Let it be, you're not well.'

'Once more – just once.'

The old man seemed to be begging. Chandan felt a stab of pity.

'One last time.'

Shivakrishnan was waiting. His eyes were bulging, the veins in his shoulders and arms pulsating. There was bright sunshine. An enormous banyan tree with all its branches in the background. Extensive fields behind the tree. Tender paddy shoots. A farmer was ploughing the land. A pond on the right. Another banyan tree. The whistle of a train in the distance. Amidst all this, a former footballer, ailing, holding on obstinately to his desire to return to his salad days forty years ago. He wanted to demonstrate how to head the ball, for the last and final time in his life.

What if he missed this time too? The horn sounded impatiently in the distance.

If he missed again, the old man would be destroyed. Let it be. There was no point. Chandan dropped the ball on the ground.

'What's the matter?'

'I'm late, the driver is honking.'

'Just once – one last time.'

Chandan had started walking. Shivakrishnan followed him.

'How long can it take, just once… I'll show you whether I can head a ball or not. You can tell them in Calcutta, I saw Shiva head a ball…yes, Shiva at sixty…It won't even take a minute…'

Chandan speeded up. Unable to keep pace, the old man stopped.

He looked over his shoulder on reaching the highway. Against the backdrop of an enormous field and a gigantic tree, he saw a frail man standing on the edge of life.

An accident had been narrowly averted. Chandan decided to follow the astrologer's advice and order a pearl ring immediately.

Rehabilitation

He was there again. For the fifth day in a row.

'Why do you think he comes here at the crack of dawn every day?' I asked Poltu. 'Yesterday he was even grinning at us.'

Bouncing the football on the ground, Poltu glanced at the neem tree. The man was sitting under it. That was where we changed our clothes, put on and took off our boots, rested after practice, ate the food we brought with us. No one else came to this field in the factory at this hour of the morning. There wasn't any way to get in, unless you knew. The entire field was walled in, but there was a crack at one spot that we used, saving both time and effort. No one lived within a quarter of a mile of the factory. It was the biggest field within a distance of four or five miles. A distant relative of mine was the foreman in this iron factory. It was on his recommendation that we had got the manager's permission to practise here every morning. Both of us were going to be playing in the first division this year, which is why our enthusiasm was high. We began practising just as it had begun to get warmer.

'Must be a madman.' Poltu didn't elaborate.

Putting the football and our bags down on the ground beneath the tree, we practically stripped to the skin before donning our football shorts. As we laced our boots, I threw a glance at the unkempt, emaciated, ageing man with the greying stubble. Both of us had taken our watches off and put them in the bags. I felt uncomfortable at the idea of the bags lying near him while we were out on the field. I considered keeping my watch on. It wasn't possible for Poltu, however, because he was a goalkeeper and frequently had to dive for the ball. I was hesitant about asking the man to sit somewhere else. Despite the palpable air of poverty about him, there was a natural confidence in his erect posture, sharp eyes and the arrogant tilt of his neck that I could not reconcile with a petty thief.

He was watching us put on our boots with the curiosity of a child. He had been dressed in a rust-coloured lungi and a white shirt all these days, but today he was in baggy denim-blue pyjamas ending well above his ankles, the kind that workers in boiler-and machine-rooms wore. His faded yellow T-shirt with a brown collar also sat loosely on him. He seemed to be wearing someone else's clothes.

'No anklets?' Both of us turned towards him at the sudden question. Poltu answered gravely, 'No need. It creates more problems.'

There was a look of astonishment in the man's eyes. Glancing at our feet, he said, 'Who says it doesn't help? Have you ever tried them?' Without waiting for a reply he continued, 'All the great players used anklets – Samad, Chhene, Jumma, Karuna. They never faced any problems. There haven't been players like them since.'

'And there won't be either, because the nature of the game has changed.' This time it was I who answered.

'What if it has! Shooting, dribbling tackling, passing…none of those have changed.' Grinning, the man said, 'All you have today are pretentious names. A youngster was explaining 4-2-4 to me the other day. It turned out to be nothing but the two-back system from our times. All it takes is for the two half-backs to drop back…'

Poltu and I exchanged glances and moved into the playing area even before he had finished talking. We usually ran several times around the pitch every day before we began practising. Poltu said in a low voice before we began, 'Wounded tiger. Another frustrated footballer.'

Both of us turned to look at the man as we ran side by side. We stopped at one point. We had left the football under the tree when we started running. The man was busy feinting past imaginary opponents with the ball at his feet. His six-foot reedy frame swayed to the left and to the right as he drew the ball towards himself with the soles of his feet, jumped over it, spun around and, pretending to take a powerful shot, kicked the ball lightly to the right and bent forward as though anxiously trying to look past someone in front of him to see whether the ball was going into the net or not. As soon as the ball rolled to a stop he raised his arms and began to laugh. It was as though he wasn't able to control his laughter at the flabbergasted expressions on the opponents' faces.

'He must have been a footballer once,' I told Poltu.

Feigning consternation, Poltu said, 'Oh my God! He won't start telling us stories about playing against the military, will he?'

'Get these stupid ideas out of your head,' I said indignantly. 'There really were some very good players in those days.'

'Yes, there were. The British were terrified of them. They would score goals from thirty or forty yards out. You won't find a trace of those goals in the record books. Maybe one goal or two, but the babus would concede five or six.' Poltu resumed running without waiting for me.

I looked at the man. Balancing on one foot, he was trying to keep the ball in the air with his other foot. It didn't work beyond three or four seconds. Finally he kicked the ball to the centre of the field in disgust. When we began shooting practice the man walked into the pitch. We had drawn the goalposts on the wall of the melting shop of the factory with a brick. The crossbar was imaginary. The shots that Poltu could not stop bounced back off the wall. The man chased the ball every time with great enthusiasm, kicking it back to me in a manner that suggested he was coaching players, and kept up a constant patter.

'No, never in the air, you must always keep the ball on the ground…lifting it means wasting it.' He raced off to retrieve the ball. 'I don't see those classic through-passes any more, the kind that Kumar-babu used to come up with.' He dashed off again. 'I was telling that young fellow, the one who was explaining 4-2-4, for heaven's sake, do you think you can play football with diagrams… keep it on the ground, don't lift the ball…yes, you have to do a lot more on the field now, I accept that, it's a lot more arduous… completely wrong, this is how you must position the top of your foot, this way, give me the ball, I'll show you.'

I gave him the ball. Poltu snarled from a distance, 'Should I count sheep meanwhile? Come and shoot, come and shoot.'

Deflated, the man quickly pushed the ball back to me. 'Football isn't just a question of taking one shot after another at the goal, you have to practise your skills too,' he said with some chagrin, although he continued retrieving the ball. Bending forward as he ran with the ball, dribbling it past imaginary defenders, he gesticulated as though he had just sent me a gem of a pass, screaming, 'Shoot, shoot!'

I took a shot without stopping the ball, which went beneath a diving Poltu's arms, hitting the wall with tremendous force and bouncing back. 'Go…o…al!' shouted the man, leaping up with his arms in the air. I was still marvelling at how flawless the shot had been. Excitedly he shouted, 'Now you know what a through-pass is. And this is what all of you have abolished from the game. What is this rubbish man-to-man play you have these days. If there's no beauty in the game, then…'

Poltu rushed up, his face red with rage. I shuddered. He had a very short temper and would start throwing punches at the slightest provocation.

'We're here to practise,' he said grimly. 'We didn't ask you to be here. Why are you troubling us? If you want to teach, find someone else. Please don't bother us.'

Poltu strode back to his position. The man had been staring at him in surprise. His face grew pale. As he walked off slowly towards the tree with his head bowed, his baggy blue pyjamas and bent figure made me think of a crumbling rock covered with slime.

When we came and sat down beneath the neem tree, the man left. As we ate Poltu began to talk of our new club secretary's daughter.

She came to the matches regularly, and went around town with the players. Just as Poltu was reeling off a list of whom she had been seen with and where, I suddenly noticed the man jogging slowly around the field. Exactly the way we did. Like me, Poltu also gazed at him in astonishment.

He ran past us after completing a round, a stern look in his glittering eyes. He didn't spare us even a fleeting glance. His narrow chest rose and fell like bellows as he breathed through his open mouth. The sight of the full head of hair dancing above the withered but lanky body like an inky mop made me want to laugh. But the very next moment I felt a stab of sadness at this childish effort from an ageing man. It was obvious that he had taken the challenge of proving himself our equal by defying his age to run around the field. I wished he would abandon this unequal contest and leave.

'He'd better not kick the bucket, or we'll be in trouble.' There was genuine anxiety in Poltu's voice. The man had stopped after one and a half rounds, and was looking up at the sky with his mouth wide open. His eyes seemed ready to burst out of their sockets. He threw a couple of covert glances at us. I rose to my feet, worrying that he might collapse. At once he began to walk at a natural pace towards the crack in the wall. This saddened me again. Poltu burst into laughter.

The man didn't show up for the next five or six days. We were relieved, assuming he wouldn't return any more. But he did come back, bringing along a flaccid football, patched in three or four places. We continued practising as usual, while he busied himself at the other end of the field, tormenting his imaginary opponents with the ball. But soon he was staring at us, the ball resting near his feet. His eyes lit up when our ball rolled towards him. About to launch himself at it, he held back, exercising utmost restraint.

'You haven't been coming,' I said out of courtesy.

'I was very ill,' he told me gravely.

To please him I said, 'Can you check whether the through-passes are all right?'

In a few minutes he began to shout, 'What are you doing? That's all wrong!' When I turned to look at him he continued, 'You have to be quick, but at a lower speed. It's the same when kicking. With the upper part of the top of your foot. The tip of the boot should be pointing at the ground – like this. And then the follow-through – this way. Try it.'

I was irritated at the idea of learning the basics of shooting from a man like him at a time when I was about to play in the first division. Ignoring him, I continued to take my shots as before. He shouted instructions a couple more times before falling silent. It was obvious that he needed a student, someone who would heed his advice, who would obey him. He must have realized we weren't going to dance to his tune.

It was raining the next day. When we arrived at the field we discovered that he had found his disciple. A plump, stupid-looking boy was standing like a block of wood in the rain, watching with great attention as the man performed his antics. We were amazed at his reckless enthusiasm. But he wasn't healthy or young enough to survive a drenching in the rain. 'He's bound to get pneumonia,' I told Poltu.

'Let him. But where did he get hold of this fat lump? He'll never learn how to play football.'

We could hear the man's instructions from a distance. As though he was lecturing in class. 'If you jump over the ball this way,' – a hop – 'it won't work. What you have to do is this…this is how you must take the ball along. Your opponent will be caught in two minds.'

The boy watched with deep concentration, nodding at everything, but the man made no effort to give him the ball. 'Now I'll show you how to pass the ball with the top of your foot.' The limp ball got stuck in the mud. The man ran up to it and dribbled it along. The boy was still rooted to the spot, the rain dripping off his chin. His hair was plastered to his forehead, and his fair skin showed through his shirt.

'Now watch how to lift the ball with your toe.' The man slipped and fell in the process. The boy didn't laugh, though; it was the man who laughed. It was pouring so much now that we stopped our practice and left. The man was still circling the boy with the ball, talking continuously.

Poltu didn't show up for practice the next day. His knee had swollen from an injury. I turned up by myself. The man was sitting beneath the neem tree. His disciple had not arrived yet. He smiled at me. 'Where's the other one?'

I explained. Then, in the course of conversation, I asked what he did, where he lived and which club he had played for. He didn't seem particularly keen on answering. All I found out was that he lived with his brother a couple of miles away. A bachelor. He had gone to the war, and then worked as a welder in the factory after being discharged from the army. Thanks to a bout of pleurisy he had had to quit his job and go back to his ancestral home to take care of the little land they owned there. Because he hadn't enjoyed that, he had come to the city to live with his younger brother. But there were problems, and no peace of mind. He was considering returning to the ancestral home.

'Yes, I used to play.' A coughing fit made him hunch over. Spitting out the phlegm from his throat, he smiled at me. 'I've always played in boots. I was with Kalighat for a year. Joseph used to play for them at the time. Have you heard of him?'

I nodded. He was about to speak but was overcome by another bout of coughing. The price of soaking in the rain yesterday. If he insisted on taking to the field to show off his tricks despite his sickness, he was going to die. I told him, 'Your student may not turn up today. Why don't you go back home?'

'No, he'll come. I'm sure he will. I've promised to make a footballer out of him, even if I have to die in the process. You can't beat my teaching technique. If you can exercise your willpower over an object, success is guaranteed.' Pausing to cough, he continued, 'And if the object happens to be raw, that is to say, young, anyone can be transformed into an outstanding player. I'm too old for it, or I'd have tried the technique on myself.'

The boy entered through the crack in the wall. Looking at a practically leafless silk cotton tree at the other end of the field, the man said, 'Trees are supposed to survive on the food they make from ingredients they absorb from their leaves. But how is that tree over there still living in that case?' His query seemed to echo his personal predicament. 'How is it surviving without any leaves?'

Suddenly I began to like the man. I sensed his regret too. No matter what teaching technique he employed, I was certain that this roly-poly pudding would never grow to be a footballer. The man was prancing around on his own, without even giving the boy a chance to kick the ball. The student certainly wouldn't have stood there like a block of wood had he been even slightly energetic. The fact was that only a dimwit would want to take lessons from the man.

I watched the man's antics for about half an hour. As soon as the boy left I offered him my food, saying, 'I didn't practise today, and besides, I'm not hungry.'

Frowning, he said, 'Why don't you practise? I'll be the goalkeeper.'

'No, never mind, I don't feel like it today.'

He didn't insist, accepting the packet of food and putting it in his pocket. He displayed neither hesitation nor gratitude. We left together. As we were walking, he said, 'You know what I think? No game on earth can be compared to football. Whether it's cricket or hockey or badminton or tennis, you need a stick. Humans with sticks. That's going back to the age of the apes. Football is a game for civilized people – it's all science. If this science can be mastered... By the way, do you have a pair of old boots? You saw how I slipped and fell yesterday. I could demonstrate better with boots.'

I shook my head, indicating I had no boots to spare. He clicked his tongue in dismay. The pallor on his cheeks was more pronounced, and they were more sunken than before. The baggy blue pyjamas were caked with dried mud. Walking with his head bent, clutching the patched ball to his chest, he looked more like a young boy than an old man. His eyes could barely conceal his excitement. In his head he was probably dribbling past his opponents one by one. When we reached the end of the road he turned in the direction of his house without saying goodbye.

The next week, I saw the boy finally practising with the ball. It seemed to me that his ageing trainer could kick harder, run faster and jump higher than him. I was surprised the boy had chosen football of all things. Half an hour later, when he had left, I asked the man, 'Do you think he'll ever be a footballer?'

'Of course!' the man said with conviction. 'I've decided to put him to the test now. I think he's ready to apply all that I've taught him in an actual game. There's a trial match in his school on Saturday – he'll play. I'll give instructions as required from the touchline.'

'Have you ever seen him play before?'

'No, and why is that necessary? What I need to see is whether he can apply all that I've taught him. There's no doubt that he's improved, or how would he get a place in the trial team?'

It was hopeless. He was trying to impose his imaginary world on the real one. The outcome could be nothing but failure. I could picture his hunched figure running up and down the touchline, while mischievous boys chased him, jeering and imitating him and tugging at his shirt. The teachers were asking for the lunatic to be taken away. I could see his glittering eyes filling with tears of humiliation and rage. He was leaving the field, his head bowed, followed by a gaggle of boys.

'Isn't it too soon for him to play?' I asked as gently as possible. 'You've only been training him a few days.'

'I've kept track, I've coached him twenty-five hours in all. Twenty-five hours of coaching is sufficient for young boys to achieve a high standard of football.'

'But this boy won't achieve any standards even with five hundred hours of coaching.'

He looked at me in surprise before shaking his head with a smile. 'You have no idea what willpower can achieve. If you have the desire to play like Samad or Chhone or Gostho Pal…or like those players I hear so much about these days…Pelé, Eusebio…you can do it.'

I didn't prolong the conversation. Let him do as he pleases, I told myself, why should I worry about it? Perhaps he'd come to his senses once he had been taught a lesson.

After that, every day during practice sessions with Poltu, I would keep an eye on the crack in the wall. Perhaps he would turn up today. Later I thought, maybe the boy had let him down so badly that he was embarrassed to meet us now.

One day I spotted him again, standing under the neem tree, watching us practise. He was dressed in a lungi and a half-sleeved shirt, his face covered in a stubble. He walked off slowly when he realized we had seen him, but I ran up to ask, 'What happened in the trial match?'

He stumbled and steadied himself before continuing to walk. 'Willpower isn't everything – some talent is necessary too. I was wrong after all.' He turned towards me. In his eyes I saw a burning desire for rehabilitation. But the way he walked away made me think of an injured beast crawling into the jungle to die in seclusion.

A few days later I ran into the boy on the road. He was watching a group of urchins even younger than him playing gilli-danda. When I asked about the man he answered in irritation, 'Who knows? Maybe he's fallen ill again.'

'Do you know where he lives?'

'I do but I can't take you there. He looks at me like he wants to burn in hell. What could I have done? He behaved so strangely at the game that all the boys began to tease him. Was that my fault?'

'Absolutely not.'

'Well, then? How could an old man like him burst into tears in front of everyone just because I played badly?'

'Can you show me his house from a distance?' I asked impatiently. 'You can do that, can't you?'

'I can,' the boy said hesitantly.

As agreed, he pointed the house out to me and left. It was practically a slum. A single-storeyed building with a tiled roof and a courtyard in the middle. A gaggle of children were shrieking and tumbling about. Next to it was an open barrel, overflowing with sludge. On one side stood a bamboo trellis supporting bottle-gourd vines. Oil-stained and torn sheets hung from a bamboo rod. A duck was pecking at scraps of food in the rubbish heap. A woman smacked a child on his back and dragged him away. She pointed lackadaisically to one of the rooms in response to my question and went off without displaying the slightest curiosity.

The door was at the back. Peeping through the window as I passed, I saw, in the corner of a room messily overflowing with calendars, trunks, tins, bowls, bedding, a mosquito net and many other things, the man sitting on the floor, leaning against the wall. He was staring at the wall opposite him. I could see him in profile, his chin lifted as though he didn't care for anything in the world. His cheekbones seemed even higher than before, making his eyes recede further into their sockets. Death was brushing its fingertips tenderly across his body, and he seemed to have surrendered to its luxury.

Suddenly he turned his head. Our eyes locked. I was only a few feet away, but there was no recognition in his eyes. A hollow, incurious, blank look. To me he seemed to be an ancient tree trunk, devoid of leaves, the colour of decaying rock, engaged in a motionless passage to rehabilitation. I smiled at him as an acquaintance would. There was no reflection in his eyes.

A Far-reaching Radiance

I didn't know Bijon Datta was in this sanatorium. I used to visit Dr Basu Roy's quarters sometimes after school, to pass some time with him if he was home. That day he said, 'Since you're mad about football, you must have heard of Bijon Datta.'

Seeing that I was wracking my brain uneasily, he said, 'Apparently he was a stand-by for the Indian football team for the London Olympics in 1948. Not that I can confirm whether that's true or not, but he speaks crudely, just like a footballer, swears all the time and is extremely stubborn. He's almost fifty but it's obvious he was strong and fit in his youth.'

I remembered hearing my elder brothers mention the name. I hadn't yet begun watching football matches when he broke his foot and stopped playing. And besides, Bijon Datta had never played for Mohun Bagan. So my ignorance about him was not surprising. Looking up his ward and bed number, I went to make his acquaintance one afternoon.

The room held just four beds. His was against the wall. Next to it was a door leading into the veranda. He was lying on his back with his arms behind his head. Not an inch shorter than six feet, possible taller. His hair was closely cropped, half of it grey, giving his head the look of a ripe coconut. When I went up to his bed his curiosity turned to surprise that blazed beneath his shaggy eyebrows.

'When I came to know you're here I thought I'd meet you.'

Trying to smile to dispel my reserve, I realized courtesy was wasted on this man.

'But why – am I film star or a test player?'

Undaunted, I said, 'I love football, I watch it regularly.'

'You've never touched a football in your life, have you?' He propped himself up on an elbow. 'It's obvious, looking at you.'

He was ninety per cent right, so I didn't have the courage to protest.

'Last year another weakling like you turned up, the son of a friend of the football secretary. I was told to try him out.' Bijon Datta grinned. 'When he came for practice the first day, I told him to run twenty laps. He couldn't continue after six. I lobbed the ball high in front of the goal and told him to head it, also told the stopper to give him a jab. Going up for the ball, he collapsed immediately, clutching his ribs. Then it was time to practise tackles. The punk had a decent dodge up his sleeve. Twice he dribbled past me. The third time he spun like a top and fell ten feet beyond the sideline. He didn't show up again.'

Slapping his thighs, Bijon Datta laughed like a motorcycle starting its engine. Two of his lower front teeth were missing.

'Football is a game for men. That's how we played it, all right? We hit them, they hit us. Both the cartilages are missing from my left knee, and the shinbone on the other one…' Raising his lungi to his knees, Bijon Datta stretched his right leg out. Some scars were visible through the thick hair on his skin. 'I had to stop playing when this foot was fractured.'

An inadvertent expression of relief must have appeared on my face. Bijon Datta asked me grimly, 'What do you do?'

'I teach at the school here. Science.'

'So you're a teacher. I'm one too. I teach football. I've studied up to Class Five.'

'Are you a coach now?'

'Shobhabajar Sporting. We were supposed to get into the first division last year, didn't happen.' His face twisted with suppressed rage. Clenching his teeth, he said, 'The motherfucker bought the game. He knew he couldn't have taken a point off us fairly.'

'Who are you talking of?'

'Ratan Sarkar. The bastard visited my goalkeeper at home with a hundred rupees the night before the match. The stopper's wife was dying, he promised to get her a bed in a hospital. He gave expensive trousers to the two half-backs. You think Pradip Sangha could have become champions otherwise? He bought five games with a thousand rupees, and the swine claims to be a coach! I've always known he's a top-class cheat, from the time we played together. The number of times he scored with his hand! He would drop to the ground in the penalty area and writhe like he had been hacked down. He bagged many penalties this way. When the goalkeeper is about to leap for the ball, Ratan grabs his pants and pulls him back. No trick was too dirty for him.'

I started laughing as I listened to him. How angry he was with Ratan Sarkar, but he didn't say a word against the players in his own club who took the bribes. Seeing me laugh, he looked at me coldly. 'Which club do you support?'

'Mohun Bagan.'

Uttering a profanity, he said, 'They quake, do you know, they quake with fear even against small teams. I have offers from three clubs. Haven't yet decided which one to take, but I'll definitely take one of them. I'll teach Ratan a lesson the son of a bitch will never forget. And I'll take points off Mohun Bagan and East Bengal. Easily. I'll bet you a hundred rupees.'

'What if Ratan Sarkar bribes your players again?' I asked.

Rage blazed from his eyes before dying down slowly. Shrugging, all he said was, 'That bastard is capable of anything. The game means nothing to him – winning is all that matters.'

Glancing at my watch, I said, 'It's time for my train. I have to go back to Calcutta now. Will it bother you if I drop by sometimes for a chat?'

'Of course not. Come every day, I'd love that. It's hard to pass the time. My wife can't visit me every day after all.'

The despair that appeared on his face made me sympathize with this unpolished but simple, short-tempered and proud man. The body language of the other three occupants of the room made it obvious that none of them liked him. There was no reason to. I wouldn't have either. But the untamed primal force radiating from his voice, the way he shook his hands or his head, the look in his eyes and his mercurial temperament, seemed very attractive to me. I said, 'I can bring you some books if you'd like to read.'

'Books!' Staring at me for a few moments, he shook his head. 'Forget it, I don't care for reading. If you could bring me some sex books, though – mind you, I tell the boys not to read them. They cause great harm to footballers, they make them very weak. Once, the night before a match against Mohun Bagan…' Pausing, he gave a wink as an explanation and continued, 'I could barely get out of bed in the morning.'

'How well did you play that day?'

'Where's the question of playing – McBride gave me marching orders within ten minutes of the start. I'd used my feet a little bit, just gently – it didn't even hurt the other player particularly. A free kick, fine, but a send-off?'

There was genuine resentment in his voice. The way he was looking at me, I had no choice but to offer a comment. 'Maybe the referee was nervous,' I said, 'so to steady his nerves he became a little too strict…'

'Of course not. McBride was a very good referee – there was no question of nervousness. The fact is that I never understand my limits, or at which point I should check myself. I don't know this at all. This has harmed me a great deal. I didn't make it to the Olympics team only because of this. I cannot flatter anyone, nor do I know when to hold my tongue. I used to abuse the bosses to their faces. I thought I'd get into the team on the strength of my performance, not through the back door by licking their boots.'

Bijon Datta's voice turned sombre. I saw a trace of regret in his eyes.

'That's how it should be,' I said. 'That's what real men do. It will keep your conscience clear all your life, you can hold your head high. And people like Ratan Sarkar will squirm when they see you.'

An expression of suppressed joy appeared on his face but there was also muffled rage there. Grinding his teeth, he muttered, 'Let me get that motherfucker once… Just wait till I get out of here.'

On my way back it occurred to me that I had remained standing throughout our conversation. Bijon Datta had not offered me a seat. It seemed to me that it wasn't a lack of politeness – he just didn't know the first thing about good manners.

I would visit him from time to time. I noticed that Bijon Datta would wait for me. Having received permission to get out of bed, he would stand on the veranda, waving as soon as he spotted me at the sanatorium gate. His complaints began the moment I drew a stool up to him. Why had I not visited him the past two days? He had developed a fondness for me. We'd sit in the veranda while he told me stories – about a goal from twenty or twenty-five years ago, about the game, about the players, about a magnificent win or a terrible loss on account of cheating. One truth emerged clearly from all his stories – football is as tough as you are, and since football is tough, life itself is tough.

One day I found him lying in his bed, and the stool next to him occupied by a plump, dark woman in a handloom sari. Her face was rotund, she had a large vermilion dot on her forehead, there was talcum powder on her neck and shoulders, and on her wrists were not only the ritual bands signalling she was married but also a set of plastic as well as gold bangles. I realized she was Bijon Datta's wife. His had been a late marriage. They had just the one son, who was about ten. 'The fellow can shoot well, uses both his feet.' He hadn't told me more than this about the boy. And about his wife, just this. 'Thank goodness I got married after giving up the game, else my football would have gone to hell. What a bitch. There's no love or anything like that between us any more. You won't understand unless you're married yourself.'

The irked expression on her face and Bijon Datta's attempt to explain something to her helplessly, waving his arms, suggested they were busy settling something personal. He hadn't seen me. I turned around right there and went back. I spent an hour with him the next day but he didn't mention his wife's visit.

A few days later, I was sitting on the same stool, waiting for Bijon Datta, who was in the bathroom. I spotted a tall woman, a widow, hesitating near the door – about thirty-five, with long oval eyes flanking a sharp nose. A sling bag hung from her shoulder. A patient immersed in his book near the door pointed towards me on being asked a question in a low voice. Coming up to me, she said softly, 'Is this Bijon Datta's bed?'

'Yes, please take a seat, he's gone to the bathroom.' I gave the stool up for her. Since it was uncomfortable to stand in silence near a woman I didn't know, I went out to the veranda. A minute or two later I heard Bijon Datta say joyfully, 'Minu!'

From the veranda I saw the woman's shy smile slowly change to anguish. As soon as she whispered something to Bijon Datta, he slapped his thigh and shouted, 'To hell with illness. I'm fine.' I couldn't hear him after this. Peeping in, I saw him talking without a pause in a low voice, laughing silently, eating an apple and even lifting the woman's hand surreptitiously to his lips and kissing her fingers.

I went in and told him, 'I'm off.'

Throwing a look at me, Bijon Datta nodded as though he were giving me permission.

I felt annoyed with him for the first time. I didn't go anywhere near the sanatorium for a week, going directly to the station from the school. Twice I saw his wife getting off the train, accompanied by the son on one occasion. I saw the widowed woman too, arriving at the station in a cycle rickshaw from the direction of the sanatorium. She bought her ticket and waited at one end of the platform, covering her face with her sari when a train from Calcutta arrived.

One day I visited Dr Basu Roy in his quarters. He was busy with some close relatives. As I was leaving, he said, 'Your friend was looking for you.' When he saw me look surprised, he said, 'The footballer Bijon Datta. He's been allowed to go out now.'

There was a pond behind the doctors' and other staff's quarters, and next to it, a slice of open land. The children played football there. I knew part of the wall by the pond was broken, allowing an exit that shortened the walk to the station by a minute or so. I was going that way when I suddenly heard a voice admonishing someone. 'Cover the left side, the left.' It was Bijon Datta, dressed in a vest and black shorts, running alongside a twelve-year-old boy who had the ball at his feet; Bijon Datta was waving his arms and giving directions to the defenders. I froze in fear. One shoulder charge and the frail boy would spin to the ground.

Reaching out and hooking the ball with his foot, Bijon Datta stood still and began to laugh. Not knowing what he should do, the boy gazed at him helplessly. 'Why are you standing there? Grab the ball from me – come on, charge me.' When the boy stepped up fearfully and tried to kick the ball way, Bijon pivoted and shielded it with his body. 'Push me, harder, harder. There's nothing to fear… Hopeless.' Sounding fed up, Bijon Datta continued, 'You can't play football if you're afraid. What does a man do when something goes wrong? Either he hits out or he dies. Hit me and take the ball off me. Football is a game of honour, a game for men.'

The boys were listening, stupefied. That was when he spotted me. Gesturing at me to wait, he told the boys, 'Keep playing. But don't forget – give it everything you've got.'

His face was red with exertion and excitement, his chest heaving frantically, the hair on his body sticking to his skin with perspiration. Coming up to me, he said, 'I couldn't control myself. How can the bee resist the flower?'

'It's wrong, what you're doing is absolutely wrong. You've begun running around even before you've recovered fully. What if there's a relapse?'

He seemed to enjoy being chided. Waving his hand, he said, 'I'll be fine. I've more or less recovered. Why didn't you come all these days, were you with your girlfriend?'

'Yes.'

Bijon Datta burst into laughter. We went up to the cemented steps leading down to the pond and sat down. A dog was curled up at the bottom of the steps, asleep. Two women were washing clothes on the opposite side. There was mild sunshine and a gentle breeze. A host of yellow flowers were in bloom. Bijon Datta wiped the perspiration off his brow.

'How's it going with your girlfriend?' I asked.

'Girlfriend?' He was genuinely surprised. 'That's my wife.'

'Not her, the other one.'

Bijon Datta looked disconcerted. Rising to his feet, he picked up a bamboo stick and poked the dog, who yelped and went a few feet away, wagging its tail, before settling down again. Bijon Datta began to slash the air with the stick as though it were a sword. The dog was probably accustomed to this. It waited instead of being scared off.

Bijon Datta came back and sat down again. 'I had planned to marry her. Orthodox Brahmin family – they were up in arms as soon as they heard. I wasn't educated, my job was nothing but a bearer's. Footballers didn't earn ten or fifteen thousand rupees those days, nothing but transport costs, not even a job like they get now.'

The light faded rapidly in the last hour of the day. Bijon Datta was looking haggard and vulnerable. Unable to look at his pale face, I turned my eyes to the shimmering reflection of the coconut tree in the water. A forlorn Bijon Datta continued, 'They used to live in the same neighbourhood but they left after this. Run away with me, she told me. I agreed but backed out eventually. Even today I don't know what I was afraid of, or why.'

'Doesn't your wife know about her?'

'I haven't told her but she must have heard from my family or the neighbours.'

'What will you do if they run into each other?' I asked anxiously.

'I'll watch the Mohun Bagan versus East Bengal match,' he said with a laugh.

I didn't prolong the discussion. 'You probably won't have to stay here much longer.'

'Yes, the temperature hasn't been caught offside for some days now. I cannot bear this imprisonment and the doctor's orders any more. Sometimes I wonder what I'm doing here. I've never been ill, not even for a day. The only time I went to the hospital was for my cartilage and my fractured foot.'

'How did you fall ill?'

'How? The doctor said it was overwork. But I've been working just as hard for twenty-five years. Do you know what he said to that? You're not a young man any more, you're older now. Of course, but I'm not an old man either. Am I?'

Looking at him, I realized that Bijon Datta would always be a young man in his own eyes. He would never be able to acknowledge his age. 'A month at the most. I'll go back and start with the boys at once. We have to get to the first division next year. The other day I saw in the papers that we lost by seven goals.'

He grimaced in pain as he uttered the last sentence but regained his composure immediately. 'The new fashion is for the half-back to go upfield and score. I never allow them to do that. They can go up just fine, but when there's a counter attack the gentlemen are unable to get back to their positions quickly. That's how they must have conceded so many goals. It wouldn't have happened if I'd been there. I once dropped one of my stoppers for four games because he disobeyed me.'

I was back the next day in a state of some excitement. Bijon Datta had just woken up and was sitting on his bed, his legs dangling. I held the handbill up before his eyes. 'Look, Pradip Sangha is playing an exhibition match here against a local eleven the day after tomorrow – that's Sunday.'

Snatching the handbill from my hand like a starving man, Bijon Datta read it breathlessly from beginning to end and said, 'I want to watch the game. How far is it? Will tickets be available?'

'It's about a mile and a half away. But you're not strong enough yet to take the strain.'

'That's for me to decide, you don't have to worry about it,' Bijon Datta answered brusquely. 'I'm sure Ratan will be there too with his team. I'll humiliate the bastard in front of everyone.'

The widowed woman entered at that moment. Biting back what I was about to say, I rose to my feet. As I went out through the sanatorium gate, I saw Bijon Datta's wife approaching, with her child. I felt a curious sense of jubilation. You can watch your Mohun Bagan versus East Bengal match now, my friend.

At the station I discovered that I had a long wait for the train to Calcutta. The widowed woman arrived soon afterwards, looking ashen and disgruntled. Throwing a glance at me, she sat down on a bench at one end of the platform.

On Sunday I went directly from the train to the venue of the match. Normally I wouldn't have bothered, for Pradip Sangha was not the kind of team for which I'd rush all the way from Calcutta on a holiday. Even though they were a first division team, I didn't even know the colour of their jersey. But I was sure Bijon Datta would be there and would create a scene with Ratan Sarkar. I was probably hoping for a showdown.

It was very crowded when I arrived. People had turned up even from distant villages, and there was a rush of buses, cycles and even bullock carts. The field had been fenced off with tin sheets. The Pradip Sangha players were staying at the house of a local businessman nearby. They would walk to the field. Youngsters were crowding around the gate through which they would enter.

Suddenly I noticed Bijon Datta pacing about impatiently a short distance from the gate. I didn't go up to him, and moved away from the crowd. Two of the students at the school where I taught hid their cigarettes and gave me sheepish smiles.

The jostling and shoving intensified as the Pradip Sangha players approached. From a distance I saw Bijon Datta moving towards a short, dark, plump man. I hurried to get closer to them.

I couldn't hear their preliminary conversation – all I saw was Bijon Datta saying something calmly, without agitation, whereupon the man looked uncomfortable and tried to sidestep him with a shrug. Bijon Datta blocked his way. Despite his surprise and annoyance, the other man said in a friendly voice, 'I heard you were ill. How are you now?'

'Very well. I'm feeling even better now that I've met you.' With a light smile Bijon Datta ran his eyes over the eager faces around them. 'So, Ratan, are you planning to buy your way to the first division championship this year too?'

'What do you mean?' Despite Ratan Sarkar's belligerence, there was fear in his eyes.

'That's just what I came to ask. Your team couldn't have earned seven points in seventeen games if you'd played fairly. Everyone is aware of your exploits.'

'What's all this you're saying, Bijon! Get out of my way.' Ratan Sarkar tried to hustle past Bijon Datta. A couple of taunts had been thrown at him already from the crowd.

A pleased Bijon Datta raised his voice even further. 'The game doesn't end so quickly. We'll definitely make it to the first division next year – and then I'll see how many games you can win with your expensive trousers and a place in the Bengal team and a hospital bed for the wife.'

'We won each and every game cleanly and honestly!' Ratan Sarkar shouted back.

'Yes, by bribing the opponent.'

'Hold your tongue, Bijon. Your coaching skills have relegated not one but two teams from the first division, you've been forced to join a second division team because no one else will have you. Now how will you survive except by maligning others?'

Bijon Datta looked like he was ready to pounce on Ratan Sarkar now. The blood had drained from his face. He was shaking uncontrollably. It wasn't good for his health to get so agitated. I tried to grab his arm but he freed himself with a jerk.

I breathed a sigh of relief as I saw Ratan Sarkar rushing in through the gate. 'Come on,' I said, 'the match will start now.'

'You can watch it if you want. I'm going back now.' His voice, which had been shaking with anger earlier, sounded fatigued now. I was frightened when I looked at his eyes. There was a strange emptiness in them. He seemed barely aware of the crowds and the commotion.

On the way back to the sanatorium in a cycle rickshaw, I asked him, 'I hope the doctor knows you're here.'

Leaning back, his body limp, Bijon Datta shook his head, saying softly, 'The doctor didn't give permission. If you want to develop pleurisy you can go, he said. I came secretly. Had to walk a long way.'

Bijon Datta began to cough. When he stopped I noticed that his breathing had become laboured. His body slumping, he clutched the handle of the seat and tried to keep his head from sinking to his chest. His face grey, he said, 'If only I were as young as you,' and remained silent the rest of the way.

When I went the next day I discovered he had had a fever of a hundred degrees since last night. The other three patients in his room had woken up several times because of his coughing fits. The doctor had said furiously that he wouldn't be at all surprised if pleurisy were to have set in.

'I should have obeyed the doctor. It wasn't a good idea to play with illness. Ratan might end up winning because of my foolishness. I've been foiled every time by my temper.' Bijon Datta tilted his head to gaze outside the window. A little later, he said, 'It's not entirely true that two teams were relegated because of me. None of the boys could play properly, no football sense at all. How much could I have done alone?'

I made enquiries with Dr Basu Roy. The sputum test was positive. Bijon Datta had lost his appetite, his eyes were sunken, he was losing weight rapidly. His wife came every day. She sat there miserably, saying softly from time to time, 'You shouldn't have gone. You knew it would harm you.'

I had never heard Bijon Datta utter terms like AP/PP, refill, PAS, thoracic and so on. He used to ignore the existence of this illness by eschewing these words. But these days he spoke about it sometimes, even though he had grown taciturn on the whole.

On my way to school one morning I spotted the widowed woman walking dejectedly towards the sanatorium. That afternoon I asked Bijon Datta with a laugh, 'What was the result of the East Bengal versus Mohun Bagan match?' A brief smile appeared on his face. Winking, he said, 'Match postponed. They're not willing to play on this pitch.'

A teachers' movement was about to be launched in Bengal in support of various demands. I was involved in the organization. There was to be a picket line in front of the Governor's House. Several days went by without my visiting Bijon Datta. When I went eventually, I found he had been shifted to a different room. Visitors weren't allowed. 'We are going to collapse the other lung,' said Dr Basu Roy.

I went again one afternoon four or five days later. I was allowed to see him for a minute, provided there was no conversation. Bijon Datta was lying on his back, staring at the ceiling. His cheeks were hollow. Only a wreck remained of a body that had once been so powerful.

'What news?' Bijon Datta rasped.

'No talking,' the nurse scolded him briefly.

Raising his hand to tell her not to worry, Bijon Datta asked me, 'Do they play every day by the pond?'

I didn't know whether they did but to please him, I said, 'Yes, every day.'

'One of the boys there – you'll see, fantastic football sense.'

The nurse said, 'You must leave now or he'll keep talking.'

As I turned to go, I heard him wheeze, 'I've decided to groom him.'

I mused about him as I walked to the station. The body lying like an ancient ruin alone in that room kept appearing before my eyes – the laboured effort to raise a withered arm, the gasps for breath in an effort to speak. I wasn't sure whether death had as yet prised open the lock of invincibility that his savage spirit of life had given him.

I was on my way to the sanatorium one evening four or five days later. The autumnal sky was an intense blue, its radiance stretching into the distance. A woman's gentle voice raised in song wafted in from one of the houses nearby. I turned the corner slowly. The road lay straight ahead now. I could see the gate of the sanatorium. Suddenly I saw the widowed woman emerging from the gate, holding the hand of Bijon Datta's son, while his wife followed with tired footsteps.

That was when I realized that he was about to die.

The Blazer

1

For twenty minutes after leaving the Talkatora Swimming Pool, the father and the son had been trying to get a taxi or an autorickshaw. Buses on different routes drove past them but they didn't know which one would take them to their hotel. On their way back from the inauguration of the Asian Games at Nehru Stadium they had taken a bus on a man's advice and ended up in north Delhi. That was when they had decided, never again.

'One of these buses is bound to go past our hotel. Let's ask the conductor and get in.' Barun looked uncertainly at his son for approval. Bolu's assent was more important to him than many other things. 'Even if it takes us somewhere nearby – waiting like this…'

'But the government should have arranged for transport. So many foreign tourists here, people from all over the country too – are they all going to take buses?' Bolu's voice held more criticism than annoyance. Barun savoured it, especially the flawless pronunciation of *government*.

Raising his eyebrows and shrugging, he said, 'Do you think we'd have to run around for a taxi quite so long in a foreign country?'

Bolu was silent.

'It's the same story all over India,' Barun ranted. 'Be it a taxi or an autorickshaw or a bus or tram, you'll never get one when you need it... What time is the match?'

Drawing back the sleeve of his blazer to check the time on his watch, Barun thought he heard a ripping sound near the underarm. The blazer was twenty-eight years old. It was still usable only because Sudha had taken care of it. But what could she do if the thread began to rot? Nor was he as trim as he used to be twenty-eight years ago. He weighed a little over sixty kilos then. Four days ago he had checked at Howrah Station – his weight was seventy-six kilos now.

Bolu ran behind a taxi, and so did Barun. But Bolu stopped after a few steps. The doctor had forbidden sudden activity. He marched up smartly instead. The passenger paid the fare and looked at them. When he saw the blazer he turned to look directly at Barun, his eyes briefly betraying his effort to make a connection. He tried to read the words on the pocket of the blazer, and then looked at Barun again, smiled faintly and walked up to the entrance to the pool.

Barun was enveloped by a sudden sense of self-satisfaction.

'Why did he look at you?'

Did the blazer not suit him? The older the blazer, the more its value. Was this one ready to be consigned to a museum?

Am I looking very old? Was the man staring at me? Do people still recognize me?

Barun looked at his son. Bolu was hungrily devouring the streets and houses, the trees and the sights through the window. This was his first visit to Delhi. When had he come for the first time? It was to play in his first Durand Cup. Which year? A smile appeared on Barun's face. Thirty-one years had passed in a flash.

'The house are so beautiful, and what wide roads and lovely trees. No deafening car horns.'

Seeing that Bolu was getting carried away, Barun said softly but seriously, 'Remember, this is India's capital, and Asia's biggest sporting event is under way. Everything has to be bright and glittering. It's a matter of national prestige. Foreign dignitaries everywhere...'

He was fretting over the tearing sound near his underarm. Where could he get the blazer repaired if it had ripped?

'I don't feel like watching the badminton, are you interested?'

'We do have tickets for one more day.'

'Padukone is out – at least if there'd been an Indian challenge... What a marvellous stadium! We couldn't even imagine all this in our day. An indoor stadium for 25,000 people – you have to hand it to Delhi.'

'Yesterday I saw a street named Copernicus Marg. Calcutta's streets should also have such names.'

'What about Shakespeare Sarani?'

'There should be one for a scientist.'

'Einstein?'

'Yes.' Bolu turned to him and smiled. 'This city hasn't turned filthy like Calcutta, with revolting statues of political leaders.'

'Correct!' Barun nodded vehemently a couple of times. He was happy that Bolu was mature for his age.

The moment their taxi drove through the gate of the new hotel constructed for the Asian Games and stopped in the portico, a waiting couple came forward eagerly. Paying the fare, Barun turned around to look at the new passengers.

The eyes of the balding, thickset, dark-skinned man were on the pocket of Barun's blazer, where it was embroidered in golden thread: 'Indian Football Team, Manila Asian Games, 1954.' The letters were discoloured and the thread had come off in places, which made the words difficult to read, even though the light shining through the hotel door was quite strong. Barun turned to face the man so that he could read properly. The man summoned the beginnings of a smile to his face and raised his eyes to look at Barun, who smiled back courteously. He noticed that the man said something to his wife as soon as they got into the taxi, after which both of them turned to look at him through the rear window of the vehicle as it started moving.

Frowning, Barun placed a foot on the steps and discovered Bolu looking at him in surprise.

'Someone you know?'

'No, not at all. Why do you ask?'

'Nothing.'

Once again he felt a burst of self-satisfaction. 'It's amazing how strong some people's memories are,' he said to himself.

While collecting the room key, Barun felt that the receptionist's eyes had settled on his breast pocket for three seconds before flying off. He'd never seen this particular young man at the counter before. He didn't look like he had the slightest curiosity about Barun's blazer. Maybe he didn't like football or perhaps he wasn't bothered about anyone except film stars. He can't have been born before the Manila Games. His father or uncle might be familiar with the name Barun Chatterjee, assuming they were even interested in football in the first place.

The sofas in front of the television set in the lobby were packed with viewers, and many were standing and watching. Bolu moved in that direction. Women's volleyball.

'Hurry up, Bolu, what time is the match?' About to lift his left wrist to his eyes, Barun stopped and looked at the wall clock in the lobby instead.

As they waited for the lift, Barun wondered who the man might have been. He'd stopped playing twenty years or so ago; the man was at least forty. He looked like he was a Bengali, maybe someone from Calcutta who had a job here. Even if he'd started watching football at seventeen, say – Bolu's age – he must have heard of Barun, maybe even watched him play. It shouldn't be too difficult to remember him – the papers published his photograph at least two or three times a year, although most of them were from the time he was twenty-four or twenty-five. Still, other than gaining weight and losing some of his hair, he had hardly changed.

Had he recognized me or was the curiosity only on account of the blazer?

His self-satisfaction persisted, however, and he felt that he too had a role to play in these Asian Games. He would have to achieve something here. Bolu's 'Do you know him?' and the surprise in his eyes seemed to show Barun the way. He appeared to be discovering his own identity after all these years. Here was an opportunity to present himself in a new way to his son. He'd never had the chance in Calcutta – people would have laughed if he had worn the blazer there. He felt grateful to the Delhi Asian Games.

Some people came out of the lift. Barun didn't notice that one of them stopped short at the sight of him before continuing on his way. His eyes were on Bolu. The boy was engrossed in the television.

2

Frowning at his son for a few moments, Barun Chatterjee drew back his sleeve to glance at his watch. Making a quick calculation, he spoke rapidly. 'Fifteen minutes…twenty at the most. Get dressed. Warm socks, full-sleeved sweater, jacket. And take your cap too. Carry the overcoat. I'll go the bathroom, meanwhile. I'm asking for tea – would you like a bite to eat? You mustn't starve – we won't be back before ten. What time did we get back last night? I'm ordering sandwiches. And listen, not those jeans. You have no idea how cold it gets in Delhi – change into your warm trousers. When we used to come here for the Durand Cup…'

Barun picked up the telephone receiver. 'I'm speaking from room number four zero five, yes, four hundred and five. Two plates of chicken sandwiches and a pot of tea…quickly, please.'

He looked at his son from the corner of his eye. Bolu studied in an English medium school. Class Nine. He was more or less fluent in English, and even his pronunciation was different. It was Barun who felt uncomfortable speaking in English in his son's presence. He had passed his Intermediate of Arts exams in 1952. He had registered for his third year in college, but that was all, he hadn't studied further.

Football had put paid to education. He'd even been abroad twice with the Indian football team, one of the visits being to Manila for the Asian Games, but he hadn't been able to master English. He'd had neither the opportunity nor the need to speak Hindi during the first thirty years of his life. He was not only shy but also perpetually worried about speaking ungrammatically and becoming an object of embarrassment for others.

With his back turned to Barun, Bolu was trying to wriggle out of his jeans. Well-built and deeply interested in the game, he played as the central striker in the school team. Let the boy play if he wanted to, Barun had no objection. Through his own efforts he had built an agency for selling paints, and a three-storeyed house which brought in a rent of two and a half thousand rupees a month. There was the plot of land in Salt Lake too. All of these would go to Bolu. He wouldn't lack for money. If he became a well-known footballer he'd have fame, recognition, honour – just like Barun had once, and perhaps still did. Still did? Did anyone recognize him now? Would they?

Bolu was his only son. Unlike today's rude and cocky teenagers, he loved and respected his parents, did well in his studies, was good-looking too, with a face like his mother's. Barun loved his son. He tried his utmost to make himself an inspiring figure to his son. He'd been successful – just last month Bolu had got him to sign two autograph books.

'I don't want to take the overcoat, it can't be all that cold.'

'No, you must. The cold is treacherous here. You won't feel it but it is… I caught a cold while playing in the Santosh Trophy here in Delhi. We were walking back from a night show… I've told you the story. My chest was congested, I couldn't play any of the matches before the final. But I scored the winning goal for Bengal in the final. Don't forget, it's an open stadium – you mustn't ignore the cold.'

Barun went into the bathroom and shut the door, emerging ten minutes later. The tea and sandwiches had arrived. Bolu was stirring the tea, a sandwich in his other hand.

'Check the tickets, make sure we have the right date.'

Quickly putting on his sweater, Barun lovingly picked up his twenty-eight-year-old sky-blue blazer from the bed. Examining it carefully, he plucked out a half-inch length of red thread with his fingertips and flicked some dust off the shoulder. Then he slipped his arms in gingerly. He could no longer button it at his stomach, and it sat tightly on his shoulders too. Barun was on tenterhooks whenever he put the blazer on, always worrying that the seam would split. 'I have to lose weight, too much fat,' he told himself every time he wore the blazer, as he did now as well.

Taking the tickets out of Barun's briefcase, Bolu scanned them quickly. 'It's okay, today's date.'

'Still a good idea to check. In Singapore once we...'

He paused. Bolu was kneeling to tie his shoelaces, not paying attention. He must have heard the story a couple of dozen times.

Finishing his sandwiches and tea, Barun looked around the room. Glancing in the mirror, he patted the locks of hair combed across his balding pate and behind his ears.

'Check whether the door to the veranda is locked.' He tugged at the locks on the suitcases to make sure they were secure. 'I know nothing will be stolen, you can trust the staff at big hotels, but it's a good habit to have. Always be careful. Let's go now.'

Before locking the door, Barun checked how much money he had in his wallet and smiled at his son. 'We'll eat at Kake Da Dhaba in Connaught Place tonight. Nice and spicy, but too rich. Once in a while it's fine, though.'

3

Out on the road they waited to flag down an autorickshaw. Stopping an empty one, Barun said, 'Nehru Stadium.'

Shaking his head to indicate his unwillingness to take them, the driver sped off. After waiting a while longer, they began to walk.

'Let's try here.'

Barun stopped in a bright pool of light at the crossing of Sansad Marg and Ashoka Road. There was enough light for his blazer to be visible.

'This is the problem, you can't get into an auto without the driver's permission.'

'Taxi drivers in Calcutta do the same thing. It's obnoxious – just shows how underdeveloped we are.'

Barun enjoyed his son's use of the words obnoxious and underdeveloped in English.

'And we're supposed to be the leader of the Third World.' Barun felt he was the first footballer in India to use the phrase Third World. How many of today's footballers could do it?

'Get that one, Bolu!'

Not only did the driver of the autorickshaw stop on seeing them, he also agreed instantly to take them to Nehru Stadium.

They had to get out of the autorickshaw nearly half a mile away from the stadium. There was a huge stream of people. They flowed along with them to reach the stadium. As they were climbing the stairs, Barun smiled and nodded at a Sikh of about his age, dressed in a blazer. The man raised a hand. His blazer said 'Tokyo Asian Games 1958'. Barun didn't have the time to read the name of the sport – possibly athletics or hockey.

'Someone you know?'

'Me? No.'

'He raised his hand.'

'Really? Maybe he recognized me.'

The football match had India playing Bangladesh. The stadium, which had a seating capacity of 75,000, was packed. They managed to squeeze in somehow. It was obvious from the conversations that most of the spectators around them were Bengalis.

'Put on your cap.'

'Later.'

'Do it now, the Delhi cold is treacherous.'

Bolu put on the cap reluctantly. His ears remained uncovered; Barun pulled the cap down over them.

India won 2-0. As they jostled their way down the stairs, someone said in response to a comment made by the person next to Barun, 'Prasoon took two shots from thirty yards out and scored with both. How can an international goalkeeper let in goals off those shots?'

'Of course they can. What terrific shots – the ball swerved so much.'

'As if you could tell the swerve from where we were sitting. What nonsense.'

Their voices rose and others turned around to look. A few steps below them, Barun leaned slightly towards Bolu and said, 'Forget thirty, I've scored against Sanjiv in the Rovers Cup from forty yards out. Sanjiv was definitely India's best goalkeeper then – one of the best in the world too.'

Barun spoke louder than he needed to for Bolu to hear. Many heads turned. Sharp eyes probed his face and then moved eagerly to his blazer. The breast pocket was hidden behind the crowd's view by Bolu, who was right in front of him. He was tall for his age.

There were a few curious whispers. 'Who is he?'

'India team blazer...which year, can you see?'

'Our fathers' generation.'

'Can you recognize him? Which club did he play for?'

'Ask him who he is. Don't be shy, ask... What's your name, dada?'

'Barun Chatterjee.'

He answered somewhat carelessly. There were no more questions. He observed the faces around him covertly. Expressionless. Discussions about the just-completed match resumed. No one gave him a second glance.

4

They had walked half a mile after leaving the stadium but there was still no taxi or autorickshaw to be found. They didn't get into a bus as Barun was afraid of where it might take them.

'Let's wait here.'

'It was the same yesterday. We had no problem getting back from Talkatora in the afternoon.'

Two taxis sped past, packed with people. An autorickshaw refused them.

'Let's go back a bit to the crossroads.'

The roads were desolate, barring a few pedestrians. Another man stood there, probably waiting for transport, just like them. He came up to them a little later and asked, 'Where are you going?'

'Hotel Olive, Janpath.'

'Ah, I'm going close by – Ashok Jatri Niwas. We can share… Do you see how pathetic the transport situation is? I've been waiting twenty minutes.' The man kept throwing glances at Barun's blazer as he talked. 'You were in the '54 Asian Games. I was a stand-by for the cycling team in '51…Jimmy Dastur.'

Shaking the man's outstretched hand, Barun looked at his face. His thick red sweater suited his fair skin perfectly. Thick eyebrows, balding in front. A scar on his forehead. Dastur was about the same age.

'We can go together. But…' Dastur began to run, still talking. 'Taxi, taxiiiii…'

The taxi stopped. After a brief conversation with the driver Dastur beckoned to them. Holding the door open, he said, 'Get in. We've been lucky, at least we got a cab.'

As they sped off, Dastur said, 'I'm from Bombay. I watch football quite often – I enjoy it.'

'I've played in the Rovers Cup eight times. Twice in the final.'

'Really! What's your name? Which club? Is this your son?'

'Barun Chatterjee...I played for both Mohun Bagan and East Bengal, from '50 to '59. Yes, my son.'

Bolu extended his hand with a smile.

'Then I must have watched you play. Your name rings...tell me, did you play against ICL in 1952?'

'Yes.'

'Did you score?'

'Yes.'

'Oh yes! Fantastic goal...fantastic! I can still see it. The right-out chipped the ball, you grabbed it, dodged past two players and then a diagonal shot, it must have been...what, twenty? Twenty-five? Am I right?'

'Forty yards.' Bolu spoke almost inaudibly, holding his breath.

Dastur's thick brows came together, indicating some confusion. 'Fo...r...ty? Is that so? Sanjiv was the goalkeeper, wasn't he?'

'Yes, forty. I remember.' Barun presented the information softly, almost deferentially, but with uncertainty and anxiety in his mind.

'Must be. But it was a fabulous goal. I can still see it.'

Dastur wanted to drop them first. Barun objected, and insisted on paying the fare. Finally they agreed to stop halfway between their respective hotels, so that no one would have to walk more than two hundred yards.

'But I'm paying the fare.' Barun was insistent. For the first time he'd met someone who remembered his goal. He didn't want to let him go.

'Baba, we could go for dinner to Kake Da right now. Why let the taxi go?'

Barun was astonished. How strange, why had this simple solution not occurred to him? During his playing days no one could have accused him of being thickheaded. But it was Bolu who had been intelligent enough to...

'Ask him to join us for dinner, Baba,' Bolu whispered in Barun's ear.

He all but leapt up. Instructing the taxi driver to go to Connaught Place, he gripped Dastur's arm. 'Mr Dastur, you must have dinner with us tonight...please, it's my son's request.'

About to refuse, Dastur smiled when he saw their faces and nodded helplessly. 'I must have got off the right side of the bed this morning. But I'm paying the fare.'

'As you wish,' said Barun, as though he were generously giving permission.

A table on the first floor of Kake Da Dhaba had just been vacated, so they didn't have to wait.

Barun held out the menu to Dastur. 'Please order whatever you want.'

'I don't eat spicy food. Naan and egg bhaji. I'm not used to a full meal at night.'

Barun looked surprised and disappointed. He had planned to repay Dastur for remembering his goal by giving him a huge dinner.

'Please eat whatever you like, I eat lightly at night.'

'We don't eat much either. You order, Bolu.'

Passing the menu to his son, he lowered his head and said softly, 'Order the way a footballer would.'

Dastur looked on with a smile as Bolu ordered with a great deal of care, after questioning the waiter in detail.

'My son plays football too.'

'Indeed! I have a daughter – she doesn't care for sports, she's learning to play the piano.'

'That's good – she's into culture. You weren't part of the Indian team after '51?'

Dastur smiled. Shaking his head, he said, 'The Indian cycling team never toured after that till I retired. After I gave up competitive cycling a team was sent to the Tokyo Olympics. There's no velodrome in the country, so no expertise either. You need to practise regularly to be able to ride at an angle of forty-five degrees – you can't develop this skill overnight. Our cyclists couldn't even compete in Tokyo, they had to scratch.'

'You should have chosen a different sport,' Bolu said gravely. He was very anxious, having no idea how the food he'd ordered would taste.

'Among other sports, football is my favourite.'

'That's obvious, or you wouldn't have remembered my goal, what kind of pass, the dodges, the shot…'

'From forty yards out,' said Bolu, holding his breath.

Dastur frowned. Stopping himself from saying what he was about to, he only muttered, 'But Sanjiv was the goalkeeper.'

Barun had heard. His face turned pale for a moment. He threw a glance at Bolu, who was frowning.

'You don't know how powerful my shots were, Mr Dastur. The Burmese goalkeeper knows – that was the only match in Manila where India was leading 1-0 in the first half. Forty yards… The newspaper clipping… Bolu, I think your mother has the file… The Chinese goalkeeper dived miraculously and saved the goal, that one was also from thirty-five or forty yards out.'

Dastur was taken aback. He hadn't expected Barun to take a casual remark of his so seriously. Barun had indeed scored past Sanjiv, but he'd have to be very credulous to believe it had been from forty yards out. But he was a guest now, and he should not say anything that could upset the host.

'I've heard a lot about your shots, in Bombay as well as Calcutta.'

'Calcutta!' Bolu was surprised.

'I've been to Calcutta many times. I have many Bengali friends. They told me how you were unjustly left out of the '56 Olympic team.'

Barun sat up in sudden excitement. Looking out of the corner of his eye at Bolu, he saw astonishment.

'You never told me, Baba.'

Barun felt a tremor in his heart. It wasn't just astonishment, his son's young face was also suffused with profound respect now. What more could he seek from the next generation? This respect would pass on down the ages. Bolu's son and his son and his son – all of them would be told how their forefather, the founder of the dynasty, was a famous and talented footballer who had played for the country but was unjustly left out of the Olympic team despite being fully qualified for it. He would live on a long time.

'What's the use of talking about all this? Is it appropriate for a man to tell his son about such a thing? That would be in bad taste. You heard it from this gentleman, maybe you'll hear it from others – that's how you will get to know.'

The food had arrived. One plate after another was set out on their table.

'So much food – this is impossible.' Dastur was genuinely alarmed.

'Eat as much as you can, let the rest be.' Barun's broad smile was radiantly bountiful. 'Who knows when we'll meet again. You must let us know when you're in Calcutta next – I'll give you my card, do ring me.'

'It's my good fortune too to get to meet such a great footballer on visiting Delhi.' Dastur lowered his head to eat.

'When did you hear about my being left out unjustly?'

'When it happened. There was some Gupta – you were declared medically unfit to accommodate him. Was that what it was?'

'Yes.'

'Who's Gupta, Baba?'

'Gupta, a Bengali, his first name is Shubhendu. You wouldn't have heard of him. Never played for India except on that Olympic team. Didn't even make it to the playing eleven in Melbourne. How could he – Rahim could tell real players from fake ones. Every time I met him Rahim saab would say, sorry Barun, it's you who should have got the Olympic blazer, but an ass got it instead. This is what happens – they cosy up to selectors, do them favours and then proudly strut around in Olympic blazers… You'll see many of them here too.'

5

The entire crowd in the lobby was around the television set. It was only 10 p.m.

'Are you planning to sit here and watch?'

'For a bit.'

Bolu joined the crowd. As Barun was on his way to the lift after collecting his key, someone called him from behind in a deep voice. He stopped and turned.

'When did you get here, you bugger? I saw you in the lift when I was going out, didn't speak to you then because I was in a hurry.'

Barun was staring as though he'd seen a ghost. The blood had drained from his face. His fingers shook uncontrollably. How extraordinary that Shubhendu Gupta was standing in front of him at this moment!

'You!'

'Yes, me. Don't you think I might want to watch the Asian Games too? Do you think I can't afford to come to Delhi because I'm a clerk?'

Exposing stained teeth, the gaunt figure ran his fingers through his salt-and-pepper hair. His orange full-sleeved shirt, sitting on the dark skin, felt like a nail being drilled into Barun's head. The tie was faded. Barun recognized it – he had one too, although he wasn't wearing it.

'Are you off to your room? Let's go sit in the bar. I'm seeing you after such a long time. What do you do these days, the same paints business?'

Before he could answer, Shubhendu steered him by the elbow towards the bar. Barun turned his head to find Bolu immersed in the action on the television. He felt a sense of relief – Bolu hadn't seen him.

'Which room are you in?' he asked Shubhendu.

'Five twenty-four.'

Most of the tables were free. They sat at one near the wall. Barun was trying to work out how to extricate himself from the situation. He had always disliked this man. Arrogant, foul-mouthed, greedy and uneducated. Alcohol, drugs – there was nothing he wasn't addicted to.

'What'll you have?' Barun glanced at his watch to indicate he was in a hurry.

'You want to buy me a drink? I thought I'd buy you one.'

'I gave up a long time ago. Heart trouble. And besides, we just had dinner.'

'Take a small one. Even if you don't drink it – else I'll be uncomfortable.'

Shubhendu ordered one large and one small rum.

'You seem to have had a few already.'

'One or two. I still have a few fans. I can't turn them down. This hotel room is also being paid for by one of them. Wanted to watch the Asian Games. He flew me here. We're in the room together, we'll go back together too. Unlimited wealth, no one to pass it on to. Smuggles gold – don't go telling anyone now.'

Barun realized that Shubhendu had been carrying a coat on his arm when he tossed it on a chair. When it fell to the floor, Barun bent to pick it up.

A blazer just like the one he was wearing. Except the words on the breast pocket were different. This one was an Olympic blazer.

'Why don't you take care of it?' Barun shook the dust off the blazer and put it on the table. He noticed one of the buttons was missing.

The waiter brought the drinks.

'Cheers.'

Barun raised his glass and put it down at once.

'I don't take care of it at all. I didn't even know I had it. Before leaving my son told me, take this along. So I did. But oh lord, when I tried to put it on I saw how baggy it looks. So I carry it on my arm. I even forgot it during a hockey match I was watching. Someone reminded me. Yours seems to fit you quite well. You've looked after yourself.'

There was neither happiness nor regret in Shubhendu's voice. His eyes were as cunning as ever. He was savouring his drink. Barun didn't know what he was plotting now. It was as impossible to read him as it had been to read his game. No defence in India had a clue where he would appear to put the ball in the net.

'Watched the game?'

'I did.' Shubhendu's disinterested reply made it clear he wasn't keen on discussing it. Draining his glass, he signalled the waiter for a refill.

'What were the goals like?'

'Like goals. Even you would have scored if you'd played today. Fourth class.'

Barun paled. Shubhendu had always referred to him as a third-class player, even in front of others. He looked at his watch.

'You're not enjoying my company, which is why you keep looking at your watch, right? Are you with anyone?'

'My son.' And immediately he remembered that the key was with him – Bolu might be waiting for him in the corridor. He leaped to his feet. Shubhendu lifted his eyes.

'What's your room number?'

'Four zero five. The key's with me.' Barun displayed the key.

'You're leaving? Not buying me another drink?'

'Of course, of course, go ahead.' Barun waved urgently for the waiter.

'Bring this saab four more large rums. And bring the bill fast… Will four be enough?'

'Yes, they will.'

'Don't forget your blazer.'

Looking at it carelessly, Shubhendu said, 'What difference does it make whether I do or not? What have I gained from playing football? It would have been better if I'd learnt to drive a bullock cart instead. Football has given you a lot. And yet, I was a much better player. I injured my knee in '54 – I couldn't go despite being selected, you went instead. And now you're strutting around in that blazer. Listen, can you give me some money?'

'Money?'

'About five hundred.'

'You think I have five hundred rupees?' Barun's voice was acidic.

'My knee gave you that blazer. Give it to the knee.'

Barun didn't reply. Paying the bill and tipping the waiter, he left quickly.

Bolu was indeed waiting. He looked questioningly at his father.

'You'll never believe it,' Barun said. 'That ass nabbed me. The one whom Dastur spoke of at Kake Da…Gupta…Shubhendu. I ran into him. What a strange coincidence.'

'Shubhendu Gupta! Who was sent to the Olympics while you were declared unfit. What's he doing here?'

'He's staying in this hotel. Showing off his Olympic blazer to people – makes me laugh.'

They changed into their nightclothes, switched off the lights, and got into bed.

'The morning's free – hockey in the evening, right?'

'Yes.'

A little later Bolu said softly, 'Baba.'

'What?'

'The Olympic blazer earns more respect than the Asiad one, doesn't it?'

Barun was silent. Bolu said nothing more.

6

In the morning, Barun left the room while Bolu was in the bathroom. Returning about twenty minutes later, he saw Bolu putting his shoes on. A waiter was taking away the empty plates.

'Are you going out? Where?'

'I'll take a walk, maybe go see the underground Palika Bazar. Want to come?'

'No, my stomach's acting up – I overate yesterday. Need some money?'

'Yes. I have to buy a belt.'

Barun gave him a hundred-rupee note. He made a phone call after Bolu left, and then went into the bathroom with the newspaper.

The phone rang about an hour later. Barun was lying on his bed, his eyes closed. He shot up and answered the phone.

'No, he isn't back yet…I'll ring you…yes, I've told you already.' Barun disconnected the phone and went back to bed.

Barun woke up when the doorbell rang. It was Bolu.

'That took a long time.'

'They're showing the diving heats and women's volleyball on television.'

Bolu had a new belt around his waist. He showed it to his father. He'd also bought a T-shirt with the Appu mascot.

'Good buys. Go have your bath now. I'd fallen asleep – it's been hectic these past few days.'

As soon as Bolu went into the bathroom and shut the door, Barun almost ran to the phone.

Bolu opened the bathroom door again and came out. Barun didn't see him because he had his back to his son. As Bolu picked up the towel from the chair and went back into the bathroom he heard the words 'come by in fifteen minutes'.

Bolu had put on his undershirt and picked up his comb when the doorbell rang. He looked at his father in surprise.

'Can you see who it is?' Barun said in an annoyed tone.

'Is Barun Chatterjee…oh, there you are, Barun.'

A frail, dark man in a baggy blazer entered. 'I thought I'd say hello. How are you? Is this your son?'

'Yes.' Irritation was writ large on Barun's face. 'I was about to go for a bath.'

'The great footballer retains his temper, I see. Do you know, my boy…what's your name?'

'Balen.' Announcing his name coldly, Bolu stared at the blazer. The very thought that his father had not been able to go to the Olympics because of this man had soured his attitude.

'Do you know, Balen, your father would practise shooting and we'd stand behind the goalposts to retrieve the ball. The slightest delay and he'd take our heads off. So many people used to stop to watch your father shoot at the goal. He'd shoot from thirty or forty yards out and the goalkeeper wouldn't even have time to dive. Even a goalkeeper like Sanjiv was beaten hands down. You know the story, don't you?'

'I do. Rovers Cup, 1952, and after that at the Manila Games too he scored against Burma from forty yards out.'

'Wonderful – you know a great deal about your father's exploits.'

Shubhendu sat down in a chair. Barun stood behind him and signalled to Bolu with his hands to get rid of him quickly.

'Of course I do. I also know how he was cheated out of going to Melbourne.' Bolu stared aggressively at Shubhendu through narrowed eyes. It was because of this man that his father had been left out of the team.

'It was indeed injustice. When I think about it I know I did something terribly wrong, something that cannot be forgiven. What did I get for depriving a worthy man?' Shubhendu's voice was thick with contrition, his head was bowed. Barun was looking at him unwaveringly.

'That blazer, of course.'

Shubhendu raised his head to look at Bolu with empty eyes. A strange mixture of deep sadness, despair and exhaustion reappeared in them.

'Yes, this blazer. Whenever I put it on I feel I'm wearing something I've stolen. I've often wanted to give it to Barun. But then I felt embarrassed too. What if he refused? He was a far greater footballer than I was. There was no one in India who was anywhere near as good as Barun in his time. This blazer holds no value for me. You know the story of the donkey dressed in a lion's skin, don't you? That's what this one is. Do you suppose I can turn into Barun Chatterjee by putting this on? The lion is always a lion, Barun is always Barun.'

A quiet happiness had appeared on Bolu's face. His combative attitude had melted away, making way for compassion, a desire for reconciliation.

'Will you have some tea?'

'No, not at this hour. I told you yesterday I'd drop by, Barun, so I did. I put on the blazer deliberately, so that you might hate me – that would be my punishment.'

'Of course not, what are you saying?' Barun finally spoke. He had been in a daze. 'What made you think I would hate you?'

'We have to atone for our sins.'

'How?'

'I'm going to burn this blazer.'

'What!' Bolu practically screamed.

'When did you start getting these peculiar ideas?' Barun all but shouted at Shubhendu.

'Last night. When I saw you in your blazer it occurred to me that I shouldn't be wearing this one. I couldn't sleep all night.'

Shubhendu suddenly leapt to his feet and tore his blazer off with a violent movement. He appeared distraught, his eyes about to burst out of their sockets. He looked around for something.

'Got a matchbox?'

'Please sit down,' said Bolu.

'What madness is this, Shubhendu?' Barun snatched the blazer away from his hands.

'Keep it, let it remain with you.' Shubhendu's face brightened. He gazed at the blazer with relieved eyes, as though a huge weight had been lifted off his shoulders. Pleadingly he said, 'Will you honour my request?'

Two streams of tears rolled down his cheeks. He was pressing

Barun's hands in his own. Bolu looked at his father. What should he do now? The man was clearly not as horrible as he had thought. Very honest, in fact. None of his friends in Calcutta would believe what had happened if he told them. It was really dramatic.

Barun looked at his son with beleaguered eyes – what should I do now?

'Keep it, Baba.'

A distressed Shubhendu kept looking alternately at Barun and Bolu.

'All right.'

'Put it on, let me look at you.'

An unsettled Barun put the blazer on simply to comply with Shubhendu's request. It was a perfect fit. Looking into the mirror, he saw a self-satisfied smile appear automatically on his lips.

'I'll go now, I'll go.' Shubhendu rushed out.

'What a strange man… Who gives away something like this?

After lunch at the restaurant in the hotel, both of them lay down. Bolu was leafing through an old sports magazine when the phone rang. Turning to look at his father, he saw Barun was asleep. Bolu answered the phone.

'Were you asleep, bastard? How was my performance? I astonished myself. Listen, you'd better keep that blasted blazer, just give me two hundred more… Hello, hello…'

Replacing the receiver on its cradle, Bolu gazed out of the window. His knees had turned to jelly, he felt on the point of collapse. His throat was dry.

'Who rang, Bolu?'

'Wrong number.'

Bolu heard his father turn over on his bed. Slumping into a chair, he hid his face in his hands. He couldn't think any more. Nor did he want to. Just one question buzzed in his head continuously – whom was this for? Whom had Baba done this for?

They were both dressed to go and watch the hockey match at the National Stadium.

'Are the tickets in your pocket? Your sweater? All right, let's go now.'

Barun went towards the door.

'Baba.'

He turned around.

'Put on the blazer.'

'What are you saying? Anyone who knows will laugh. I never even went to the Olympics…'

'I don't care if they laugh, I'd like you to wear it. It fits you perfectly.' Bolu lit up with excitement. 'Put it on. He did say it belongs to you.'

As they left the hotel in search of an autorickshaw, Barun wearing the blazer, Bolu said effusively, 'You're looking just like an Olympian.'

Reddy

Amar had not considered the possibility that the fellow might actually turn up. He certainly wouldn't have given him his name and address in that case.

Here's what happened. Having graced the chief guest's chair at the final of a tournament in Contai, he was returning the next day to Calcutta in a rich businessman's car. The businessman was a fan not just of the Juger Jatri football club but also of his. The man was gratified at the privilege of hosting Amar for the night and grateful for the opportunity to have driven him home.

But his Ambassador did not appear quite as beholden. Snapping its fan belt on Bombay Road, it left Amar stranded on the highway. Two trucks did not heed his attempts to stop them, but a Kharagpur-bound Maruti drew up even without his trying to flag it down. One of Amar's countless anonymous fans. The driver hitched a ride to buy a replacement belt in Mecheda. Amar remained to guard the car.

Farmland stretched out on both sides of the road. A searing heatwave had been followed by three successive days of rain. Apparently the sowing of paddy had been delayed by the late arrival of the monsoon. Some women were planting seeds. Having watched them from the car for a while, Amar got out and began to walk towards a cluster of huts with thatched roofs. A narrow path paved with bricks meandered from the highway towards the village. At the top of this road were a sweet shop, a grocery, a cycle repair shop and a tea shop. Two men sat on a bench fashioned from bamboo strips and posts, drinking tea.

A woman was behind the shop counter, while a boy of about ten was pounding lumps of coal. Sitting on the bench, Amar ordered a cup of tea. The woman looked as rickety as her shop. He could tell that her striped handloom sari had once been purple in colour, just as he could tell that she had once been fair and even lovely. Biscuits and slices of cake were stored in dirty jars, with cigarettes and bidis on one side. There was a line of vermilion in the woman's hair. Amar surmised her husband was at work somewhere, perhaps busy with sowing.

His first instinct on sipping the tea was to pour it out of the cup. He held back only because it would disappoint and upset the woman. Many people wondered how he could have such a gentle disposition and yet tackle opponents ruthlessly on the football pitch. Amar had been playing in the first division for eight years. A number of players had felt the impact of his elbow on their teeth and mouths, or of his boots on their stomachs, ninety per cent of these incidents being deliberate. Amar was a rough footballer, but outside the field he was soft-spoken – a complete gentleman.

As he sipped his tea, he noticed a framed photograph on the fence that passed off as the walls of the shop. The dust and grime around it made it impossible to identify the subject. Trying to hazard a guess as he rose to his feet to pay for his tea, he leaned forward to peer at the photograph. He realized it was a football team. What he discovered on rubbing the dirt off the glass with his fingertips startled him. This was the 1955 team of Juger Jatri, which had toured East Africa. The same picture was hung in the club tent, although that one was four times as large. It had been taken in Nairobi.

What was this photograph doing in a place like this? How had it got here in the first place? Unable to suppress his curiosity, Amar asked the woman. It was the boy who replied that his father was one of the people in it, pointing to the fourth person from the right in the back row.

The shortest of them all, the man was dressed in a blazer and tie, with a receding chin and brushed-back hair. Although the photograph was discoloured with neglect, his eyes stood out. They were fierce and intense, signalling a reckless, headstrong person. Amar had never seen him. But then the photo had been taken three years before he was born. He asked the boy what his father's name was.

Sudhakar Reddy. Amar couldn't possibly remain indifferent to this, and so he duly exclaimed, 'What!' He had heard old-timers talk of Sudhakar Reddy. Juger Jatri had persuaded him to move from Hyderabad. At the time Calcutta's football pitches had no other left-back like him. When it came to sticking to the quarry like a leech and snatching the ball, many people felt that Reddy's modern-day counterpart was Amar Bose. Amar had not gauged how high this praise was.

He felt a thrill at unexpectedly tracking down this man. The snapped fan belt now seemed like a blessing in disguise. Where was Reddy? The boy said he was in bed with a fever; he hadn't gone to work. Amar said he wanted to meet him. The boy took him to his father. On the way Amar learnt that his name was Gopal and his mother's Sabita. She was Bengali. Gopal had been born in this village. Amar had heard that Reddy used to stay at the club's boarding house, where he had become involved in drinking, gambling and whoring. He'd sunk into debt as well. But he had never skipped practice. He couldn't have sat out more than six matches during the six years he had played for Jatri. The club had won at least two major tournaments every year in that period. His abilities had declined after he fractured his leg while playing in the Durand Cup. Jatri had bid him goodbye with a bonus of two thousand rupees.

This was all Amar knew about Reddy. But although he found it strange that a Telugu from Hyderabad was living with his wife and son in a village in Medinipur, he kept his curiosity to himself. A dilapidated mud hut with a low thatched roof. Two openings by way of windows in the earthen walls, with bars made of cane. There was a damp smell. A brick column functioned as one of the four legs of the cot.

Dressed in a lungi, Reddy was lying on his side. He turned over when Gopal nudged his shoulder, sitting up at the sight of the stranger.

Greeting him, Amar said, 'I've heard of you. I play football for Juger Jatri too. The fan belt of the car snapped. I saw your photograph while having a cup of tea. So I thought I'd meet you.'

Reddy had a greying stubble of at least ten days, sunken cheeks, matted white hair. Poverty had raked the flesh off his entire frame. Amar felt that only his eyes blazed as strongly as ever.

Perhaps because Reddy was unused to being greeted, he did not return Amar's greeting. In unaccented Bangla, he asked, 'You play for Jatri? Which position?'

'Left stopper-back.'

'What's your name?'

'Amar Bose.'

There was no reaction on Reddy's face. He stared at Amar.

'You have a fever, I believe.'

'Not just a fever, the pain in the knee has flared up too. It's hard to walk.' Reddy drew his lungi up to bare his right leg up to the knee. It was shrivelled to the thickness of a bamboo pole. 'Fracture.' He put his finger on his knee. 'Durand semi-final, '59. Sukhlal of Services kicked me.'

'Didn't you get it treated?'

'What treatment are you talking of? Where are the doctors here? How will I afford the medicine? I work as a daily labourer at the truck kiln – no work no pay.'

'How long have you been here?'

'About fifteen years. My wife's family lives here. I was in Kharagpur earlier. I used to be a sweeper at the railway hospital, that's where I married Gopal's mother.' As he spoke Reddy swung his legs over to place them on the floor and grimaced in pain as soon as he put his weight on them.

Amar was saddened. What a wretched state for a famous footballer to be in. How much would Reddy have earned had he been playing now? At least a lakh and a half, just like Amar did. He wouldn't be suffering this way had he been playing these days. Amar felt he had benefited from being born later. And the resultant sense of security made him compassionate and generous. 'Come to Calcutta and get your leg treated,' he said. 'I know a good doctor, I'll make the arrangements. You won't have to pay.'

Reddy looked wistful. His eyes misted up. He bent over and gripped Amar's legs below the knees.

'What are you doing! Don't embarrass me, please.' Amar helped Reddy to his feet.

'Do something for my legs, sir. A man can't do anything without his legs. You play football, you know what it's like.'

'You've played football too. I've heard you were very well known, you even made it to the selection camp for the Melbourne Olympics.'

'And, sir…'

'Not "sir", Amar, just Amar.'

Reddy looked at him doubtfully. 'But I'm a labourer now.'

'So what, you're nothing less than an elder brother for me – we're all members of the football family. Our generation flows from the tradition yours created. It's my duty to take care of you.'

Amar felt a sense of contentment about what he'd said. A feeling of exhilaration, much like the happiness of winning the championship in the last match of the League, overwhelmed him. Finally he had an opportunity to do something as a human being.

Writing his address on a paper bag, Amar said, 'Can you find your way to Behala?'

'I can. I lived in Calcutta for six years, after all. I've been everywhere, from Shyambazar and Belgachhia to Ballygunge and Tollygunge. Ghosh used to live in Kalighat, our goalkeeper Antu

Ghosh, Braja Datta in Shyampukur, Milan Sur in Uttarpara. I've been to their homes many times.'

'In that case you shouldn't have a problem.'

With the driver back and honking, Amar didn't stay longer. The boy had run out of the room. He came back to say, 'The man in the car is looking for you.'

Amar returned to his new house in Behala, the image of a moist-eyed Reddy gratefully bidding him goodbye imprinted on his brain. At dinner that night he told his father Chittaranjan, 'A strange thing happened today. I suddenly discovered someone who used to play for Jatri thirty-five years ago, a terrific player. No one knew of his whereabouts all this while – everyone assumed he was dead. And do you know how it happened?'

He told the story of meeting Reddy in great detail to his parents, wife and younger sister, ending with, 'I've asked him to visit me. I'll get Dr Tarun Datta to treat him.'

'I'm glad you have.' Chittaranjan nodded his approval. 'Every generation is indebted to the previous one. Paying back this debt is humane.'

Everyone at home was looking at Amar as though they had discovered a new hero.

Amar told his colleagues in office the story of how he discovered Sudhakar Reddy. He informed his club too. Most of them merely looked at him and said, 'Really?' Even in the Jatri tent, the revelation elicited just surprise and little else. Salil Mandal was the only one among those visiting the tent regularly who had played with Reddy. He displayed keen interest.

'Let me know if Sudha turns up. He was a very talented footballer. He was the left-back and I was the left-out. We had an excellent understanding. He'd draw his hand back as though he was going to slap someone, and I'd start my run. I knew at exactly which point the ball would land at my feet, and it always did. His passes were as precise as a computer's.' Salil Mandal's memories made him effusive before he sobered down, saying, 'He was always something of a bohemian. He blew up all he earned on gambling and drinking. His home was in Guntur, but he never went back. He would stay on in Calcutta, telling us there was no one back home. Completely uneducated, but he picked up Bangla very quickly. Rabi-da was the club secretary then. He got Sudha a job at a cement warehouse owned by a friend of his. But they sacked him in six months for drunkenness.'

Amar said, 'The club should have taken care of his treatment when he broke his leg. It's a moral responsibility.'

Salil Mandal smiled sadly. 'Back then there were no good doctors in Calcutta for such injuries. A major injury meant the end of your playing career. Sudha did get some treatment, though. I'm sorry to hear he's still in pain. If you can help him, Amar, I'll bless you with all my heart.'

Amar was touched by the older man's heartfelt anxiety. Mandal had requested Amar to take care of a 'very talented footballer'. He would definitely honour the request.

The Calcutta football season was over. Jatri had emerged as the runners-up in the League championship. A bitter, annoyed Amar returned to Calcutta during Durga Puja weighed down under the burden of disappointment of fans and officials after a semi-final defeat in the Durand Cup in Delhi.

The players were to leave for Bombay next to play in the Rovers Cup and practice was on. It was then that Sudhakar Reddy arrived at Amar's house one cold November morning with a rations' shopping bag. Amar was about to leave for the club grounds.

'I'm here, sir,' said Reddy with a broad smile. 'You asked me to come, remember?'

Amar gazed at him for a few seconds, swallowing his astonishment. He'd completely forgotten. He said uneasily, 'But I'm going for practice now. Can you wait at home till I return?'

Amar introduced everyone at home to Reddy, who had shaved, combed his brushed-back hair which now hung to his shoulders, and was dressed in a synthetic bush shirt with a floral pattern and baggy jeans, with sandals. His eyes were shining with expectation and enthusiasm. Amar felt a stab of sympathy. Drawing his mother aside, he said, 'Give him something to eat. He's very poor, feed him well.'

After the practice session three journalists were quizzing the coach and captain in the club tent. Four of the players would not be able to accompany the team to the Rovers Cup because they had to go to Cuttack two days later for an office tournament. Who would be in the squad for Bombay, then? Getting their answers, they turned to Amar, a senior player, who said, 'I'm going to give you some news that will startle you. I know you'll pounce on me for details.'

The three of them surrounded Amar eagerly. There was a famine when it came to news at this time of the year. There was no possibility of breaking news from local cricket. No test matches, the Durand Cup had ended, the Calcutta teams hadn't yet left for the Rovers Cup, and there were no upheavals in international sports either.

'A famous footballer of yesteryears.' Amar paused to create a dramatic silence. When the expected levels of curiosity appeared on the journalists' faces, he said, 'Sudhakar Reddy, the footballer from Hyderabad who once earned Jatri tremendous respect and a number of trophies, is now poor and penniless, close to succumbing to starvation and lack of medical treatment in a village right here in Bengal. I found him. He's in my house right now.'

After answering the journalists' questions, Amar ate breakfast at the club and then left for office on his scooter before returning home in the afternoon. The house was a new construction, and it wasn't complete yet. There was a three-room flat on the ground floor that was to be rented out. The tenant had been identified too, but the tiles had not yet been set on the floor and the electrical fittings and wiring were also not in place. The work would begin after he returned from the Rovers Cup. On the first floor the woodwork was being polished. Completing the work in the house was another of Amar's worries, along with losing in the Durand Cup and finalizing the lease documents. And now Reddy had turned up.

Back home Amar discovered Reddy had gone out after lunch. His bag was lying in the corridor. Chittaranjan said, 'There's no telling how long the treatment will take. We could make arrangements for him to stay in one of the rooms downstairs. He can manage even without electricity.'

Amar rang Dr Tarun Datta that evening from a medicine shop in the neighbourhood. What he heard was cause for concern. The doctor was in Madras to attend an international conference of orthopaedic specialists. His family did not know when he would be back. Should he ask Reddy to stay till the doctor came back, or should he ask him to leave?

His mother said, 'Now that he's here he might as well stay a few days.'

'Maybe the doctor will be back in a day or two,' his father added.

But Amar was to fly to Bombay the day after tomorrow.

'We're here, aren't we? We'll make sure he stays here till you get back. He can stay downstairs and have his meals with us, it's no problem,' Chittaranjan reassured his son.

One of the three reporters turned up the next day, along with a photographer. Sitting on the sofa on the first floor, Reddy gave them an interview. They photographed him in different poses with Amar, who then walked them down the road.

'No footballer can be expected to do what you're doing for Reddy, Amar.'

'I've hardly done anything…'

'There's no need for modesty. You've set an example. We must let people know there are still good human beings left in this world.'

'To tell you the truth I had tears in my eyes when I saw him. Even beggars live in greater comfort, I think.'

'You're a little too soft-hearted.'

A wave of elation surged over Amar. The agony of not winning either the League or the Durand Cup seemed to be washed away.

How fortunate the fan belt had snapped that day, he thought to himself, for he would never have run into Reddy otherwise. Nor would he have earned all this praise. He must take care of Reddy.

Returning home, he found Reddy sitting in a ground-floor room lit by a candle. 'Why don't you go upstairs and watch television?' he said.

'No, sir, I'm fine here.'

'You're sirring me again.'

Reddy smiled. Amar handed him two ten-rupee notes, saying, 'Keep this. You never know when you may need some money. Good to have some with you.'

Reddy raised the hand holding the note to his forehead in a gesture of gratitude. Something seemed to burst in Amar's heart at the sight.

The first thing he saw on the sports page of the newspaper the next morning was the photograph. He was standing with his arms around Reddy, their cheeks touching. But he was astonished by the report below it.

Was this what he had told them? That Reddy was begging on the side of the road? Amar was having a cup of tea at a tea shop when Reddy came up to him to ask for some money. Amar felt he looked familiar, that he must have seen him somewhere. Then he remembered the face in the photograph hanging on the clubhouse wall. When he asked the man his name, he learnt this was the famous footballer Sudhakar Reddy, a former legend of Calcutta football.

Besides, it seemed Reddy had not wanted to come to Calcutta for treatment for fear of being marked absent at the brick kiln where he had got a job. Amar had been to his village twice to fetch him but had failed. Finally he had had to promise Reddy he would get him a job in Calcutta if he were to be sacked. Only after this had Reddy come to Calcutta. Dr Tarun Datta would examine his leg next Wednesday. An entire paragraph had been devoted to Amar Bose's generosity.

Amar's first instinct was to write a letter to rectify the inaccuracies in this report. But everyone at home said, 'Why bother? They've changed some details to make it more dramatic but this *is* roughly what happened, isn't it?'

'But what must Reddy have thought?'

'What must Reddy have thought?' Chittaranjan said in surprise. 'It's not like he can read. He's a beggar for all intents and purposes – do you suppose he has any self-esteem?'

Abandoning his intentions of writing a letter, Amar left for Dum Dum Airport in the afternoon to fly to Bombay. Before leaving he told Reddy to treat the house as his own, to ask for anything he needed. Would he like a little more money over and above the twenty rupees? Reddy joined his palms obsequiously and shook his head. No need.

That same evening at nine-thirty Reddy was brought home drunk by some of the young men in the neighbourhood. Everyone was confused and embarrassed. One of the young men said, 'We recognized him because of his picture in this morning's papers with Amar-da. He was such a great player once. He collapsed on the road in front of us. It would have meant a loss of face for Amar-da if we hadn't brought him home.'

'Thank you, boys,' Chittaranjan said, his voice subdued. 'Amar's gone to Bombay today. You've read about Reddy in the papers. Please keep an eye on him.'

They left after laying Reddy down on his bed. The next morning Chittaranjan told him the details of the incident. 'You have an image to maintain too. These boys haven't seen you play but they've read about you in the papers. They helped you only because of your former glory. Please don't drink any more.'

Reddy listened in silence, his head bowed. Apologizing, he said, 'It was after a long time. I overdid it.'

In the afternoon he went out, telling Amar's sister he was going to visit his old friend Antu at Kalighat. Returning in the evening, he went to bed in the darkened room downstairs. He didn't eat dinner, saying, 'Antu's dead, I feel terrible.'

Reddy went out again the next afternoon. He said he was going to meet Ghulam Nabi at Park Circus. He couldn't quite remember the location of the house but he would find his way.

Reddy returned at eleven at night. The streets were deserted. Chittaranjan was waiting on the first-floor balcony. Reddy got out of a taxi, which left without waiting to be paid. Chittaranjan went downstairs to open the door.

'Nabi's son drives a taxi, he dropped me.' Reddy was slurring his words and weaving a little. 'They stuffed me with food. Look, Nabi gifted me a warm shawl.' He held up a plastic bag. 'I didn't ask for it, he gave it to me on his own. He's made a lot of money.' Reddy smiled and went into his room.

The next day Chittaranjan said, 'You drank again?'

Reddy looked at him in wonder. 'How could I not? One minute to go in the game. I dribbled past two…no, three of them and sent a through straight to Nabi's feet. He was entering the box from the right. He took a left-footed shot without stopping the ball. It went into the net exactly where the crossbar meets the upright. That goal gave us the IFA Shield. I've never seen a goal like that. Nabi was talking about that goal and pouring us a drink. How could I refuse!' When a triumphant memory from thirty-two years ago began to play out before your eyes, Reddy couldn't believe it was possible to honour it without celebration.

Chittaranjan didn't prolong the conversation. All he told his wife was, 'Amar's made a big mistake.'

Jatri had entered the Rovers Cup final. Underlining a couple of paragraphs in the match report, Chittaranjan handed the newspaper to his daughter-in-law. 'It's about Amar. Read it out to your mother-in-law.'

Amar's wife read the lines out loud for her mother-in-law's benefit. 'Less than thirty seconds were left for the final whistle when Amar grabbed the ball midway in his own half. He raced up the pitch, dribbling past three defenders in succession and pushing the ball towards Sunil before running towards the penalty spot. Then, without even stopping Sunil's return-pass, he took a sudden shot on the run, dispatching the ball to the far corner of the net. Five seconds to full time. An incredible goal. The Dempo players could do nothing but stare at their own goal in disappointment. Jatri has not won with such a spectacular goal in living memory. Amar Bose did it single-handedly.'

All three of them were bursting with pride. Chittaranjan said, 'Give me the paper. Let me read it out to him.'

Reddy was soaking his shirt in a bucket filled with soap water. Chittaranjan read the report out to him. Dipping his vest as well and then squeezing the water out of it, Reddy said, 'Sir is a great player. I've heard people here say so. My regret is that I haven't seen him play and I don't know if I will either.' Reddy looked forlorn. His mass of grey hair moved as he shook his head.

'The regret is natural. How will people like us who have never played football know how to judge this goal? Only you can do that.'

'In that case' – Reddy's eyes began to blaze – 'Nabi's is the best goal I have ever seen. No, sir must have scored a wonderful goal. The papers won't lie, I'm sure it's a fantastic goal, but…' Reddy paused.

'But what?' Chittaranjan made no attempt to conceal his hostility. It seemed to him that Reddy was unwilling in his heart to accept praise for Amar.

'Not even the greatest player in the world can take a first-time shot on a moving ball unless it lands up in the right place at the right time. Nabi admitted as much the other day. Yes, he did. Salil used to believe it too. He would take me to dinner whenever he scored a goal from my pass.' Reddy's through-passes probably began to rerun before his eyes from the distant past. Plunging his arms into the bucket of soapy water to squeeze the dirt out of his shirt and vest, he wiped his eyes on his shoulder.

It was the Rovers Cup final between Jatri and Kerala Police. The match would be shown live on television everywhere in India. Reddy went out before the game began. Jatri was leading by a goal till two minutes before the end. Then Kerala Police earned a penalty. Joseph had dribbled past Amar to enter the Jatri penalty box when Amar tripped him from the back. Needless to say, the players surrounded the referee with appeals, arguments and jostling. Then the referee showed Amar the red card. Kerala Police scored from the penalty and it was 1-1. The channel stopped telecasting the match and switched to other programmes before extra time began.

A brooding silence reigned over the house. Everyone spoke in low tones and trod softly. The maid was scolded for a clatter with the dishes in the kitchen. Chittaranjan drew a chair to the veranda. At that moment there was no way of finding out the result of the match in extra time. His wife joined him on the veranda. Chittaranjan whispered to himself, 'Amar had no choice but to trip him. But a red card? You have to keep your cool at such moments, you have to be careful... Losing a player at this stage is a big loss.'

'He was playing well, they conspired to...'

'Be quiet.' Chittaranjan cut his wife short bitterly.

There was a power cut. All of them were on the veranda, staring into the darkness. Winter had arrived but without its bite. They were wearing light sweaters. A battery-operated emergency light glowed in the corridor behind them.

Amar's sister said, 'They'll have the result in the television news. The transistor batteries are dead.'

'The newspaper offices must know. If only we had a phone.' Chittaranjan sounded rueful.

'We've applied,' said Amar's wife.

Suddenly there was a sound of firecrackers up the street. A joyful clamour. This was a neighbourhood of Jatri fans.

'Do you hear, Baba?'

'Yes, they've probably won.'

'Should I find out?'

'I'll go.'

Chittaranjan practically ran out into the road with a torch and, returning five minutes later, began to dance like a little boy, raising his arms and chanting, 'They won, they won!' He said, 'Nishith scored with a header from a free kick in the eighteenth minute of extra time. They found out from the newspaper office.'

'At least Amar doesn't have to feel guilty now.'

As they were talking at the top of their voices, a discordant uproar could be heard on the road, coming closer. All of them went back out to the veranda.

At least a dozen people had gathered in the dark outside their house. One of them shouted, 'We won't spare him today, Uncle! He's abusing Jatri, saying Amar-da is no footballer.'

'No, sir, that's not what I said!' Reddy's scream was slurred.

'He's completely drunk, Uncle. Another word against Jatri and we'll bury him alive.'

'When you take a shot you can score a goal…but you must get the ball before you can shoot. Am I right or not? You think Jatri is a team worth talking about? Tchah, you call that a team? If I could today…if my leg was all right…can you hear what I'm saying? My through-passes would have left Amar standing. I watched the match on television at Salil's house, he gave me money for food…'

'We don't know when this bastard was a great player, Uncle. Don't let him stay in your house any more. Throw him out today. What a nuisance.'

Chittaranjan leaned over the railing in the darkness. 'Amar will be back tomorrow, let him come.'

'If my leg had been all right I'd have danced rings around them… Amar would have conceded a dozen penalties.'

'Shut up, swine!'

There was the sound of a slap, and of someone falling.

'Let it be, don't beat him up,' said an upset Chittaranjan. 'Help him into the room instead.' He went downstairs to open the front door.

The next morning, the maid peeped into Reddy's room on her way to fetch the milk in the morning and ran back upstairs. 'He's gone, his bag too.'

Stopper

1

'Oh, it's you! All right, why don't you sit down right here?'

It wasn't so much a request as an instruction. The young journalist gulped and nodded. Perching on the rickety iron chair, he tried to look confident by leaning back and crossing his legs, wiping his neck with his handkerchief and taking a cigarette out of a packet – only, on second thoughts, to put it back again.

A few limp figures lay scattered on the ground about ten yards away. Some of them lay flat on the grass, some on their stomachs, some spreadeagled. The perspiration on their skin had now dried, leaving it with a pallor and a coarse texture like that of dried bricks. Almost surreptitiously, they shook their fatigued limbs or heads, their eyes blank and expressionless.

One of them was rubbing ice into his thigh with great concentration. Twice, a plump man in a dhoti and kurta squatted before him to tell him something but could elicit no response, for the player's attention was focused on the ice.

One young man who had been lying on his stomach, his head in the crook of his arm, suddenly sat up and shouted harshly, 'Keshto, when the hell are you going to get the water?'

A mild grumbling emanated from the rear of the tent in response.

The young journalist glanced at the club tent. He could see an area with a cement floor, flanked by light wooden doors with springs that were kept busy by the constant opening and closing because of the onslaught of people. The back of the tent was open, offering a view of another tent and a tube well. Seven or eight people were sitting on the floor around a circular steel table, upon which rested several cups of tea, and arguing at the top of their voices. One of them munched on a slice of toast, his eyes shut. The fan whirred. You could tell it was stifling inside the tent.

'Tea for you.'

The journalist started. A boy in a vest held out a dirty cup of tea, two biscuits balanced precariously on the saucer.

'For me? I…'

'Kamal-babu sent the tea,'

The journalist accepted the cup and, sipping his tea, began to mentally organize the questions he had come up with over the past few days.

'How many times did I tell you to guard the right? But no, you had to cut inside.'

'What could I do?' Shambhu kept saying. 'Can't cope, can't cope, help me out here, Balai. How do you expect me to cover the wings as well as the midfield?'

'If only Salil hadn't been injured – he was playing so well. Imagine taking that shot of Sukalyan's on your chest – my God! I half expected his ribs to be fractured.'

'How bad is the injury?'

'Who knows. Kamal-da took him inside to give him some medicine.'

'His pet! Medicine for him, ice for us.'

'Talent! He's brimming with talent. We're brimming with cow dung. Anyway. Why go where we're not welcome? Five-thirty sharp tomorrow at Basusree, okay?'

'You still owe me twenty-five paise.'

'What twenty-five paise?'

'Convenient memory loss! Didn't you borrow it for the *Dilko Dekho* ticket?'

'Wow. Some memory you have. Twenty-five paise is peanuts.'

The journalist's ears were flapping. The lanky player who'd been lying down on the ground all this while, with his arm over his eyes, made a noise which he choked back almost immediately, catching the journalist's eye.

'Result?' the journalist asked softly.

'Five.'

The journalist tried to express sympathy by summoning up a sorrowful expression. 'They could have scored a dozen – just didn't, that's all.' The player smiled wanly.

'First game of the season?'

Nodding, he sat up, swallowing visibly and licking his dry lips. He had a reedy chest, collarbones that stuck out and legs devoid of any ripple of muscle. The journalist was unable to picture him anywhere except between the goalposts.

'Sorry to have kept you waiting so long. Did they bring you a cup of tea?'

Kamal Guha drew up a chair next to the journalist.

'Some more tea?'

'No, no, I don't drink tea that often.'

'Good. Too much tea isn't good for health. I can count the number of cups of tea I've had in the past twenty-five years. Footballers have to look after their health, first and foremost, else they cannot expect a long playing career. I've been playing first division football for twenty – yes, twenty – years.'

The journalist was already taking notes.

'How old are you now?'

'Guess.'

'If you've been playing for twenty years in the first division, you must be at least forty.'

Kamal's eyes betrayed disappointment. 'That's based on calculations. But how old do I look?'

Frowning, the journalist scanned Kamal the way a talented student scans an abstruse mathematical problem. Curly, thick, short hair, turning grey around the ears. Three or four creases across the forehead. The journalist was reminded of a close-up of Stanley Matthews across two pages of a book, with the caption? 'The face of thirty-five years of tension in football'. Matthews had five creases on his forehead, one below his lips, and just beyond that, in the aftermath of some huge earthquake, two waves had crashed on to his face. And then, all the way to the corners of his eyes, his skin was wrinkled like the coastline. But Kamal Guha did not have Matthews' fatigued eyes that seemed desperate for rest. Instead, his were bright and deep-set – rebellious, challenging.

Tilting his notebook as he looked at Kamal's Guha's eyes, the journalist jotted down the words 'angry', 'blunt' and 'sentimental'.

He found nothing distinctive about the appearance of this medium-sized Bengali footballer with a complexion the colour of tea with too much milk in it. His voice was on the heavier, harsher side. All you noticed when he walked was that he carried his spine like the Shahid Minar – tall and erect. He never hurried.

'Twenty-eight. Thirty at the most,' the journalist said hesitatingly.

Unexpectedly, Kamal Guha broke into a belly laugh, its intensity increasing when he saw the journalist's uncertainty. This made two policemen from the cavalry who were returning from duty to rein in their horses and glance at them.

'You're overdoing it. My official age at work *is* lower than my real one, but even I didn't dare take so many years off. If you don't mind, how old are you?'

'Twenty-five.' Clearing his throat, the journalist tried to look dignified.

'Come, let's do ten rounds around the field,' said Kamal Guha, arching his eyebrows.

'How would I be able to do that?' the journalist protested. 'How would I ever keep up with a footballer? Would you be able to write an article like I can?'

The amused expression slowly left Kamal Guha's face.

'You're right, I wouldn't be able to. But why did you want to know how old I am? To get a sense of what I'm capable of physically, right? If I said twenty-five, you'd expect me to be able to run at least a hundred metres in eleven seconds, wouldn't you? But if I changed it to forty, the eleven seconds would climb to fifteen. But if we were to race each other, and I beat you, would you not accept me as twenty-five? Dates do not make your age – your physical prowess does. I'm twenty-seven now, you see.'

Quickly writing down the word 'humbug' in his notebook, the journalist asked, 'What was the last match you played before retiring?'

'Retire? Me? Even last year I played the second halves of two matches. I'll play this year too, if need be. The knee injury Salil picked up today could sideline him for a month. I may have to play. As a stopper, you play in a limited space – not a major problem.'

'Stanley Matthews did play first division football till about fifty, didn't he? Why, he played for England for twenty-three years.'

'You're talking of a legend. That too a winger! I cannot imagine playing in that position at that age. I began as a right-in.'

'Which club?'

'Here at Shobhabajar Sporting for the first two years, then another two at Bhabanipur, followed by a year at Aryan, four at Juger Jatri, one at Mohun Bagan, two more at Juger Jatri, and then back to Shobhabajar. I began during the two-back era and then played my way through the three-back and four-back periods. It was Poltu-da who moved me from right-in to stopper.'

'Poltu-da who?' asked the journalist, his pen raised.

'You wouldn't know him. Poltu Mukherjee, my guru. He stopped playing in 1935. He was Dukhiram-babu's protégé, used to play for Aryan. But he was addicted to the card sessions here at the Shobhabajar tent. Went bankrupt gambling. Cards, horses and, of course, liquor. But what he also did was create footballers by the dozen. Whatever football I've learnt, whatever recognition I've got, is all thanks to him. I will never be able to repay my teacher's debt. You could say he literally plucked me off the roads to make me what I am. Day after day I stayed at his house, ate at his table, even passed my exams thanks to him.'

Jumping up suddenly, Kamal Guha proceeded to roll up his shirt. Even as he stared in surprise, the journalist wrote the word 'disciple' in his notebook.

Having bared his body up to the neck, Kamal Guha turned around and asked, 'Can you see, there, below the neck, near the spine?'

The journalist noticed a two-inch scar. 'Yes, looks like the mark of a boot.'

'Not a boot. He slashed at me with a bronze dining plate.'

'A plate!' said a new voice.

As he turned his head to see who had spoken, the journalist felt a shiver run down his spine. A gorilla in clothes stood behind him. A complexion like ebony, a hairline that started barely an inch above the eyebrows, button eyes sunk in their sockets and a lower lip thick enough to give his face a permanent pout.

Turning around to face the journalist again, Kamal Guha parted his hair. 'There's another one here. Proof that he used to wear clogs.'

'You never told us you'd been beaten up like this.' The newcomer's expression didn't suggest either fear or awe. His face was virtually flat from forehead to chin, as though someone had smashed it in at birth. His voice reflected his thoughts.

'Payment for football lessons. I was literally thrashed into education. The plate landed on my neck after he saw me come out of a cinema hall. The clogs were after seeing my exam results.' Kamal Guha's voice became sombre. The whites of his eyes glistened. 'He was all that a guru should be. You can't even imagine learning that way any more. Now they ask you how much you'll pay before they've even learnt to take a shot properly. If you ask them why they didn't come for training, they accuse you of treating them as servants.

That's why I don't say anything any more. They're rotten already. The dedicated ones need no urging.'

Kamal Guha spoke to the other person, who was looking at the ground.

'You must go to the doctor today. Now. The knee's much too delicate to be ignored. It's finished the career of many a talented footballer. Do you have the money for a taxi?'

He nodded.

'Show me,' Kamal Guha said sceptically.

'I'll manage,' the player said quickly. Kamal Guha held out a five-rupee note from his pocket.

'But I can take a bus.'

'Don't you disobey me.'

It wasn't just the player but also the journalist who quailed before the authority in his voice. Accepting the money, the player bent to touch Kamal Guha's feet in respect. Kamal Guha put his hand on his back lightly, and watched as he walked off, dragging his left foot.

'He's serious about the game. Good material. Hasn't studied much, not too sharp, but a loyal soldier. He'll follow orders with his life if necessary. You need players like these too. Let's see how much he can be moulded.' For the first time, Kamal Guha sounded tender.

'Are you his coach?' The journalist brandished his pen.

'Coach? Oh no. The club has a coach with a degree from the National Institute of Sports. But Salil is my protégé. Lives in a slum with eight brothers and sisters. I help as much as I can. Everyone wants to live forever, but there comes a time when you know you're done. You can only live on through your progeny. Even footballers have to give up the game eventually, but they can go on by choosing their own replacements. Salil is mine.'

'How many children do you have?'

A cloud of pain and despair passed fleetingly over Kamal Guha's face. 'Just the one son. He's seventeen, doing pre-university classes. I got married very young.'

'Whom does he play for?'

'No one. He's never even touched a football. He hates the game. Doesn't even watch my matches. Never has. Strange, isn't it?'

'Isn't your wife interested?'

Kamal Guha shook his head tiredly. 'Wasn't, not isn't. She died ten years ago, but not for a day did she reconcile herself to my being a footballer. It was from her that Amitava learnt to detest football. He talks of politics, argues about it with his friends, sings, tries to write poetry…but has never ever discussed football.'

'Strange,' said the journalist, and wrote 'sad life' in his notebook.

Lost in thought, Kamal Guha stared at a neon advertising sign in faraway Esplanade. The journalist waited patiently. Evening had descended. The footballers who had hitherto been lying around here and there had since showered and were now busy polishing off mutton stew with bread. Snatches of conversation could be heard from within the tent.

'Any idea what happened in the Kalighat game…'

'No way, players like that won't last a week in Calcutta. Just see how they mess up once the rains start…'

'I'm willing to wager a hundred chips Nimu will never score off a header…'

'Who're we playing next?'

'Why did you chip the ball to Gopal instead of giving it to Sridhar, you think Gopal can beat Nayeem in the air…'

'Do you have any more questions?'

'Plenty,' the journalist replied after some hesitation.

'For instance?' Kamal Guha asked without curiosity.

'Everyone assumed you'd be selected for the 1956 Olympics, but you weren't included. What was the reason? You played four times in the Santosh Trophy, twice against the Russians, you had the reputation of being India's finest stopper. So many mediocre players made it to the Asian Games and the Merdeka, but not you. Not even once. Why?'

'Any other questions?'

Kamal Guha still didn't sound interested. The journalist now thought it necessary to use more aggressive tactics. 'Why is it that we no longer get footballers like you? Are we capable of playing ninety-minute games? Would it be better to shift the football season to winter?'

The journalist paused; the phone in the tent was ringing. 'Telephone for you, Kamal-da,' someone shouted.

'Coming, ask them to hang on a minute,' Kamal shouted back.

Quickly he turned to the journalist and said, 'Answering all these questions will take time. Why don't we meet again?'

'May I visit you at home?'

'You can. Any weekend morning,' Kamal Guha replied before disappearing in the direction of the tent.

Staring at his notebook for some time, as though he were trying to digest its contents, the journalist frowned in deep annoyance as he walked out through the door in the fence, taking a last look behind him as he left. Kamal Guha could be seen through an open window, hunched over the phone he was speaking into.

'Aru? Aruna? What's the matter? What! How did Poltu-da fall? Blood pressure…what's the doctor saying? No, I'll arrange for the money, call the doctor. Yes, I'm coming over right away.' Putting the receiver down, Kamal addressed the club's joint secretary, Abani Mandal, who was the only other person in the room. 'Need some money immediately. At least a hundred.'

'ONE hundred! Where am I going to get that kind of money from?'

'I don't care from where. I don't care how.'

'It's easy to say that, but how? I don't need to remind you just how much cash you will find in our cashbox.'

Gripped by an impotent rage, Kamal was unable to speak for some time. Abani was right, but he needed the money. None of the people hanging round the club or playing cards were the kind to be carrying a hundred rupees in their pockets.

2

Over the past fifteen years Kamal had changed jobs twice, homes six times and clubs six times too. Having played for Shobhabajar Sporting, Bhabanipur, Aryan, Juger Jatri – twice, on either side of a stint in Mohun Bagan – he was now back at Shobhabajar. During this period he had lived in Dorjipara, Ahiritola, Shyampukur, Kumartuli and Shyampukur again, before moving to his current home in Bagbajar. Although his club was named after the locality it had been born in, there was no longer any trace of the club in that neighbourhood – just as Kamal had never visited Faridpur, the area in which he had been born, since leaving home at the age of three. Shobhabajar Sporting now existed only in its tent on the Maidan and in the Beleghata residence of Keshto-da, or Krishnaprasad Maiti.

The last time Kamal set foot inside the Juger Jatri tent was seven years ago. He had signed the transfer form to move from Mohun Bagan on an advance payment of one thousand rupees, with the total agreed fee being five thousand rupees.

Having received only four thousand rupees by the end of the year, he asked Gulo-da for the rest on returning from Delhi after the club lost in the Durand Cup quarter-final. Gulo-da – club vice-president Pratap Bhaduri – was the most influential person in the club. Besides making such decisions as what players would eat after morning training, what the team composition would be for every game, who would be signed on by the club and at what price, Gulo-da and his coterie also controlled the selection of the club's general secretary, football secretary and even the president. All tickets for charity matches or cricket test matches allotted to the club quota went directly to Gulo-da, who regulated their distribution to members. He was a member of three or four subcommittees of the IFA and the CAB. The owner of a small press, Gulo-da owned two houses, both less than a year old, in Bhabanipur and in Kasba.

He always spoke in a soft, deferential tone.

'What! They haven't paid you yet?' Kamal was taken aback by Gulo-da's astonishment.

'It's criminal. Criminal. I'm going to talk to Tapen right away.'

Sending for the accountant, Tapen Roy, Gulo-da put on a show of anger. 'Is it true that Kamal hasn't been paid his dues yet? This can't be allowed. Please pay him immediately. Kamal is the pillar of our defence. How can we remain a strong team by weakening him?'

'I hope I'll get paid before we leave for the Rovers Cup, Gulo-da,' Kamal said warily.

'Why don't you work it out with Tapen?' said Gulo-da as he started dialling a number on the telephone.

Despite three successive visits, Tapen Roy didn't make the payment. Kamal didn't travel with the team for the Rovers Cup, sending word to the football secretary that the pain in his knee had worsened. All that Gulo-da had said in response was, 'Indeed!'

Just before the transfer window opened the following season, Gulo-da sent for Kamal. As soon as he arrived, Gulo-da handed him ten one-hundred-rupee notes with a broad smile, saying, 'Here you are. How can Jatri survive if someone like you is going to get upset? With ten years of first division football behind you, with Bengal colours and India colours, it doesn't suit you to be childish. If you make a fuss about money like some upstart footballer... You should be setting an example, they must learn from you how to love their club. You must be dignified. We're counting on you to get us a good team this year – have you thought of names?'

Gulo-da pointed to the chair across his desk, resuming as soon as Kamal had put the notes in his pocket and sat down. 'Where *are* the players? Take Debu. He dropped by asking for his money. So I told him, before you take the money, can you calculate for me on a piece of paper exactly how many minutes you were on the field, how many yards you ran, how many mis-passes you made, how many times you couldn't receive the ball, how many open net opportunities you missed? It's all very well for the members to want us to win the Calcutta League and the IFA Shield, but all the good players have been snapped up by Mohun Bagan and East Bengal, haven't they? How can we win without good players? If a couple more of our defenders could play the kind of football Kamal Guha plays even twenty-five per cent of the time, we'd win every trophy in the country. Class – it's all a matter of class. How many players of your class do you suppose the Calcutta Maidan has? Kamal, you must sign up the very first day of transfers.'

'But we haven't discussed money…' Kamal began.

'Do we have to bargain about that? The same as last year, of course.'

Kamal signed up for Juger Jatri on the very first day of transfers. And then, he was made to warm the benches during the first seven games. In the eighth, with Jatri leading 5-0 against Sporting Union with ten minutes to go, Bibhas Sen, the coach, said, 'Kamal, warm up.'

Kamal's head jerked. This ten-minute offer was like rubbing salt into the wound of the humiliation inflicted by having to join the reserves on the sideline, like some rookie footballer, in full sight of thousands of spectators.

'And why now, after all these days?' Kamal asked in an abnormally cold voice.

'Don't be upset, my friend, you know how little I have to do with all this. One man controls everything, as you know very well.' Looking round furtively, Bibhas said, 'Gulo-da told me before the game to put you in for the last ten minutes.'

Rising from the bench, Kamal looked back at the gallery. Gulo-da was seated in his reserved spot on the top row as usual. Kamal walked up to him, took off his jersey and said, 'I'm no longer as young, nor my game as sharp. But so long as Kamal Guha plays football on the Maidan, he'll strike terror in this jersey.'

Tossing the jersey into the lap of a speechless Gulo-da, Kamal walked bare-chested to the club tent, doggedly evading the curious glances of hundreds of people on his way. As he was leaving, having changed into his own clothes and packed his boots and kit, an explosion of joy rose into the air, hitting a crescendo as the final whistle was blown. Halting in his tracks, Kamal muttered through clenched teeth, 'One day I'll change those cheers to wails of mourning.'

Kamal didn't set foot anywhere near the Juger Jatri tent after that. On the very first day of transfers for the next season, he signed up for Shobhabajar Sporting. Shobhabajar was one of the five or six bottom-ranking teams that inevitably formed a cartel and fixed matches amongst themselves to share points and ensure survival. They had to play Jatri that season after conceding eleven goals in three matches. Kamal played the match and single-handedly ensured that the Jatri forwards couldn't go beyond the penalty box each time they attacked. The match ended 0-0, an ominous silence descending upon the crowd after the final whistle. Staggering out of the playing area, supported by two teammates, Kamal said, 'If only I had the strength, you'd have heard a war cry.'

In the return match, Shobhabajar confronted Jatri with fourteen points from twenty-five games. Jatri was then trailing behind Mohun Bagan, East Bengal, Mohammedan Sporting and Aryan, just ahead of BNR. They had no hopes of becoming champions – it was just an exercise in honour.

At half-time, club members began flinging shoes, bricks and wooden missiles at Gulo-da, accompanied by obscenities. A voice could be heard rising above the din, 'Why was Kamal let go?' The score was 0-0. At that point, a companion of Gulo-da's went off for a chat with Krishna Maiti, the Shobhabajar secretary.

As Kamal took the field in the second half, he was amazed to see that Sidhu, who had played splendidly as goalkeeper, saving three certain goals, was being substituted by the greenhorn Bharat. Within five minutes of the start of the second half, the Jatri left-half took a casual shot at goal from thirty yards out. Kamal watched with a shudder as Bharat suddenly stopped short in his attempt to save the shot, which promptly bounced over his head and entered the net.

Ten minutes later, the ball was with Kamal, and two Jatri forwards were rushing towards him. Shielding the ball from them, he passed it to the right-back, who was in the clear. But without any thought, the right-back returned it to him immediately. The Jatri left-in swooped in for the challenge. Kamal was left with no choice but to either concede a corner or give a backpass to the goalkeeper. He did the latter, only to find Bharat essaying a showy dive and letting the ball into the goal after it had grazed his fingertips. Shobhabajar lost 0-2. As he left the ground through a narrow passage between the stands, someone shouted, 'What happened to your threats to Juger Jatri, Kamal?'

Three days later, Kamal took Bharat aside and asked, 'Why did you do that?'

Bharat went pale. Trying in vain to argue, he finally admitted, 'Keshto-da said that if I wanted to play regularly for the team, I'd have to let in two goals. And that if I agreed, he would put me on straight away. I couldn't resist the temptation, Kamal-da. I've spent six years as a reserve player – played only four full matches.' Stooping, he grabbed Kamal's knees. 'Forgive me, Kamal-da, I won't do it again.'

'How many attacks can you defend against, stopper?' Kamal asked himself.

The next year, during the first match against Jatri, Kamal was forced to trip a Jatri forward a yard outside the penalty box. Blowing his whistle, referee Radhakanta Ghosh ran up to mark out the penalty spot.

'Penalty? Whatever for?' asked Kamal in utter surprise.

'No, no, it's a penalty.' Radhakanta placed the ball on the penalty spot.

'The foul was nowhere near the box!' Kamal tried to argue in a display of obstinacy.

'No arguments. I am quite sure of it.'

'I see,' said Kamal sarcastically. Pretending not to have heard, Radhakanta blew his whistle. Kamal shut his eyes and clamped his hands over his ears, waiting for that tragic cheer.

An enormous sigh swept over the football ground. Kamal opened his eyes to see Bharat on the grass, clutching the ball to his chest with both hands. Shobhabajar then pounced on Jatri with twice the ferocity. A minute before half-time, the right-winger made a wonderful run up the touchline and crossed the ball beautifully. The right-in, positioned at the edge of the penalty box, received the ball on his chest and pushed it forward. But as soon as the left-winger tried to slip in between two Jatri defenders and put the ball in the net, Radhakanta ran up, blowing his whistle. Offside. Kamal asked himself, 'How will the stopper prevent such attacks?'

Juger Jatri eventually won 1-0. Just before the last minute of the match, the ball was lobbed into the Shobhabajar goalmouth in a free kick. Bharat punched the ball as far as the Jatri right-winger, who headed it back towards the goal. As Bharat back-pedalled to grab the ball, he found himself rooted to the spot. The Jatri left-in was hanging on to his shorts. The ball went into the net without a challenge.

After the match was over, as the Shobhabajar players were waiting for the crowds to thin down, Kamal spotted Rathin, went up to him and smiled sarcastically. 'We won 1-0 today.'

'I'm Jatri's football secretary this year,' said Rathin with a wry smile.

'Oh yes, I'd forgotten. I should have said, the referee won today. Instead of winning games this way, why don't you get a good team? Win the game on the field, not off it.'

Ignoring the barb, Rathin asked, 'How long do you propose to torment us in this way?'

'Me? This proves you don't know the first thing about football. Ask your Gulo-da. He knows, which is why he used to make me warm the bench two years ago.'

'You make me envious. How well you're playing still. And look at us – already become old.'

'But you've got your life in order as a trade-off, haven't you? I heard you have a very good job at Progressive Bank. Why don't you get me a job?' Kamal laughed. 'I'll stop troubling Jatri. Can't compete with big teams like yours on the field, after all.'

'Are you serious about a job? Come to the tent then, let's talk.'

'Sorry, Rathin.' Kamal's face hardened. 'I do need a job, I've been unemployed for the past two months. But I won't enter the Jatri tent.'

Kamal walked away without another word. That was five years ago.

3

An old green Fiat was parked on the road in front of the Juger Jatri tent. Kamal instantly recognized it as Rathin's car. Promoted about six months ago to the position of departmental head, he now earned seventeen hundred a month and was quite powerful at the bank – something that he constantly tried to convey through his behaviour. Moreover, Rathin was handsome, although a newly acquired paunch made him look less young than he once used to.

That day five years ago, Kamal had asked Rathin for a job in pure jest. But Rathin had telephoned him at the Shobhabajar tent the very next day, asking Kamal to see him. Kamal was extremely surprised. Having resigned from his four-hundred-rupee job at Bengal Jute Mill in a fit of rage two months ago, he was in dire straits. So he went to the bank to meet Rathin, who told him, 'You have to play for the office team. I've spoken to the secretary of the sports club. Put in an application as quickly as you can, they're recruiting for the dispatch department.'

'What's the salary?' Kamal asked.

'What if I said one hundred?' said Rathin, raising his eyebrows. 'After two months without a job even fifty rupees a month is better than nothing, isn't it?'

Kamal didn't prolong the conversation but went back with an application the very next day. The job he got now paid him, after five years, 461 rupees a year. Kamal knew his educational qualifications would never have got him this job had Rathin not helped. Kamal Guha didn't have even half the reputation that he had enjoyed between 1955 and 1960. The days when his football skills could have got him a job were over. That he had still got a job at all was thanks to Rathin.

As he was about to enter the Jatri tent for the first time in seven long years, Kamal suddenly realized the surprise his entry would create. What if someone tried to insult him? Still, he was only there at the invitation of the football secretary and hadn't come to ask for money for himself. So, Kamal told himself, I needn't feel as though I've betrayed myself.

Veteran members of the club were chatting with one another on the benches scattered around outside the entrance. None of them noticed Kamal. The first person to lock eyes with him inside was Tapen Roy, the Juger Jatri accountant. With him were two other people, one whom Kamal knew as a notorious acolyte of Gulo-da's.

'Oh, hello Kamal.'

'Where's Rathin? He telephoned me to meet him here.'

'Yes, he asked me to give you a hundred rupees.'

Tapen pulled a currency note out of his shirt pocket and held it out. Kamal felt he had been waiting for him.

'Doesn't he have to sign a voucher?' Gulo-da's acolyte asked, bustling about.

'No, this isn't the club's money,' Tapen said dismissively. 'Since Kamal won't touch Jatri's cash, I'm giving it to him out of my own pocket.'

'I'll return the money to Rathin tomorrow,' said Kamal, 'Where is he now?'

'He's talking to the players inside. We're playing Kumartuli tomorrow.'

Kamal hesitated. He felt he should meet Rathin before he left. But if he was discussing tactics for the next day's match, it wouldn't be right for an outsider to barge in.

'Playing this year too, Kamal?' asked Tapen, concealing a yawn behind his palm and adding, almost sotto voce, 'How much longer?'

Kamal merely smiled.

'Have you seen Kamal's body, Tapen-da?' asked the acolyte. 'You won't find any of today's players looking as fit.'

Pretending not to have heard, Tapen continued in the same vein. 'The four-back defence system has probably given a new lease of life to ageing players. Longer career, more money. How much are you getting from Shobhabajar?'

'Not a penny.'

Tapen frowned briefly.

'Free service in this day and age?' The acolyte was surprised. 'Of course, Kamal plays only two League matches every season.'

'Just two?' exclaimed Tapen. 'Why not the rest?'

'These last two years the only matches Kamal has played were against us.' The acolyte blinked. 'He couldn't shake Jatri though. We earned full points each time. He may have flung the Jatri jersey on the ground to show his protest, but he hasn't been able to fulfil his threat. Football isn't a solo game, after all.'

'You had to manage players, officials, referees, everybody, to get your full points,' Kamal wanted to retort but couldn't. Rathin entered through the swing door, followed by four players. 'Ah, how long have you been here?' he asked Kamal. 'Has Tapen-da given you the money?'

Tapen nodded. 'I'm going to Tollygunge,' Rathin said. 'You're heading for Naktala, aren't you, Kamal? If you can wait a few minutes, we could go together.'

'I'll wait in your car,' said Kamal. 'Please hurry up.'

'No need to worry about returning the money, Kamal,' said Tapen softly.

'Why?'

'I'll ask for it when I need it. I'll be happy to think I could be useful to you when you were in need. I'm pleased that it was Jatri you turned to when you were in trouble.'

Kamal grew pale. 'I asked Rathin for the money, not Jatri. And it's for someone else, not for myself.' He was about to add that he would return the cash if it didn't belong to Rathin, but didn't get the chance because Poltu-da's face suddenly swam up before his eyes. He felt as though he had been flung into a bizarre cage which, despite being open on all sides, would not let him escape.

Maintaining his gentle smile, Tapen Ray said, 'Telephone me at home if you need more money. It's our duty to contribute to Poltu Mukherjee's treatment as well. This isn't a loan, Kamal, this is my… our…tribute to Poltu-da.'

Kamal suddenly felt helpless. He seemed to be alone in the penalty box, with two of the opposition's forwards bearing down on him with the ball. He didn't even have the time to look around for support.

In the car, neither of them spoke for a while. When they were close to the Victoria Memorial, having passed Brigade Parade Ground to the east, Rathin said, 'You didn't play the last two office matches.'

'These matches are meaningless. I don't like playing them. Besides, I had to see how the new players were shaping up in Shobhabajar's practice matches.'

'But the bank has given you a job to play for the office team.'

Kamal remained silent.

'People are talking. Besides, you never stay beyond three-thirty or four, even though your work isn't complete.

'Who told you? Ranen Das, I'm sure.'

'Never mind who told me. I've made enquiries – they aren't lying.'

The traffic policeman had raised his arm. Rathin braked. He would now turn right to enter Harish Mukherjee Road. Kamal was staring at the policeman. Rathin took the turn, changed gears and said mildly, 'You have to realize that your reputation and your brilliance are both things of the past. You cannot take – or expect – the advantages that today's rising stars can. You have to put the job before everything now. You're no longer different from anyone else.'

'I'm no different from anyone else,' Kamal repeated in a whisper.

Pain flashed briefly over Rathin's face before being replaced by a hard expression.

'How can you say I am no different from clerks like Bipul Ghosh, Ranen Das or Notu Saha, Rathin? I've played for India, I've contributed to the nation. I gave my best years to nothing but hard work and struggle, with no time for education, no concern for security, no attention to my family. What sacrifices have they made, tell me. By what logic can I be no different from them?'

Rathin was silent. He seemed to be concentrating fiercely on driving.

'I still want to do something for football. I want to nurture players. That's why I leave office early. The office league is pointless.'

'Kamal, players are remembered in our country only so long as they can be seen on the ground. After that they sink into public forgetfulness. New heroes appear, becoming everyone's darling. See what's happening with Prasoon Bhattacharya now at Jatri – he's everyone's hot favourite. But remember how fans had once upon a time beaten up the same Prasoon's father after accusing him of taking a bribe and tanking the IFA Shield final? Do something people will remember you by.'

'I'm getting old, Rathin. I no longer have the ability to do anything like that. A footballer's only asset is his body, after all.'

'Focus on your job, then. Even the union was opposed to your getting the job. Everyone wanted a new player, someone young, to get the job. You know, of course, about Apurva – plays in the second division league. We got him to play eight matches for the office team last year. He played quite well but hasn't got a job yet. The committee members want big names. Four names from East Bengal and Mohun Bagan came up. I argued that experience shows that players like these never give their best in office matches. Teams lose despite them. The company doesn't benefit at all. It's players on the decline who offer better service. I had to lobby with the assistant general manager for you. Now if you choose not to play, where does that leave my credibility? With so many people talking about it, if you still stay away from the games I'll have to take disciplinary action against you.'

'But it will not be possible for me to stay in office till five o'clock or play for the office team on Shobhabajar's match days.'

Rathin's face betrayed irritation.

'Your track record with jobs is quite poor. Can you imagine what will happen if you lose this job at this age? I don't think you'll get another one. Have you any idea how many unemployed people we have in this country?'

'No, I don't. I don't want to, either. Stop the car here,' Kamal almost shouted in annoyance. Surprised, Rathin braked immediately.

'I could drop you further down the road.'

'No, this is fine. And I'll return your money in the office tomorrow.'

Getting out of the car, Kamal slammed the door unnecessarily loudly and marched off in the opposite direction towards the bus stop.

4

Kamal got into a suffocating, crowded bus, and while holding on to an overhead rod, he remembered the old days.

Thirteen years ago, the first time that he played for Juger Jatri, Rathin was the right-back and Kamal, the stopper. As captain of Calcutta University, Rathin had brought home the Sir Ashutosh Trophy from Lucknow that year. As a player, he was slightly better than average. He used to address Kamal as 'Kamal-da' back then.

Rathin was a favourite of Gulo-da's. A new international tournament named Merdeka had just begun in Malaysia. The Indian team was going to participate. Twelve players from Bengal had been picked for the training camp in Bombay, three of them from Jatri:

Rathin, Aminullah and Sunit. People were told that Kamal had not been sent for the trials because he had a knee injury. And not only that – he had an eyesight problem as well. Both were lies.

Kamal was slightly injured in the match against Eastern Railway. He was rested in the next game, with Rathin taking his place as stopper. He played quite well. In the subsequent match, against Aryan, Jatri lost 0-1. Misjudging the flight of a high cross, Kamal failed to head it away. The centre-forward, who had been lurking behind him, scored. It was after that match that the rumour about Kamal's eyesight had been spread.

Kamal ran off to complain to Poltu Mukherjee.

'They're going to drop me completely, Poltu-da.'

'Oh dear, dropped completely!' Poltu-da laughed heartily, leaning back in the chair outside his door, where he had been reading the newspaper. 'Dropped? Why, no, I can see you're very much upright.'

'No, Poltu-da, it's not a joke. I'm not enjoying this any more. I'm going to stop playing.'

'Not enjoying this? Let me take care of that. Go run to Jadavpur Station and back. Now.'

Paying no attention, Kamal said, 'I'm really going to give up the game. So terribly unfair, this Rathin is nowhere near as good as me…' He stopped.

Poltu-da sat up in his chair, his nostrils flaring, anger gathering in his eyes.

'Aru!' He called his daughter in a stentorian voice. 'Come here, Aru.'

As soon as Aruna emerged, he said, 'Get my walking stick.'

Kamal stepped back instantly. 'Are you planning to go out now?' Aruna asked in surprise.

'I asked for my stick!' Poltu-da shouted.

Seeing Kamal looking as scared as a little boy, Aruna concluded it may not be a good idea to fetch the walking stick. Scenes like these had been familiar to her since childhood. 'Should I get the thick one, Baba?' she asked in jest.

Poltu-da didn't reply. As soon as Aruna went back inside the house, Kamal ran off swiftly without another word. Poltu-da watched him retreating till he was no longer visible, walking to the kerb and raising his chin to look even further.

People on the road looked on in surprise. Many of them knew Kamal. It was beyond their wildest imagination that such a famous footballer would be running in his shirt and trousers on a crowded street at eight in the morning.

Returning to his chair in exhaustion, Poltu-da covered his eyes with his left arm. When Aruna emerged from the house to place her hand on her father's forehead, he lowered his arm. Two thin streams of tears were flowing down his cheeks.

'He's been terribly hurt. Life is full of blows, but why do they have to come so unfairly?' Poltu-da covered his eyes again.

Much later, Kamal's red, perspiring face peeped through Poltu-da's kitchen window.

'Aru!'

Aru stopped what she was doing and raised her eyes.

'Kamal-da? He's still…'

'What? Still?'

'Yes, he's got the stick in his hand. Are you sure you went as far as Jadavpur station?'

'I swear by football.'

'Let me check.'

Returning in a minute, Aruna said, 'Come round to the front door. He doesn't have the stick any more.'

Poltu-da was busy sewing a button on to his shirt. Throwing a glance at Kamal, he asked, 'Have you eaten?'

'Yes.'

'How's your son? How old is he?'

'He's well. He'll be five in September.'

'More practice, better practice. There *will* be disappointments, you have to conquer them. Do you suppose you can become a great player just by representing India? You become great when you experience within yourself a special joy, a special tranquillity, where despair cannot reach. If you want to give up the game, it can only mean you haven't achieved greatness.'

Kamal stood rooted to the spot, his head bowed. He experienced an unfamiliar combination of feelings – distress and tearfulness.

And now, as he recalled all those events from thirteen years ago during this four-minute walk from the bus stop to Poltu-da's house, a strange feeling of compassion and pain swelled in Kamal's breast.

Lying back against three pillows, Poltu-da extended his hand towards Kamal.

'I'm all right,' he said softly.

'He's not allowed to talk.' Aruna directed her instruction at Kamal.

Kamal looked at her. Dressed in the white sari of a widow, she had spent the past five years since her husband's death at her father's house, along with her son. She was a teacher in a primary school now. Poltu-da had gone bankrupt financing his other three daughters' marriages. His wife had died two years ago. Besides his youngest daughter Aruna, his household included only a widowed sister. Both of them stood forlornly at his bedside, while Aruna's son Pintu sat on one side of his grandfather's bed.

'How is he?' Kamal whispered to Aruna. 'Has the doctor been?'

'He has. Said there's nothing anyone can do.'

'What about medicines?'

'He prescribed some. We didn't get them. Baba said not to.'

'Give me the prescription.' Kamal stretched out his hand.

Poltu-da had been looking at them. Now he spoke in a tired, measured tone. 'No need to waste any more money on me.'

Kamal gently lowered his outstretched hand.

'Didn't anyone else drop by?' Aruna shook her head at his question. Four of Poltu-da's protégés had played in the Indian football team, and another fifteen for Bengal.

'Balance, Kamal – never lose your balance. I couldn't hold on to mine, which is why I have no legacy to leave behind – besides you.' Ruffling Pintu's hair with his right hand, Poltu-da continued, 'This whole world revolves around balance. We walk thanks to our balance, we run, dribble the ball, even think because of it. Never lose yours – whether in your behaviour or in your state of mind. I no longer care who visits me. I always knew you'd come, and you have.' After a pause, he said, 'Look after them. This is my last wish.'

'Poltu-da, since you'll insist on talking as long as I'm here, I'd better go.'

'You can't, can you?' Poltu-da said with a smile. 'What if I just asked you to stand here before me? And I will just look at you and all those scenes will flash before my eyes – your ball control, you looking up as you stroke the ball forward with your feet, and then looking around. For some reason I was always reminded of Abhimanyu, that follow-through of yours after a shot, that dodge – leaning to the right, swaying to the left, and then instantly back to the right, without dropping your speed. Can you do it still?'

'No. I've grown old too, Poltu-da.'

'No, you haven't. You can if you try. Will you?'

Kamal looked in wonder at Poltu-da. His eyes were sunken into his emaciated face. But how brightly they shone! That was how he used to look at people twenty years earlier.

'Will you show me what I've taught you?' Poltu-da's voice held not the command of yore, but an entreaty.

An invisible string, such as one that controlled a puppet, forced Kamal's hand to his head. Moving his hair out of his eyes and bending to look at Poltu-da, he said, 'I will.'

Spotting a rubber ball beneath the bed – probably Pintu's – Kamal drew it out with his feet. Seeing him dribble it around with the soles of his feet, Pintu got off the bed to approach Kamal and suddenly stretched out his small foot. The ball was deflected towards the wall. Nobody except Pintu laughed.

Unknown to himself, Kamal crouched like a taut bow, as though his opponent were trying to snatch the ball from him. His eyes fixed on Pintu, Kamal rolled the ball around with the sole of his foot, left and right, forward and backward, as he moved all around the room. Pintu kept kicking at the ball indiscriminately, without being able to connect even once. Suddenly taking a half turn, Kamal stood opposite Pintu, bent his body to the left, waist upwards, then to the right, and then back upright again. Losing his balance, Pintu fell on the floor and looked around in surprise, then sprang up and buried his face in his mother's lap in embarrassment.

Kamal paid no attention. Gradually, he forgot about the room, about its inhabitants, even about Poltu-da, who was on his deathbed. He felt as though he was back on the pitch, the crowds in the galleries greeting his exploits with cries of rapture. Like a rampaging god, Kamal danced and swayed all over the room with the ball at his feet, lost in his own world, dodging past his imaginary opponents one by one. He bounced the ball on his feet, then on to his thighs, sending it to his head, then back down to his thighs and feet – the ball played all over his body.

Poltu-da watched, his eyes fixed on Kamal, his face wreathed in a smile. Then he shut his eyes slowly.

A few minutes later, Aruna said softly, 'Kamal-da, I think Baba just passed away.'

5

Kamal returned home at nine in the night, thirty-six hours after he had left home to go to office the previous morning. His eyes were bloodshot, his hair unkempt and his body bent over with fatigue.

He lived in a two-room flat on the ground floor, with one room for himself and one for Amitava. The maid did all the housekeeping, including the cooking, and left at ten o'clock every night. Ten years ago, when Shikha had died, the seven-year-old Amitava had been taken away to Guwahati by Shikha's mother. He had returned two years ago to live with his father.

At first, their relationship had been similar to that of two new students at school. Two years later, there was still no intimacy between them. They spoke very little, avoiding one another as much as possible, not even entering each other's rooms. Once, however, Kamal had gone into Amitava's room looking for a pen to sign for a registered letter he had received. He found the pen tucked into a notebook half filled with scribbled poetry and, beside it, peeping out of one of the books lined up on the desk, a photograph of his wife. The photograph used to be in the drawer of Kamal's dressing table. Kamal was saddened. He'd have been happier had Amitava asked for his mother's photo instead of stealing it. Kamal loved his studious, serious, soft-spoken son, although he felt a sense of discomfort at Amitava's frail appearance and thick glasses. Amitava addressed his father very formally, although Kamal would have preferred him to be informal.

Two other boys were chatting in Amitava's room. Kamal shot a glance at them on the way to his own room. He threw himself down in the armchair, shutting his eyes. One by one, the events of the past twenty-four hours swam before his eyes. The sobbing, the chores, the phone calls, the cremation, the return to Poltu-da's Naktala home. Poltu-da's sons-in-law were present, but none of them were well-off. The hundred rupees had been very useful.

Kamal opened his eyes at the sound of footsteps. It was Amitava, with the other two boys behind him.

'These are friends of mine from college, they've come to say hello.' Amitava's embarrassed tone sounded repulsive to Kamal. In a tired voice, he said, 'Can we meet another day? I'm out of sorts both physically and mentally.'

They left without another word. Kamal shut his eyes and fell asleep in ten minutes.

Like every day, he was awake at five in the morning. He'd neither switched off the light, nor changed out of his clothes. Kamal sprang out of the chair.

In half an hour he had put the kettle on to boil, knocked on Amitava's door as he did every day and was waiting at the dining table. By the time Amitava took a seat, the tea was ready.

'My guru passed away the day before, which is why I couldn't come back home.'

'Who?' asked Amitava with a frown.

'Poltu Mukherjee.' Kamal watched Amitava silently as he spread the jam on his bread. 'You haven't heard of him though.'

'No. I know nothing of football, actually.'

'Poltu-da was…' Kamal said animatedly, 'like in literature…'

He became nervous when he saw Amitava's eyes dancing in amusement behind his thick lenses.

'Like Tagore?'

'No, not that great.' Kamal felt squashed. To get out of the hole, he said in desperation, 'But he was my Tagore.'

'Then you must be very upset.'

Kamal remained silent.

'Were you upset when my mother died?'

Kamal looked sharply at Amitava, who lowered his eyes and took a sip of tea from his cup.

'Your mother could not adjust to my life, to my ambition. The wife of a footballer has to make many sacrifices, tolerate a lot. She lacked the strength. She didn't like my going off to training camps or to play in tournaments away from home. We had frequent quarrels. It was against her wishes that I went to play in the Rovers Cup for Jatri. That was when it happened.'

'You had been sent a telegram after she was taken to the hospital. But you didn't come.' Amitava levelled his accusation against Kamal in a cold, harsh voice. Kamal heard the unspoken 'Why not?' ringing in his ears. The tender grief on his face was seared by rage.

'I've told you this before. The telegram was delivered to our manager Gulo-da. He chose to keep it from me, for we were playing Hyderabad Police in the semi-final the next day. Jatri couldn't have played that match without me.' Kamal looked sharply at Amitava as he spoke.

As before, disbelief was writ large on Amitava's curled lips. Kamal had not yet managed to convince him that he would have dropped everything to rush to Calcutta had he received the telegram.

Leaving the dining table, he went to his room and ran his hand over his stubble as he looked in the mirror. But he didn't feel like going to office, which meant he didn't need to shave. Kamal picked up a pair of scissors to carefully remove a few grey strands from his beard.

He could hear the front door open. The maid, perhaps, or the morning newspaper being delivered. Kamal put down the scissors to pull some money out of his pocket. The maid, who did the daily shopping, would start grumbling if there was a delay.

'Kamal-da.'

Salil stood at the door, shuffling his feet.

'What is it, Salil? Why are you here at this hour?'

'I came from the ground. Went for practice.'

'Don't you have an injured foot?'

'It's nothing, the doctor said, just needs some rest.' Salil sat down on the bed. Kamal felt that he had come to say something else.

'So Poltu-da's passed away.'

'Hmm. He was seventy-three.' Kamal observed Salil in the mirror as he trimmed the grey strands in his beard.

'Is there something you want to tell me?'

Salil looked down, dragging his big toe across the floor for a while before saying hoarsely, 'We haven't eaten anything for two days, Kamal-da. There are eight people in our family.'

Kamal had no idea how to respond. He frequently heard stories like this among footballers. Initially he'd feel a sigh welling up in his breast, but now all that happened was a tightening of the jaw.

'I've got a job with a cardboard factory, eighteen rupees a week. They want me to start today.'

'And football?'

Salil lowered his eyes again and remained silent. Kamal saw tears coursing down his cheeks. As he slunk out silently, Kamal thought of calling him back but didn't.

Salil was face-to-face with the first major crisis in his life. The battle between football and family had begun for him. Between ambition and love. If he was passionate about football, if he was consumed by the desire to be a great footballer, he would have to be ruthless, breaking out of the chains of everyday life. Bengalis were far too tender. Most young men could not do it, being swallowed up instead in the all-consuming belly of the daily grind. Salil would have to decide for himself. Giving him money out of pity would not help him become a footballer.

Kamal was reminded of his own situation. After his mother's death, his father forced him into marriage so that there would be a woman at home to look after the family. He was only twenty. He had to wage a peculiar battle with Amitava's mother. But his son wouldn't understand that. His friends may have been interested in meeting his father, but Amitava himself was oblivious to his father's reputation. Not once had he said, 'Can you get me a ticket? I'd like to watch you play.' For years, Kamal had longed for his son to watch him.

'The tailor will deliver the trousers today, Baba.'

'Today.' Kamal headed for the drawer, key in hand. 'How much?'

'Twenty.'

For a second, as he handed the money to Amitava, Kamal remembered that Salil was taking a job for just eighteen rupees a week. Amitava and Salil were roughly the same age.

6

In the afternoon, Kamal went over to the Shobhabajar tent. Everyone had heard of Poltu Mukherjee's death. Kamal had to answer several inquisitive questions. Saroj, the Shobhabajar coach, said, 'Kamal, we're playing Rajasthan tomorrow. Shall we work out the team now?'

'What's to work on? Play the same team as the last match. Why mess around early in the season?'

'Salil says he'll play. But I don't think he's fit. He was limping after a couple of fifty-metre sprints this morning. When I asked him to do a few spot jumps, he couldn't.'

'Let him rest for at least a couple of weeks.'

'But who's going to play as right-stopper? We have no one for that position. You know just what Satya and Shambhu are capable of. We could move Swapan back from the half-line, but who'll feed the forwards then? Whatever else Rudra can do, ball distribution isn't his forte.'

'Well, then?' Kamal looked worriedly at Saroj and smiled wanly. 'Me, in other words?'

Saroj nodded.

'But I've put my foot to the ball barely once or twice this season. Done no training to speak of.'

'That doesn't matter,' replied Saroj enthusiastically. 'Experience will take care of it all. The biggest problem with my defence is the lack of experience. You saw during the Mohun Bagan match, didn't you, how all four defenders stood in the same line, with each through-pass completely opening them up. They spread out the game to cover a lot of space, and our defenders ran so hard to keep pace that they ran out of steam in half an hour. They didn't even think about slowing down the game, about holding on to the ball.'

'They'll learn on the job. All right, I'll play tomorrow. Tell the boys to come to the ground in the morning. I want a spot of practice with them.'

'On a match day?'

'Just a little. I want to practise a couple of moves. Don't worry, I won't keep them more than an hour.'

Saroj looked grim. Kamal realized he didn't approve and that, as coach, his ego was smarting. Switching to a soft, friendly tone, Kamal said, 'Small clubs like ours have no resources to speak of. Our players are raw, unpolished. Towards the end of the season such clubs have to fix their games to survive in the first division. Have you thought of the outcome of trying to get them to play artistic football? You don't want your first year of coaching in the first division to be your last, do you?'

Saroj's face fell for a moment, then grew stern. 'I want them to play good football, Kamal-da. Even if Shobhabajar were to be relegated as a result, I wouldn't have any regrets, not even if I had to sink with them. But I'm not going to surrender right at the beginning.'

'Are the club officials aware of your plan? Does Keshto-da know?'

'If they did, they'd throw me out this very minute.' Saroj didn't try to hide his smile.

'There's no need to tell you this, but I'm still tempted to. I've probably played more football than you have, I'm probably more experienced. Let's say I'd like to discuss a couple of things with you.'

'Kamal-da, you don't have to say all this, there can be no comparison between you and me,' said Saroj humbly. 'I have so much to learn from you.'

'Would you say we have the players to play the kind of football you want the team to play?'

'No,' came the prompt reply.

'Then all we'll do is lose one match after another. And eventually, the club will be forced to play the dirty game of match-fixing to get a few points for survival. There's no point in trying artistic football, Saroj. Put off your dreams till you get a team capable of it. The club comes before style. Get hold of players first and prepare them. Defence first, counter-attack afterwards. That's the best strategy everywhere, even for life.'

'Status quo ante, in other words?'

'Yes. But even so, we have to try to further strengthen our defence. All your tactics, during the entire seventy minutes, must be aimed at occupying and covering space. You get more time to control the ball if you get it in free space. Denying your opponent space is to deny him time, which is why we use tight man-to-man marking these days. There were many flaws in the three-back system, which I've played in. The four-back system has plugged those gaps. Wingers used to get up to twenty-five yards of free space earlier, which the four-back system can reduce to five. But, as you must have noticed, Shobhabajar cannot manage even with four defenders.'

'Do you want to play with five, then?'

'Something like that. How about a roving defender behind the four regular defenders? One of the forwards, even two, can be made to play in midfield. We need a 1-4-3-2 formation.'

'You want a Catenaccio defence. In other words, you want to kill football.'

Saroj flew into an obdurate rage, which was just what Kamal had feared.

'We wouldn't have let in five goals against Mohun Bagan and lost two points had we used this formation. We'd have earned one point at least. Would that have been so bad? You put too much emphasis on midfield play, but it's lost its relevance. The battle is at the head of the penalty box, to narrow the attacking angle so that goal-bound shots can be blocked. Why don't you understand that scoring is the only objective for teams, for that's the only way you can win. Shobhabajar may not have the ability to score goals, but we can prevent other teams from scoring, can't we?'

'Our thoughts are not in sync, Kamal-da. So long as I continue to coach Shobhabajar, I want the team to play according to my ideas.'

Saroj's firm, uncompromising tone made it clear that he wasn't willing to argue any more. 'Fine,' said Kamal lightly, looking away.

'But you're playing tomorrow, aren't you?'

Kamal nodded, smiling.

7

Having stayed away two days, Kamal was back in office. Ranen Das wasn't anywhere to be seen. The familiar, diminutive figure of Bipul

Ghosh had, however, occupied his seat at the stroke of ten, like he did every day, and was busy writing the name of his favourite god in red ink. The five-storeyed office building, where nearly four hundred and fifty people worked, was humming with noise. No one did any work before ten-thirty. There were just three people in the dispatch department, where Kamal worked.

Completing his daily ritual, Bipul Ghosh enquired, 'Didn't see you the last two days. You weren't ill, I hope?'

'A relative died. I was busy with that. Do you have a leave application form, Ghosh-da?'

Bipul Ghosh gave him a form. Filling it out, Kamal took it himself to the leave section on the third floor. There was a crowd of younger employees around Anupam Ghoshal. Anupam was the right-winger for Juger Jatri, and fast making a name for himself. Rathin had got him a job here. He had scored a hat-trick against Kumartuli the previous day.

'Do you suppose Anupam couldn't have got more goals? When Prasoon dodged past three defenders at the beginning of the second half and tried to selfishly score all by himself, Anupam was in the clear, only five yards from goal. Anupam would have scored if Prasoon had given him a pass. Wouldn't you, Anupam?'

'You can never tell in football.' Anupam smiled slightly.

'Why blame Prasoon. How could he pass to Anupam? He was clearly offside.'

'Rubbish! Were you offside, Anupam?'

'Their left-back and I were on the same line,' Anupam said grimly, looking away.

'There you are! I've always said Prasoon is the most selfish of them all. Never lets go of the ball, wants to score himself every single time. Jatri has scored far fewer goals than it could have, thanks to him. We may have scored five against Bally Protibha, but if Prasoon had sent all the passes to Anupam that he should have, there would have been five more. I doubt whether Anupam got the ball more than three or four times from Prasoon. Am I wrong, Anupam?'

'Never mind all that.' Anupam laughed disinterestedly.

'Yes, cut the rubbish. It hardly matters whether Prasoon passes the ball to Anupam or not. The next match is against Eastern Railway. Anupam, I'm giving you advance warning, my nephew's very keen on watching the match.'

'It's very hard to get people into the stands these days, Satya-da. Even the number of day slips is limited.'

'I don't know all that. You simply have to organize something.'

'Let me see what I can do,' said Anupam, making his way to the desk of Nirmal Datta, the section head. Anupam usually left the office after spending a few minutes chatting with Datta.

'Anupam, you must play just as brilliantly against East Bengal too.' Anupam merely smiled as he passed.

They suddenly spotted Kamal, who was waiting at a distance, holding his leave application.

'Casual leave, Kamal-babu? Leave it here on this desk.'

As Kamal was about to leave, having deposited his form, someone asked, 'What do you think of Anupam, Kamal-babu? Isn't he a fantastic footballer?'

'Yes, fantastic.'

'Have you watched all his games this year?'

'Not a single one.'

'But didn't you say he's fantastic?'

'I said it because all of you were saying the same thing.'

'No, it's not a joke. Seriously now, don't you think he's got something in him? You can evaluate him better than we can, after all.'

Kamal thought for a bit before replying gravely. 'Don't judge a player only by his performance. You have to take into account his attitude, his thinking, his devotion to the game. Maybe he does play well, but when a person who's in the clear five yards from goal says he's not sure whether he could have scored, I wouldn't consider him a footballer of quality.'

'But the world's greatest players have failed to score from even a yard, haven't they?'

'I don't know if they have, but you will never hear them say they're doubtful whether they can score from five yards. This "whether" – this uncertainty, this lack of self-belief – is not something that will ever escape their lips. If you were asked how much two times two is, would you ever wonder whether the answer is four or not?'

Having spoken out on an impulse, Kamal noticed the shades of dissatisfaction on his listeners' faces.

'You're right, but you know what, having done arithmetic from childhood, it's as natural as breathing now, which is why the answer to two times two will be four all my life. But football isn't like that – you perfect it at a particular age, give it up at another. However great a player may be, he cannot play at the same level all his life, can he? Can you stop Anupam today the way you used to stop a Chuni Goswami or a P.K. Banerjee or a Balaram once upon a time?'

The words carried more than a hint of derision. Kamal felt his temples throb. 'Toothless old lion,' someone quipped from the back.

Although tempted to check who it was, Kamal restrained himself with great effort and said, 'So long as one hasn't cheated on one's education, the skills that one has acquired with hard work never disappear, even with old age.'

'You mean you can play just as well now as earlier?'

'No. But I can probably play well enough to stop the Anupams of the world.'

Surprise showed on everyone's face, transforming quickly, via disbelief, to laughter. Kamal felt he had overdone it.

'Aren't you just asking to have your nose rubbed in it, old man?'

'We'll see what happens when Jatri plays Shobhabajar in the League,' said Kamal through clenched teeth.

As he reached the head of the stairs, Kamal heard someone shout in the large hall he had just left, 'That was a challenge. We have to let Anupam know.'

Ranen Das waved him over to his own desk as soon as Kamal returned to his department. 'And where were you all these days? Can't you give advance notice before disappearing? Three people have to do the work of twelve here. How can we cope when one of them stays away? And then you'll be transformed into a footballer after three o'clock.'

The horrible mood in which Kamal had returned from the third floor remained intact. 'I took leave because I needed to,' he said bitterly. 'I have the right to take leave too.'

'You do? Leaving at three o'clock every day is also part of your rights, is it?'

Kamal didn't bother to respond. He didn't care for Ranen Das at all. He wasn't at his desk most of the time, preferring to gossip in the canteen or the union office or elsewhere in the office, and was perpetually sniffing around for overtime wages. He had studied up to Class Eight and now earned eleven hundred rupees after thirty years of work, but never bought his own cigarettes. Ranen Das was the head of the dispatch department.

Notu Saha, the games secretary, arrived at his desk around two in the afternoon, clutching a register.

'I came looking for you yesterday, but you weren't here. We're playing Bengal Tube this afternoon at the Bhabanipur ground.' Notu Saha extended the register as he spoke. It had the names of the players, with Kamal's listed as the third. Everyone had signed next to their name.

The first thing Kamal remembered was that Shobhabajar had a match that afternoon, which he *had* to play. But Notu Saha wouldn't let him off on those grounds. He recalled what Rathin had said: *You haven't played two office games in a row...people are talking...even the union had opposed the idea of giving you a job...I had to lobby with the assistant general manager.*

Looking at his name, Kamal tried to decide what he should do. Shobhabajar needed him too – he was on the players' list. But while that match was more important, this one was linked to his livelihood. He could, of course, tell Notu Saha he wouldn't play. But that would mean giving up forever on leaving office at three o'clock.

'Why don't you sign? We have to leave soon,' said an impatient Notu Saha.

'Can't you leave me out of this one?'

'No, we have no one in defence. Just Anupam among the forwards. Gobindo is on a week's leave, Jahar is injured – we've barely managed to put a team together.'

Kamal signed without prolonging the discussion. He could see the expression on Saroj's face – helpless, overcast with rage.

8

The Progressive Bank van dropped them at the ground at four o'clock. Observing that Anupam kept looking at him from the corner where he was seated, Kamal surmised he must have heard something. He felt uncomfortable. After changing into his playing kit, Kamal discovered that Anupam hadn't. 'Isn't Anupam playing?' he asked Notu Saha.

'Says he'll play only if needed. Famous player, after all,' Notu Saha said sarcastically, suppressing his annoyance. 'You had better not say anything or his fans in the office will give us hell.'

Kamal smiled, recalling that he too had thrown his weight around once upon a time.

Progressive Bank was down 0-3 at half-time. Bengal Tube had made only four attacks, but scored off three of them. Only their right-winger and centre-forward were playing a decent game. Kamal could have blocked both of them if he'd wanted to, but he chose not to. Twice he tripped over his own feet like a greenhorn when trying to tackle, and another time rose to head the ball a second or two late. That was enough for the three goals.

As soon as he came off the pitch at half-time, Kamal saw Anupam in playing gear, chatting with a few of his fans. He smiled to himself.

Notu Saha ran up to him in irritation and anger. 'How could you let in those goals? Even the junior league players don't make those charges the way you did.'

Kamal sat down on the grass without a word, picking up a bottle of lemonade.

'I have no idea why people say you used to be a great player.'

Lowering the bottle from his lips, Kamal said softly with a smile, 'We won't let in any more goals. Now tell the one you call a great player to score thrice.'

'I'm not worried about that. Anupam will score half a dozen easily enough. But, for heaven's sake, don't let in any.'

Putting the empty bottle down, Kamal stood up. The Bengal Tube players were resting a little further away. Kamal had noticed that their left-half, not very tall, had little control over the ball, was unable to give proper passes, and kicked out at opponents aimlessly. But he had amazing stamina and was fearlessly pugnacious. As a result, he chased the ball everywhere like a demented bull about to gore his enemy, which made more than one player step away hastily as soon as they saw him.

'You're playing very well,' Kamal told him. 'You've stopped Progressive single-handedly.'

The young man scratched his head in pleasure and embarrassment. Praise from Kamal Guha wasn't easy to come by.

'But you're going to be in trouble now.'

'Why?' he asked alertly.

'Anupam's coming on. Says he'll score five – Bengal Tube's no football team.'

The face turned sullen with rage,

'I'd love to see how good a player you really are.' Kamal walked away.

The second half commenced and the ball stayed midfield for the first five minutes or so. Having waited for the ball, hands on hips, near the right-hand touchline for some time, Anupam finally gave up and moved in, hoping to get a pass.

He got one almost immediately, dribbling past first one and then a second player. The left-half was charging at him from a distance of about forty yards. With three defenders before him, Anupam had stopped to find someone to pass to. As soon as he spotted the left-half approaching him like a bulldozer, he quickly pushed the ball to the centre-forward and moved away. The left-half ran on for another fifteen yards before he could apply the brakes, and then charged at the ball again.

The centre-forward hadn't been able to hold on to Anupam's pass. The ball drifted out to Kamal, who controlled it with casual touches in a tight space as he looked around to see where Anupam and his bodyguard were, before dispatching it with marvellous accuracy to a spot midway between them, so that Anupam would have to make a run to receive it.

Just as Anupam was about to put his foot to the ball, another foot reached the spot, followed by a sound like a tyre bursting. The ball was deflected to the middle of Progressive's half. Kamal provided three successive through-passes to Anupam – all of them, needless to add, closer to the left-half than to the intended recipient. What everyone saw was that Anupam either couldn't receive the pass or stopped his run short of the ball. When he moved from the right wing to the left, so did the left-half. Several people outside the pitch smiled covertly, while Kamal saw rage, irritation and hopelessness writ large on Anupam's face.

Kamal passed the ball to Anupam again. Tube seemed to know that every pass would head for Anupam, and had put three men to police him. Instead of moving even a single step towards the ball, he ran up to Kamal and shouted, waving his arms, 'Why me every time? Isn't there anyone else to pass to?'

Feigning astonishment, Kamal said, 'But they were saying in office you couldn't get more than three goals yesterday because Prasoon didn't give you enough passes.'

Anupam didn't say another word. He began running around the pitch, trying to work himself free of the left-half's clutches, with just one thought running through his mind: not to get injured. Kamal began to move up with the ball. Approaching Tube's penalty box, he turned as if to pass the ball to Anupam again but then, suddenly, twisted the other way, dribbled past a defender and scored from sixteen yards. None of the Tube players had expected him to make the shot himself instead of passing to Anupam. When the ball was entering the goal, kissing the right post, the goalkeeper was still positioned near the left post, looking at Anupam.

Three minutes later, Kamal scored again, in exactly the same way. Now Tube shifted its attention from Anupam to Kamal. With four minutes to go, the score was 3-2 in favour of Tube. Kamal moved up with the ball again, drilling a pass to the right-in after dodging past three opponents. He promptly gave it back to Kamal. Anupam's policeman was charging at him. Waiting with the ball, Kamal sidestepped him at the last moment. The left-half turned back to repeat his mad charge. Kamal positioned himself for a right-footed pass, crying out, 'Anupam!'

Anupam moved up to the left, expecting a pass, three of Tube's players following him. Kamal stroked the ball with his left foot between two defenders, into the space in the middle of the penalty box. And the right-in, who would normally blast ninety-eight out of a hundred such passes completely off target, managed to score this time.

Notu Saha ran up to Kamal after the match, his hand extended. Kamal stopped in his tracks and told Anupam, 'Prasoon knows when to pass and when not to pass. Just as you have to play with the ball, there's also a very important game to be played off the ball.'

Patting Anupam on the back and brushing aside Notu Saha's hand, Anupam strode off to the tent.

On his way back, he heard on the tram that Shobhabajar had lost 0-3 to Rajasthan.

9

As soon as Kamal got into office the next day, he heard that Rathin had sent for him.

Rathin was talking on the phone when Kamal entered his cabin and signalled to him to take a seat.

'So,' said Rathin after his phone conversation ended. 'I believe you played brilliantly yesterday.'

'Who told you?' Kamal tried to imagine who could have informed Rathin already.

'Never mind who. You let in three goals so that Anupam would be forced to play, sent through-passes he couldn't reach, then scored to save the team. Congratulations! Brilliant! Talk about killing three birds with one stone!'

Kamal smiled tightly without a word.

Rathin's face was like thunder. 'It's hard to believe a senior player would embarrass a junior on the field like this. How unsporting!'

Kamal sat up straight in shock, his anger throbbing in his eyes.

'What's the matter? I'm unsporting just because Anupam plays for your club?'

'That's not the issue. If you turn a promising player, a rising star, into a laughing stock, it causes a psychological setback. Anupam is playing an extremely important role on the Jatri forward line this year. Jatri has won the IFA Shield but has never been League champion. I want to get Jatri the League during my tenure. The team is playing like a well-oiled machine. I don't want the smallest part of the machine to go out of order. I will not allow it.'

Kamal looked at Rathin's balled-up fist, poised for a cruel blow. 'May I leave now?' he asked dispassionately.

Rathin looked at him unflinchingly. Kamal did the same.

'I trust I have made myself clear.'

Nodding, Kamal pretended he had just remembered something.

'I'm afraid I haven't been able to pay back those hundred rupees yet – I'll do it as soon as I get my salary next month.'

'I'm not bothered. Jatri isn't dying for a hundred rupees.'

'How much will it die for, then?'

'Meaning?'

'Five thousand?'

Rathin's jaw hardened. Noticing this, Kamal said, 'I don't think Juger Jatri is a particularly sporting club.'

'You may go now.' Rathin pointed to the door.

As soon as Kamal returned to his desk, Bipul Ghosh whispered, 'What happened yesterday at the match? The boys are fuming. They're claiming you sabotaged some very famous player of ours, that you monopolized the ball.'

'Yes.'

'How famous is he?'

'Very famous. Apparently he earns eight thousand.'

'Eight! Good God! I make eight thousand now, after fourteen years of pen-pushing seven hours a day. And these boys make that much just kicking a ball around. Add the salary too.'

'Good for them. Let them make their money. Football isn't any easier than pen-pushing.'

Kamal began to sort the mail in order to put an end to the conversation. Every single detail of each letter had to be entered in the register before putting it in an envelope and sending it off to the dispatch clerk for fixing stamps and posting. A mistake would mean a letter going to the wrong person, and then his job would be at stake.

Ranen Saha had been hard at work all this while. Without raising his eyes, he asked, 'Leaving at three o'clock again today?'

'Why?' asked Kamal.

'For scoring two goals yesterday.'

Kamal laughed.

The telephone call from Aruna came shortly before closing time. 'Kamal-da, I need to meet you. This school in Beleghata is looking for teachers. Can you introduce me to your club secretary? He's on the school committee. If I get the job, I can give this one to Baruna.'

Kamal told her he'd talk to Keshto-da that day.

He normally walked to the Maidan after work. On his way, what Rathin had said, the change in his attitude and, most of all, the word 'unsporting' kept hammering away inside Kamal's head.

'Here you are. Brilliant. I was planning to go to your place.'

Startled, Kamal realized it was the journalist. 'Why?' He smiled.

'I forgot to ask. Have you retired?'

'What? Where did you hear that?'

'I was at the Juger Jatri tent yesterday. Pratap Bhaduri was saying you've retired, apparently.'

'Really? What else have you heard?' Kamal continued walking.

'Someone from Jatri went to watch your office league match yesterday and Pratap Bhaduri was overheard discussing you with him. Hearing about how you made life miserable for Anupam, the man said that he believed you had now retired, and that Jatri should give you some money seeing that you played for them for so many years.'

'Did he say how much?'

'No.'

'I'm playing Shobhabajar's next match.'

'So you haven't retired.'

Kamal strode ahead without a reply, leaving the surprised journalist amidst a crowd of people.

Kamal ran into Satya and Balai at the entrance to the Shobhabajar tent.

'Why didn't you come yesterday, Kamal-da? Saroj-da waited till the last minute for you.'

'They wouldn't let me come at the office,' Kamal said defensively. 'How did it go?'

'How indeed. Swapan played instead of you. Three goals were let in thanks to him.'

'You'd have died laughing if you'd seen the last goal, Kamal-da.

Shyamal Bose from their team had already scored two goals. When their right-winger was moving up with the ball, Swapan ran towards the corner flag to tackle him – but then suddenly turned and went off to guard Shyamal Bose inside the penalty box. Obviously the right-winger simply scored himself. Astonished, we asked him why he did that. Do you know what Swapan said? What if he'd passed the ball to Shyamal Bose and he'd got a hat-trick?'

Satya burst out in laughter. Balai joined him. 'So you see, Kamal-da, Swapan didn't let the hat-trick happen. No harm letting in goals, but allow a hat-trick? Never!'

Kamal laughed too. Then he spotted Bharat inside the tent, looking at them. 'Sorry, Bharat,' he said, walking up to him.

'We wouldn't have lost yesterday if you'd been there.'

'What could I do, we had an office match.'

'This is my ninth year with Shobhabajar, Kamal-da, seventh as the first goalkeeper. I've never seen a team as lousy as this year's. They're not even fit for the third division. These players possess neither skills nor football sense. All they're capable of are obscenities and fouls. The referee warned three of our players – Balai, Satya and Sridhar. However stupidly he may have played, Swapan at least played his heart out.'

'Who's the next match against? Bata?'

'Yes.'

Saroj emerged from the secretary's room, his face growing grim as soon as he set eyes on Kamal.

'Couldn't make it, Saroj.'

'I know, you were playing for your office team.'

'I will definitely play the next match. Doesn't matter if it means losing my job.'

'Sorry, Kamal-da, the line-up's ready. Swapan will play.'

'Look, Saroj, a rumour is being spread that I've resigned. I have to play to prove it wrong.'

'The team cannot be changed.' Saroj raised the grimness of his tone. 'You can play some other match.'

That the greenhorn coach of a minor team like Shobhabajar could speak to him this way was beyond Kamal's imagination. He entered the secretary's room without prolonging the conversation.

Krishna Maiti didn't bother to buy provisions worth more than three or four rupees for home-cooked meals. The sole desire of his life was to surreptitiously consume the food that his tongue craved. Right now he was wrestling with an entire roasted chicken. When Kamal sat down opposite him, he only offered him a glance, without a word.

'The next match is against Bata. I want to play, Keshto-da.'

'Of course you will.'

'Saroj has left me out.'

'What!' Krishna Maiti shouted. 'Saroj, Saroj!'

As soon as Saroj entered, he said, 'Kamal will play against Bata.'

'But…' Saroj started, giving Kamal a dirty look.

'No buts. Kamal is the seniormost player on the circuit. The top teams still quake with fear when he plays. If he wants to play, he must.'

'But Keshto-da, I've put a lot of thought into the line-up, keeping in mind a particular pattern of play. Besides, Kamal-da hasn't practised at all with the boys.'

'Practice!' Keshto-da almost choked. After he had regained his composure, he said, 'You can have it all – pattern, practice, everything. Just do as I say. Kamal will play.'

'Fine.'

Saroj threw another fiery glance at Kamal as he left.

'The gentlemen are doing us a great favour by coaching the club, you see, Kamal. Eventually we'll have to fix matches for points to avoid being relegated. Life was so peaceful when there was no promotion or relegation.'

'They're recruiting teachers at that girls' school where you're a committee member, Keshto-da. Someone I know has applied. Can you help, please?'

'Who is she?'

'Poltu Mukherjee's eldest daughter.'

Frowning, Keshto-da seemed lost in thought as he licked his fingers. 'I can take care of it,' he said. 'But there's a condition. Our first game against Juger Jatri is on the seventeenth. You have to get us one point. If you can ensure that the match is drawn, she'll get the job.'

Kamal stared at him in helpless surprise. He could not understand why such a peculiar condition was being set.

'How can you do that, Keshto-da?'

'It has to be this way. Get me the point, and I'll try my best. I want to take revenge on Gulo. Last year he had agreed to give seven hundred rupees for repairing our tent if we let Jatri beat us, and if we voted for a replay of their abandoned match against Kalighat. We didn't have to lose by choice – they scored four goals anyway. And we did vote for the replay, but Jatri lost the vote. So he didn't pay. If you can take a point off them in the first match, they'll be so scared during the return match that I'll extract the right price, with interest. So it's entirely up to you whether Poltu Mukherjee's daughter gets the job or not.'

Unable to talk, Kamal could only look at the eyes blinking behind the glasses. He too wanted very much to deprive Jatri of a point. But his desire was at odds with Krishan Maiti's. And the most uncomfortable and worrying part of the whole thing was the condition that had been set. He couldn't take a point off Jatri single-handedly. At his age he no longer had the stamina. Both his agility and his speed were on the decline. You cannot fight against a young team with experience as your only weapon. And more importantly, if Aruna's chances of getting a job depended on the outcome of the match, he'd be under additional pressure.

The shimmering image of an old man floated up before Kamal's eyes. Trying to listen closely to what he was saying, he muttered, 'Balance. Yes, Poltu-da, mustn't lose my balance.'

'What do you mean, balance? I want a point.'

Standing up, Kamal said in a tired voice, 'I'll try.'

10

Kamal felt a light frisson run through his body as the referee blew his whistle for the match to start. His last match had been played on this very pitch – the Mohammedan Sporting ground – in the first round of last year's IFA Shield. And he hadn't returned here since then. Over the past twenty years, he had felt this tremor every single time the referee had blown his whistle. But his nerves always recovered after that brief sensation. And then every cell in his body prepared for an explosion.

Kamal felt himself ready that day too. Bata had started indolently. As they tried to attack down the centre of the field, right-half Satya charged in and dispatched the ball towards the corner flag on the right. Kamal was irritated at Satya foolishly wasting this opportunity. Although Rudra, the winger, standing near the centre flag at the time, couldn't possibly have got to the ball, he still expended some energy in chasing it.

Kamal chose to play within the eighteen-by-forty-four-yard area of the penalty box. Twice he had to challenge an advancing forward and succeeded both times, sending perfect passes to his own forwards. Whenever the raw Swapan abandoned his position to run around helter-skelter, Kamal shouted instructions to him. Even when he had clear ground before him, he resisted the temptation to move up. They were hardly fifteen minutes into the match, and Kamal had already grown confident in his role.

Just two people were watching the game from the general stands, while the Howrah Union members' stands had fewer than fifteen in them. These were people who came every day, regardless of the match, and stayed on into the evening. The Mohammedan Sporting side of the members' stands had a few people. The match was meandering in the midfield. To his irritation, Kamal noticed that quite a few of the Shobhabajar players seemed to have no inclination whatsoever to play seriously. They didn't challenge the opponent on the ball, didn't stretch for a tackle and didn't chase anyone who dribbled past them. Kamal felt the pressure piling up on him. The dam in the midfield was springing one leak after another, and Bata's attack kept building like a flood.

But Kamal was nevertheless amazed by the way Swapan, the right-back, was playing. In fact, he was wherever the ball was to be found. While he was becoming somewhat of a laughing stock with his random tackles, leaps and movements, Kamal realized that he was making an impact and so didn't stop him from leaving his position vacant any more – although the resultant hole on the right wing remained a huge danger.

Shobhabajar earned a goal kick in the first minute after half-time. As he placed the ball in the goal area, Bharat told Kamal, 'Satya, Shambhu and Balai have started their tricks. Please tell Rudra to fall back and look after the right side, Kamal-da.'

'Let's wait and watch a little longer,' said Kamal before taking the shot.

But Bata earned a penalty within a minute. Balai, the left-back, held on to the ball with both hands – quite unnecessarily, as Bharat would have got to it easily. 'What on earth?' Asked Bharat in astonishment.

'Got it all wrong. Thought you weren't in position, that the ball would go in,' a crestfallen Balai replied, wiping the sweat off his forehead dramatically.

Muttering something unintelligible, Bharat took his position, angrily fetching the ball from the goal after the penalty and flinging it with disgust to the ground.

'Balai,' said Kamal sternly, 'move up and play as right-winger. Rudra, fall back.'

'Why should I change my position?' Balai asked arrogantly.

'Because I say so.'

'Who're you to order me around? Nobody except the captain or the coach has the right to issue orders.'

Kamal walked away. 'What the hell is he saying?' Satya shouted at Balai.

Humiliation and rage roared inside Kamal's head. He began his battle with just Swapan and Pranbandhu on either side. Rudra had fallen back anyway, as there was no question of scoring now. Shobhabajar was simply using its seven- or eight-member army to fight off more goals.

But fifty minutes into the match, the defence began to break down with fatigue. Satya, Shambhu and Balai were committing unnecessary fouls all over the place. Bharat had made fantastic saves from two of the three free kicks, and fisted out the third for a corner. Gritting his teeth, Kamal tried to plug the holes in the penalty box, shouting out instructions to Swapan and Pranbandhu. Bata was attacking with six, sometimes eight players at a time. And sure enough, they scored three more goals in quick succession.

'Kamal-da, I'm done for,' Swapan panted. Although Kamal sympathized, this wasn't the time to show it or to ask him to take it easy. Shobhabajar had let in four goals already, and Bata was outnumbering them in attack two to one. This battle between unequals was impossible. The match had been reduced to a farce, with Bata toying with their opponents instead of scoring.

'I'm twice as old as you. If I can, why can't you?'

Nodding a couple of times with glazed eyes, Swapan ran off towards the ball. If only Salil were here, Kamal reflected. Pranbandhu, Swapan and Rudra were all crowded into the penalty box now. The forwards – Debidas, Gopal and Sridhar – had fallen back to the half-line. Kamal began doing what he hated, what he had never wanted to do – sending the ball into the stands as soon as he got it, so as to waste some time. With no spectators, retrieving the ball took time.

The final score was 0-4. Swapan collapsed as soon as the match ended. Pouring a glass of water over his head, Kamal threw a glance at Saroj, who averted his eyes. 'Just chicken chowmein won't do – a plate of chilli chicken each too,' Balai told Saroj with a laugh.

Kamal leant over to check Swapan's pulse. It was abnormally rapid. It seemed to be over hundred and fifty a minute. Smiling wanly at Rudra and Pranbandhu, who were squatting by him, Kamal said, 'Let him rest a little more. I'll get down to practice with the two of you starting the day after tomorrow.'

As he changed after showering, Kamal overheard a conversation between two of the executive members.

'Saroj did say you can't flog dead horses. Modern football needs so much more energy.'

'I just cannot understand Keshto-da's soft spot for him. How can we have a team without young people, what use is a coach without them? They're switching to power football all over the world and yet here we are…'

'Saroj says he cannot be held responsible if there's going to be so much interference.'

'And no one can overrule Keshto-da. We're doomed.'

They lapsed into an embarrassed silence when Kamal emerged, and then one of them hurriedly said, 'Four goals, eh?'

'Yes, four,' Kamal answered without a flicker of expression and sidestepped them to walk away. Outside the tent, he saw Saroj having a cup of tea at the canteen counter. About to call out to him, Kamal hesitated. He wanted to say a few things to him but thought it better not to get into an argument and attract a crowd. So he left instead.

Grasping an overhead handle in the jam-packed bus, Kamal noticed a middle-aged man who had been glancing at him repeatedly. 'Straight from the match?' the man finally asked.

'Yes.'

'What happened?'

Kamal felt an agony like that of a dozen needles piercing him. Weighing up the option of pretending not to have heard, he realized he couldn't ignore the other man's expectant expression. 'Four-nil,' he said softly, adding, 'We lost.'

His face crumpling with pain, the man turned to gaze out of

the window, refusing to look at Kamal any more. Kamal felt like crushing the handle he was gripping. This man had probably watched him play ten or twelve years ago, but couldn't watch football regularly these days. Even so, he had not forgotten Kamal Guha. His may have been one of the shoulders upon which Kamal had been borne aloft after many a match.

Consumed with an impotent rage and dissatisfaction with himself, Kamal walked home.

As soon as he sat down at his office desk the next morning, he was greeted with large chalk writing on the surface of his desk: '4-0. And the score against Juger Jatri will be the same.'

Kamal looked at the words for a while, without wiping them off.

'Bunch of hooligans. Wipe it off, Kamal-babu.' Bipul leaned towards him from his desk.

'Never mind.' Kamal smiled wanly.

'Why don't you skip the match against Jatri?'

Kamal stiffened. Being a well-wisher, Bipul did not want him to face further humiliation. Taking it for granted that Kamal wouldn't be able to hold Jatri back, he was offering friendly advice. 'You don't have confidence in me, do you?' Kamal asked, his eyes lowered.

'No, no, it's nothing like that. I neither watch nor understand football. But young people these days, you know what they're like – they don't know how to show respect where it's due.'

'But I *will* play against Jatri,' said Kamal with conviction. 'I have to, for another reason as well.'

An hour later a bearer deposited an envelope on Kamal's desk. It turned out to be a memorandum, issuing him with a warning for having left office early the previous day without seeking the departmental head's permission. Any repeated occurrence of such behaviour, he was told, would warrant further proceedings in accordance with company policy.

Rathin had signed the memorandum. As he folded the letter to put it back in its envelope, Kamal spotted Ranen Das smiling slyly. 'Balance, I must retain my balance now,' he told himself.

11

Kamal went to bed as soon as he got home from work. He was feverish, his body warm. Having fallen asleep, he was woken by Amitava's voice.

'Don't you want dinner? It's quite late.'

As he sat up, Kamal felt his entire body aching. Amitava noticed that his eyes were bloodshot.

'Have you eaten?'

'No,' replied Amitava after a spot of hesitation. 'I thought we could eat together.'

'I'm not eating, I think I have the flu.'

Kamal called out to Amitava as he was about to leave.

'Can you lend me your alarm clock? I need to be up early tomorrow, have to go for practice.'

'Practice!' Amitava looked at him with wide eyes. 'But you have fever.'

He stepped closer and placed his palm on Kamal's forehead to check. 'Nearly a hundred degrees.'

Sensing Amitava's lean fingers on his forehead, Kamal said with his eyes shut, 'I *have* to play.'

'Even if you're ill?'

'Yes. You can't play if you don't practise. I have no more time to waste.'

'But…' Amitava's silence held a stream of questions.

'I've looked for perfection all my life.' Kamal smiled. 'But in vain. Everyone wants to be perfect in their own field – mine's football. I had wanted to be a footballer knowing full well I'd never be a complete man. But the sad part is that your time as a footballer is finite. A footballer can bank only on his stamina, on his youth – and the time granted to him is far too little. What can a mediocre footballer like me possibly achieve in such a short span of time without hard work?'

'But you're ill.'

'So what? The challenge has been thrown. I have to accept it. So much humiliation has come my way – how will I live out the rest of my life if I cannot even the score?'

Getting out of bed, Kamal stooped to pull out a dusty pair of dark blue running shoes from underneath and started brushing them. 'You love football so much?' asked Amitava suddenly.

Nodding, Kamal responded after a pause, 'Yes. And I've had to pay the price for it. I've lost a great deal, and haven't got enough compensation for it. I've swallowed plenty of taunts and jeers in my life, but I will not retire before I pay back the idiots, the scoundrels, the arrogant. I will play, come what may, even if it kills me.'

'What if you cannot? You said time is running out.'

'I am afraid to think of that. I have to succeed, I will do it all alone if need be. I know that when I send out that pass with perfect timing, there'll be no one to receive it. My perfect through-balls will be wasted because no one will be able to control them. I'll get passes, but sent so clumsily that I won't be able to make use of them. I'll have to cope with a hundred shortcomings on the part of my fellow players and adjust to them. None of them is in tune with the rest, each of them plays his own game. I have to make them communicate with one another – which means that we have to practise together.'

'And that will make you successful?'

Kamal saw curiosity blazing in Amitava's eyes. Never before had they had such a long conversation. Kamal felt that Amitava was enjoying talking to him. The terrible indifference and suppressed loathing with which he used to talk to his father previously had been replaced with a childlike curiosity. Kamal realized that he no longer felt feverish and that the aches in his body had vanished too.

Examining a skipping rope, he asked, 'Successful? What do you think?'

Amitava stiffened.

Kamal looked on anxiously.

'I understand nothing of football.'

'Why look at it as football? Situations like these can arise anywhere. What does a person who's alone, without any support, do to be successful then?'

Amitava was silent.

Kamal felt his excitement ebbing away. 'Communicate.' He spoke slowly. 'That's what I do on the field during a match. But I cannot do it when I'm back home. I feel very lonely here.'

Seated on the bed, his eyes on the floor, he continued, 'I said a lot of things. Perhaps neither of us knows what they mean. I realize you don't love me, that you hate me. But I love you.'

Tears glistened in his eyes. His voice was heavy. Still, Amitava stood there like a statue. Kamal kept his eyes on the floor.

'Some day or another, I will have to stop playing football. What will I live for after that? Whom will I live for?'

Kamal finally raised his eyes from the ground, hoping to detect a response in Amitava's expression – only to discover that he was no longer there. He had left the room quietly without saying anything to his father.

Kamal left home with his kitbag at five-thirty in the morning. By the time he had jogged all the way from Baghbazar to the club tent, only three of the players had arrived. The three of them – Swapan, Rudra and Shibshambhu – kitted themselves up quickly.

'Straight to Victoria along Chowringhee, then a turn to the west along the tram tracks to the south of the race course to Prinsep Ghat. Northwards along the river, then turn past the Mohun Bagan ground, around Netaji's statue, and back here.' Kamal traced the route for them before they started. They nodded obediently.

As they were running along Chowringhee, Bharat leapt off a bus. They stopped in their tracks.

'You're out already, Kamal-da? I wanted to join the practice too.'

'We'll be back in an hour or so. Get ready in the meantime.'

The four of them resumed running. After a while, Kamal asked Swapan, who was running next to him, 'How much is seven multiplied by twelve?'

Astonishment was writ large all over Swapan's face. What kind of ridiculous question was this during training? After failing in Class Eight, Swapan had neither been anywhere near his school nor tried to involve himself in any problem that required him to perform such calculations as these. He started muttering the seven times table to try and answer Kamal's question.

'Eighty-four,' he answered eventually.

'Does your family come from across the border?'

Swapan gave him a wide grin.

They were running westward now, behind Victoria Memorial, having crossed Rabindra Sadan. Kamal launched a similar attack on Rudra. 'Can you recite "Twinkle, Twinkle, Little Star"?'

'No, I don't know that one.'

'"Baa Baa Black Sheep"?'

'Don't remember.'

'Can you remember the square of eleven? Or any scientific facts about India's climate? Answer – you took your college exams just last year, didn't you?'

Rudra's brows furrowed as he ran. He tried his best to remember the answers to these long-forgotten questions. Meanwhile, Kamal was busy interrogating Shibshambhu on grammar and Swapan on simple mental arithmetic. He had picked up this technique of getting the mind and the body to work in tandem from Poltu-da. Indeed, this was how he used to train Kamal – who had obeyed with complete dedication. He used to say that when the body tires, the brain can no longer function, but that footballers had to learn to apply their minds despite their exhaustion on the pitch. For that, the brain had to be prepared, which in turn meant rigorous training. 'Never keep your brain idle when running,' he used to say.

Spotting a laden truck as they ran beside the river, Kamal said, 'Chase the truck – let's see if any of you can catch it.'

The four of them started sprinting together. Failing to catch it after a seventy-metre chase, they stood panting. A bus went past them. 'Catch this one, Swapan,' Kamal said suddenly.

'Again?' asked a flustered Swapan.

'Quick.'

Kamal asked him to stop after he'd run with all his might for twenty-five metres. Then he got Rudra and Shibshambhu to set off on sudden sprints as well, chasing a bus or a truck on the road. Finally they resumed their run, Kamal in front. Near Eden Gardens, he said, 'Let's climb trees.'

Choosing a tree, he said, 'Let's see who's the first to get to those branches up there and swing.'

All four attacked the tree together. Swapan shouldered Kamal aside and shinned up the branches before the others, followed by Rudra. When Kamal followed Shibshambhu to the edge of the branch and then leapt twelve feet down to the ground, Swapan approached him looking apologetic. But before he could speak, Kamal said, 'I like it, use the shoulder charge the same way during the match.'

When they reached the Shobhabajar ground, Bharat was kicking the ball high into the air and practising plucking it off the opponent's head – all by himself. Spotting them, he shouted, 'Come and help me, one of you.'

'All in good time, need to rest first,' answered Kamal, sprawling on the grass. He'd run ten or twelve miles since leaving home that morning. Nobody went in for such intensive training halfway through the season.

After an hour and a half of passing, trapping, one-against-two tackling, heading and shooting, Kamal realized that he had to go to office. He would have to be careful from now on – not just about when he left, but also about attendance. Besides, there was a match against Mohammedan Sporting in two days – the boys couldn't be made to sweat any more. Kamal showered at the tent, ate breakfast at the canteen and walked to his office.

In the afternoon, Notu Saha informed him of a match against the Reserve Bank of India the next day. 'Not well, can't play,' said Kamal.

Notu Saha departed with an unhappy expression.

12

Juger Jatri had eighteen points from fifteen matches; Mohun Bagan had twenty-four from fourteen, East Bengal twenty-six from fourteen, and Mohammedan twenty-five from fifteen. Shobhabajar had six points from sixteen matches. As the first half of the League neared its end, footballing circles were rife with rumours that Shobhabajar was certain to be relegated to the second division. Bally Protibha, Sporting Union, George Telegraph and Kalighat were all two or three points ahead of Shobhabajar.

The day before the first match against Juger Jatri, as Kamal was waiting for his turn in the office lift, someone behind him asked, 'Playing tomorrow, Kamal-babu?'

Controlled derision radiated from his voice. When Kamal didn't respond, the speaker became agitated. 'What's the point of losing whatever little reputation you still have left? Haven't you played enough matches already?'

The lift doors opened and the people in the queue entered it, Kamal among them. As the doors were closing, he heard the man, still standing outside in the queue, say, 'It's people like him who give the game a bad name, you know.'

Kamal didn't leave his chair at lunchtime. Who knew who might hurl another taunt at him? He kept working with full concentration, looking up with a start when someone suddenly came up to his desk and asked, 'How are you, Kamal?'

It was Tapen Roy from Juger Jatri. Instantly he went pale, remembering the one hundred rupees he had borrowed.

'How's the football going? I hear you're practising a lot,' said Tapen, drawing up a chair to sit on.

'I haven't been able to return your money yet, Tapen-da. I will as soon as I get my salary next month.'

'Money? What money?' Tapen feigned astonishment.

Kamal spoke even more diffidently than before. 'I haven't

forgotten. It's just that I cannot afford to pay back a hundred rupees all at once.'

Staring at Kamal for a while, Tapen professed to remember with great difficulty. 'Oh, *that* money. I'd forgotten completely. Never mind, you don't have to return it.' He lowered his voice to a whisper. 'I know very well just how much money Jatri owes you. Who else but I have been witness to how they cheated you out of it. They can't sue you to claim this money. Take what you can.'

Kamal instantly became wary. Years of football had taught him how to size up people in these circles. He was suspicious of Tapen Roy's sudden arrival and friendly behaviour. 'What brings you here?' he asked cautiously.

'All in good time.' Tapen took out a packet of cigarettes, lit one, exhaled and continued, 'No one should forget the kind of service Kamal Guha has given Juger Jatri. But what has Jatri given him in return? Nothing at all. There's been a lot of discussion at the club about this. There was a committee meeting. It has been decided to hand you a cheque for five thousand rupees after Jatri's last League game.'

'Jatri's last League game is with Shobhabajar.'

'Is that so? Even better. But before that we need your approval – whether you'll accept it or not. Of course, I must tell you the whole thing will be finalized at the committee meeting scheduled for day after tomorrow.'

Kamal looked at Tapen. His eyes looked earnest, sincerity glowing in them. Smiling internally, Kamal said, 'I'll let you know after tomorrow's match against Jatri.'

'So you're playing tomorrow.'

'Yes.'

Taking furious puffs on his cigarette, Tapen appeared to be thinking. 'Five thousand rupees is not a small sum of money these days. Don't squander the opportunity with a rash decision. Jatri didn't have to give this money to you, they just decided to. It will not only mean showing you their respect, it will also earn Jatri the confidence of other players, don't you think?'

Kamal nodded.

'Clubs these days, you know, Kamal, are bloodsuckers. And the players are no better either – they talk of nothing but money. But Jatri is not one of those clubs. You can't have a club that doesn't have a spiritual relationship with every player.' Tapen appeared to be suppressing strong emotions. Kamal was silent.

'So you're not going to tell me right now whether you'll accept the money?'

'No. I'm going to think about it after tomorrow's match.'

After Tapen had left, Bipul Ghosh craned his neck and exclaimed, 'Five thousand rupees! What was that all about?'

'A test. When you play as a stopper, attacks come from all quarters. This was one of them.'

'Meaning?'

'We're all stoppers, Ghosh-da. Some on the field, some off it. We just keep on defending. I had to defend this time too – against greed. That man had come to bribe me. We're playing against their team tomorrow. Mr Majumdar's team. They're playing for the championship this year, playing quite well, too. They might even become champions. But he was here because they want to remove all obstacles on their way to the title. They consider me an obstacle.'

'Bribe? No, you must play well tomorrow. Play a fabulous game. Teach them a lesson.'

Bipul Ghosh's face was glowing softly with conviction.

'Hope you're coming to work tomorrow,' Ranen Das asked from a distance.

'Why?' Kamal asked in surprise.

'You know the reason very well. And I'm telling you right away that I can't let you leave before five.'

'I know that. But I'm taking the day off tomorrow.'

As soon as he entered the Shobhabajar tent on his way back from the office, Krishna Maiti grabbed his hand. 'Gulo must be taught a lesson, Kamal. The scoundrel made off with the money after getting his way. We have to take a point off them, and you're our only hope. Everyone is opposed to the idea of you playing, but I will insist on it.'

Kamal felt nervous. 'But Keshto-da, you can't bank on me alone. Football is a team game,' he said worriedly.

'You can be the entire team if you want to. Besides, remember that job for Poltu Mukherjee's daughter? If you can get us a point tomorrow, I will guarantee a job for her.'

Suddenly feeling drained, Kamal didn't prolong the conversation by arguing. A lot depended on tomorrow's match. Whoever he met now would pile another ton of responsibility on him. Kamal took a chair and sat down close to the railing outside the tent.

Bharat came up to him. 'Kamal-da, there's something I have to tell you. It's very important, but I can't tell you here. Why don't you come outside – I'll meet you outside the Town Club tent in about five minutes.'

Bharat marched out. Kamal looked around in surprise. Satya and Debidas were sharing a joke near the canteen, while Swapan was having a snack at a distance. Inside the tent, people were chatting around the table, as usual. What could Bharat possibly have to say to him in confidence?

As soon as Kamal reached the Town Club tent Bharat said, 'Kamal-da, two of our players are throwing tomorrow's match.'

Kamal froze. 'Throwing the match! Who?'

'Jatri had sent their people to my house this morning. Shambhu was with them. Jatri has promised suits. Shambhu and Satya have been to Ghulam Ali's tailoring shop to be fitted.'

'Why didn't you go?'

Bharat merely smiled. So did Kamal. Clapping Bharat on his back, he said, 'Don't tell anyone right now. After the match.'

'Any news of Salil? We'd have managed better with him in the team.'

'Salil has a job now, which leaves him no time for football. It probably never will. But, Bharat, I suspect we will be in the same situation tomorrow as in the match against Bata.'

'I have no idea,' Bharat said doubtfully. 'We don't even have an extra player or two whom we could use to replace Satya and Shambhu.'

'So it's up to Lady Luck tomorrow.' Kamal smiled wanly.

'Yes, Lady Luck.'

13

Juger Jatri beat Shobhabajar 5-0.

Kamal lay face down in his darkened room, the continuous ticking of the alarm clock hammering away inside his head. Covering his ears with his hands, he groaned indistinctly. The terrible screams still rang in his ears. The clock could be hurled on the floor and smashed into a thousand pieces, but what of the screams that came with those five goals?

When he was walking out through the narrow passage between the stands, people spat on his head, stones rained on his back. He even heard someone shout, 'So, Kamal, didn't you claim you could stop Anupam?'

Anupam had scored three goals today, although he hadn't got a hat-trick. Kamal banged his head on his bed several times, a whimper involuntarily escaping his lips.

'Well, Kamal, time to give up the dream of striking terror into the Jatri jersey.'

Gulo-da's smiling face and biting words seemed to rise out of the mattress. The mattress could be torn to shreds, but the words?

'What can I do? Go ask the man who decided the team composition. If he wants ancient players on his team, he can have them. Talk about whims! You'd expect some sense, some logic, wouldn't you?' Kamal could see a quiet glow of satisfaction in Saroj's eyes as he heard him speaking to someone after the game.

As soon as the final whistle was blown, Bharat ran up to Shambhu and slapped him. Shambhu kicked him back in retaliation. 'Did they score because of me? No, because of him, because of that man,' Shambhu screamed as they were being separated, his finger stabbing at Kamal like a hunter's knife. Kamal left the ground without looking around.

'You let me down. I'd banked on you.' Kamal suddenly remembered Keshto-da's disappointed, annoyed tone. Aruna probably wouldn't get the job, after all.

He didn't even have a face-saver at his disposal. It was the Bata match all over again. Just that Jatri was more skilled, more relentless, more motivated. Kamal only had to shut his eyes to see the scene again: Anupam and Prasoon moving up on either side of him, while the Jatri right-back came up with the ball across the untenanted midfield. Swapan and Rudra were out of their depth trying to stop the opponents.

Kamal had decided to keep Anupam tied down today. But Prasoon was by Anupam's side continuously, leaving Kamal helpless. Wherever the ball went, Prasoon was on hand to lend support to his teammates, so that there were always two forwards to take on the challenge from a Shobhabajar defender. Strapped for people, Kamal hadn't been able to solve the problem of whether to shadow Jatri's forwards or protect the turf. And besides him, only Bharat knew why there was a paucity of people.

But people would accuse him of trotting out excuses if he said that now. There was no way he could do that. Nor was there any other escape route. He would have to hear the barbs and abuse for days to come. Burying his face in his pillow, Kamal began to tremble.

Suddenly someone switched on the light in the room. Kamal shot upright.

'Kamal-da, it's me.' It was Salil, a hesitant, troubled smile on his face.

'Why are you here?'

'I heard Shobhabajar lost 5-0 today.'

Kamal looked at him without a word.

'I want to play, Kamal-da. I'm not going back home. I don't want to go to work any more, I want to play. All I need is two meals a day and somewhere to sleep.'

Kamal stood up.

'I'm not going to think about my family. I can't save them. I...'

Salil fell against the wall, clutching his stomach as Kamal kicked him.

'What have you come here for? To show pity, you rascal? To help because we lost by five goals? To deliver me from damnation by agreeing to play?' Kamal kicked him again. As Salil lay sprawled on the floor, Kamal rained kicks on his back, his head, his body. Raising him by a fistful of his hair, Kamal punched him in the face.

'Don't hit me, Kamal-da, I'm going, I'm going.' As Salil sat up, Kamal grabbed his hair again and started shaking him.

'Why have you come, why, why?'

Salil gaped at him. Blood trickled from the corner of his mouth and from his nose, and tears from his eyes. Before he could answer, Amitava appeared at the door and said, 'Let him go.'

Swiftly entering the room, he struck out at Kamal's hand, which was still clutching a handful of Salil's hair.

'What do you want here?'

'Why are you beating him up?'

'Do not interfere.'

'You expect me to just watch and not protest while you beat someone up? Just take a look at him. Even animals are treated better.'

'No, no, Kamal-da didn't beat me up,' Salil appealed to Amitava in a gravelly voice, his hands raised. 'Kamal-da never beats me up, he only punishes me.'

'Quiet,' Amitava said, silencing Salil. Bending forward, he stretched out his lean hand to touch Salil on the shoulder. 'Come to my room – we need to clean you up and put some antiseptic on that.'

Amitava paused on his way out to throw a glance at Kamal. Kamal's face was vacant, with only an unfamiliar expression of failure showing on it. He seemed to have aged ten years. Stooping, he walked slowly to his bed and sat down. Looking blankly at Salil, he ran his fingers through his hair in a distracted way.

Trying to stand up, Salil groaned in agony and then collapsed, clutching his stomach. Trying again, he slumped once more, looking helplessly at Kamal. Kamal stared at him expressionlessly.

'But I can see the scar on your head, Kamal-da.'

Kamal did not respond. Trying to smile, Salil crawled out of the room. Kamal kept running his hand through his hair. Much later, Amitava came back into his room and said softly, 'Go to sleep.'

Kamal looked up and fixed his eyes on Amitava's face. His gaze gradually regained awareness of his surroundings. His face crumpling in pain, he whispered, 'I'm finished.'

Amitava switched off the light and left the room, shutting the door behind him.

14

Kamal was a defeated man from that day onwards – in appearance as well as state of mind. He stayed slumped in his office chair all day long, not talking unless he needed to, and returning home directly after work. He no longer set foot on the football ground. Aruna had telephoned him at office, but he had refused to speak to her, instructing Bipul Ghosh, 'Tell her I haven't come to office.'

Kamal ending up not receiving the taunts and jeers he had so expected. Everyone seemed to have assumed that the outcome was a foregone conclusion. Scorn would have been preferable to such indifference. As soon as he received his salary, he went to Rathin's cabin and laid a hundred-rupee note on his table, saying, 'Here's the money I borrowed.'

'I didn't lend you anything. Return it to the person you borrowed it from.' Rathin then turned his attention back to his work without another look at Kamal.

Unsure of what to do, Kamal decided to hand the money over to Tapen Roy personally. He set off towards the Jatri tent after work, arriving at the same time as the Jatri players who were returning from the Aryan stadium after a 2-0 win over BNR. There was quite a buzz in the tent, with about a hundred people milling around within and without. Pausing at the edge of the crowd, Kamal cast his eye around for Tapen.

'Oh, Kamal-babu, it's you.' Dayanidhi, the veteran groundsman, came up to Kamal.

'I'm looking for Tapen-babu – do you know where he is?'

'He's probably inside – why don't you go in?'

Kamal entered hesitantly.

He found Tapen Roy blocking the door to the players' dressing room, telling a few young men loudly, 'Now now. They're tired. Don't bother them now.'

Kamal stepped up. Surprised at seeing him, Tapen nevertheless addressed him quite normally. 'What is it, Kamal?'

'I need to talk to you.'

'You can see how bad things are, I dare not budge. We'll have to talk here.'

Taking the hundred-rupee note out of his pocket and holding it up, Kamal said, 'I came to give this back to you.'

A thought seemed to run through Tapen Roy's mind. 'Keep the money,' he said carelessly. 'You couldn't give the club a single trophy through all those years. What favour do you expect to do the club with your money now? Jatri's a certainty for the League this year. The only important games left are the ones against the Big Two. The fireworks alone will cost ten thousand. I don't have the time to worry about a hundred rupees.'

Kamal's knees trembled. The screams of a million goals echoed in his head. But he managed to speak calmly. 'I'll come to watch the fireworks. But you must take the hundred rupees back. I will not remain in Jatri's debt. I do not want to.'

A crowd had gathered around them by now. Entering the tent at that moment, Gulo-da walked towards them, his curiosity aroused by the crowd.

'What's going on? Oh, it's you, Kamal.'

'I'd borrowed some money when I needed it. I came to return it, but Tapen-da refuses to take it.'

'You remember that money, Gulo-da, you remember telling me not to ask for it back,' Tapen reminded him quickly.

'Ah. All right, take it if he wants to return it,' Gulo-da said mildly. 'Jatri's last match is with Shobhabajar. If Kamal promises not to play, we'll take the money back.'

'What if Kamal Guha plays? Jatri will still score ten goals against Shobhabajar,' said someone in the crowd.

'That's what I mean. I won't be able to take the sight of Kamal's team – a player as great as Kamal – conceding ten goals.' Gulo-da smiled. 'It's going to be painful for Jatri too. Don't forget, Kamal belonged to Jatri once upon a time.'

'You're right, Gulo-da,' someone else spoke up in agreement. 'Kamal-da, you mustn't play that day. Jatri's honour is tied to your honour.'

Kamal smiled wanly. They'd decided to humiliate him with compassion. He wanted to tear the note into shreds, fling the pieces in the air and shout, 'I'm not done, not done yet.' But at that moment an old man's voice whispered in his breast, 'Balance, Kamal, never lose your balance.'

Looking around dejectedly, Kamal replied dully, 'Take the money back. I have no wish to play any more.'

Forcing the currency note into Tapen's hands, Kamal left the Jatri tent. He felt numb, his knees wobbling like jelly and threatening to collapse under him. The desire for vengeance was trying to rekindle itself within his breast. The depression and hopelessness that had enveloped him all this time was beginning to be dispelled as he chafed under the agony of humiliation. As he walked aimlessly through the Maidan, Kamal didn't realize he had arrived at the Shobhabajar tent. Hearing someone call his name, he saw Bharat and Salil standing outside the canteen. Bharat came up to him, although Salil did not.

'Are you ill, Kamal-da? You look unwell. It's been so long since you've been here that I was thinking of visiting you at home.'

'What's new at the club?' Kamal asked, evading Bharat's question.

'What do you expect? It's the same story as every other year. We got three points from three draws, but we're not out of danger yet.' Bharat was living under the threat relegation from the first division. 'What's the use of being a first division club, Kamal-da?'

'Is Salil playing these days?'

'Don't you know? He played the last four matches, played rather well. Bottled up Habib completely during the match against East Bengal. All the papers wrote about him.'

'Is that so? I don't read the papers any more. Anything else happening?'

'The other thing that's happened is very funny. You remember Satya and Shambhu going to Ghulam Ali for measurements for the suits they'd been promised? When they went to try out their suits a week later, they heard that Gulo-da had left instructions only to take the measurements, but not to actually make the suits till they heard from him. Gulo-da hadn't telephoned again. Satya and Shambhu are bristling with rage – they'd never imagined they'd be made fools of like this. They can't tell anyone either – they just have to swallow the whole thing. Now they're telling everyone they'll show Jatri in the return match.'

Kamal only smiled faintly. 'Where's Saroj? Is practice going well?'

'What practice? Saroj-da hasn't been anywhere near the tent in the past ten days. We heard he's got a job in Jamshedpur or Durgapur or some such place. Salil, Swapan, Rudra and a few others kick the ball around a little every morning. Keshto-da lets us have only a cup of tea and two slices of toast every morning.'

'Is Salil still doing that job of his?'

'His father came looking for him. Salil's quit his job. He's left home too. Nobody knows where he lives. We've asked, but he refuses to tell us.'

'Tell Salil to come see me.'

As Kamal was about to leave, Bharat said hesitantly, 'We don't see you here any more.'

'Yes, I don't enjoy it any longer. It's time to get out. Did anyone telephone for me?'

'No idea.'

15

As soon as he returned home, Kamal heard the maid grumbling. 'Why should I have to wash other people's clothes? Doing the dishes used by other people wasn't part of the deal. I can't do all this extra work unless you pay more.' Etcetera, etcetera.

'Who on earth are these other people?' Kamal asked curiously.

'What about that friend of your son's who's staying here?'

'Friend? Staying here?'

'Why, don't you know?' As the maid's eyebrows shot upwards in astonishment, Kamal didn't prolong the conversation.

That night, Kamal thought he could hear people talking softly in Amitava's room. But the next morning, as he was passing by his son's room, a close look inside revealed nothing. He decided to ask Amitava about it.

As he was leaving for office, Amitava asked him for twenty rupees. Having already given him forty rupees that week, Kamal asked with some discomfort, 'You're asking for money quite frequently these days. Given my salary, I cannot cope if we go on like this.'

'A friend of mine is ill, he needs medicine…' Amitava gulped.

'The maid was saying a friend of yours has his meals here.'

'A couple of times, yes. He won't any more.'

Giving Amitava the money, Kamal said, 'Your friend's meals are no problem.'

Over the next few days, Kamal noticed changes in Amitava. His grave demeanour had been replaced by a cheerfulness, there was a spring in his step, he broke into song at times, one morning he even woke Kamal with a cup of tea at his bedside. Embarrassed, Kamal said, 'I'm getting lazy now that I've given up football. Must start morning exercises again.'

'You've given up football?' Amitava asked in surprise.

'Yes.'

'Why?'

Kamal left for the market without answering. That evening, he heard at the Shobhabajar tent that Balai and Ambrose had both been red-carded for fighting during the match with Mohammedan Sporting. Sridhar's old knee injury had been aggravated, making it impossible to even stand, let alone play. Everyone was worried stiff, their brows furrowed. Shobhabajar couldn't even put together a team of eleven players. Abani Mandal, the assistant secretary, ran up to him. 'I was planning to come to you, Kamal-babu. You simply have to play the three remaining matches.'

'No,' said Kamal sternly. 'I won't play any more.' And he walked out of the tent, leaving a bewildered Abani Mandal behind him.

Kamal returned home in a disturbed frame of mind. Despite the sorry state that Shobhabajar was in, he had refused to play. And this was the club with which he had begun his career in the first division. It felt like a betrayal. He could easily play the remaining three matches, couldn't he? The last match was against Jatri. Gulo-da's taunts rang in Kamal's ears. Before handing over the hundred-rupee note to Tapen Roy, he had said, 'Never again for Jatri.' But the desire for revenge that had burned in his head at the time had now been reduced to cold ashes.

Amitava's room was dark. Entering his own room, Kamal

changed into his nightclothes and lowered himself into his armchair. Thousands of images and memories from twenty years of football were swimming around in his mind. Again and again he could see Poltu-da and could hear him say, 'More practice, better practice. There *will* be disappointments – you have to conquer them. If you're thinking of giving up the game, that can only mean you haven't succeeded in achieving greatness.'

No, I haven't, Kamal told himself over and over again. I haven't succeeded, I haven't, I haven't. I have not achieved fulfilment. There's so much I've left undone.

He heard the sound of Amitava's door being opened and the light being switched on. Kamal remembered that he hadn't been able to find his skipping rope that morning. Had Amitava taken it for some reason? He went to ask him, putting on his slippers as he got up. As he was leaving his room he thought he heard a shuffling sound coming from next door and called out for his son. Entering Amitava's room swiftly, he saw someone disappearing under the bed, a pair of legs still visible.

Kamal was about to cry 'Thief!' but bit his words back at the last moment. The legs seemed familiar, as did the section of the trousers he'd managed to catch sight of. It was Salil.

About to enter the room with some slices of bread in his hands, Amitava halted in his tracks, and then stiffened, on seeing Kamal sitting on his bed, leafing through a book.

'Bread? Haven't they cooked tonight?'

'Not feeling too well, so…'

'So much? This looks enough for two people.'

'Got some for tomorrow too.'

Kamal went on leafing through the book, while Amitava surreptitiously ran his eyes around the room.

'You hate footballers. Like you hate me.' Kamal spoke softly but clearly. 'You've held me responsible for your mother's death and have never been able to accept me. We have never had a father–

son relationship. I admit that I neglected the relationship and gave football a greater place in my life. All I want to know is whether you still hate me.'

Amitava answered after a pause. 'I don't understand why you're bringing all this up now.'

'Curiosity. Don't you ever feel like watching the man who neglected your mother to play football?'

'Yes, but not for that reason. I do feel like watching the man who's about to bid farewell to the game he loved all his life because of humiliation and disrespect.'

Kamal's eyes were boring into Amitava, who stood unmoved.

'Only for that reason?'

'No. I have become curious after finding out how crazy people can get because of their love for the game.'

'Found out from whom? From Salil?'

Startled, Amitava looked at Kamal, astonishment written all over his face.

'Why have you given him shelter?' Kamal asked sternly.

'He amazes me. The other day, after that terrible beating, he sobbed, "I won't get a scar like Kamal-da, there's no cut on my skin." He wanted shelter, which I gave him. In this room. He leaves at dawn, returning in the afternoon, then goes out again and returns late at night. He has abandoned his family. Through him I have understood many things I never did before.'

'What have you understood? What?' Kamal stood up in agitation. 'I wasn't to blame. Football is not just a physical thing, it's got to do with the mind too – have you understood that?'

'I will after I have seen you play.'

'You want to see me play?' Kamal lowered his outstretched arm. Amitava nodded.

The next day, Kamal telephoned the Shobhabajar tent from his office. 'I'm going to play the match against Jatri.'

16

Armed with cymbals, conch shells and crackers, the Jatri fans had filled the stands of the East Bengal ground. The club flag could be seen flying every ten metres. Juger Jatri would become the Calcutta League champions today. For the first time ever. They needed two more points. East Bengal were one point behind; Mohun Bagan, three; Mohammedan Sporting, six. All of them had one game to go. If Jatri won, they would be beyond reach. If they drew, however, East Bengal would have a chance to catch up in their last game against George Telegraph, whom they had beaten 4-0 in the first leg.

A single tentative voice was heard in the stands. 'What if Jatri were to lose today? You never know in football, do you?' But the same person seemed to have regained his composure a few moments later. 'Who but P.C. Sorcar or Pelé can beat Jatri today? Remember how we beat Shobhabajar 5-0 the first time round?'

'Shobhabajar will field the same team,' said another self-styled expert. 'The closer you get to the end of the season and the rains, the more tired these teams get, and the worse they play. I think Jatri has the opportunity today to score a record number of goals and win the League.'

'Tell me, will Kamal Guha play this match too? He played the last one.'

'Who knows? Haven't seen his name in the papers for a while. And what if he does play?'

'Don't you remember what he'd said when he left Jatri?'

'To hell with what he said. Anupam and Prasoon will have him for lunch today. Can you tell me how many people have survived their arrogance? Not Ravana, not Duryodhana, not Hitler – and you think Kamal Guha will?'

The only people supporting Shobhabajar today were in the East Bengal members' enclosure. They harboured a faint hope – what if Jatri lost? If they did, neither P.C. Sorcar nor Pelé would be able to prevent East Bengal from becoming League champions.

'Impossible. Can't happen. Jatri can't lose. Whom does Shobhabajar have? They've got it in the bag.' Hand-wringing all round.

'If we can beat them with lung power, today's the day. Should we?'

'Of course.'

'Oh yes, we have to get them to win, by hook or by crook. Didn't we ensure Sporting Union lost to us the other day?'

'Tell you what, Shobhabajar isn't the kind of team you can cheer to a win. Jatri must have paid off a couple of players. Sixteen years I've been watching these games.'

'That's a Mohun Bagan supporter! What's he doing here?'

'Never mind. Our interest is common today. You do know what interest means?'

'Four years of high school, my friend. You think I don't know interest and moneylending?'

Jatri's members had occupied the stands reserved for Aryan members. People were gathered around the gargantuan figure of the 'Field Marshal', famous for smoking four cigarettes at the same time, holding them in his gigantic fist. Each drag was followed by an exhalation of smoke like that from a jute mill chimney. Normally he only smoked this way after Jatri had won the game, but today he had started early.

The Field Marshal was followed by two minions lugging an enormous pot, with fifteen kilos of mutton in it, to be distributed after the game. There was a stampede for seats near the pot.

'Very hungry today, why not finish it off right now? We know the result, don't we? Why wait?'

'No, no, not now.' The Field Marshal waved them away. 'Only after the official victory.'

In one corner were a handful of spectators who had turned up with entry passes issued by Shobhabajar. Most of them, of course, were Jatri supporters at heart. It was Bipul Ghosh's first day at a football match, his entry pass having been provided by Kamal. Next to him was Amitava, alone and silent. Salil had given him a pass. It was his first day at a game too. Behind him were Aruna and Pintu. Kamal had visited them the day before, standing for a long time before Poltu-da's photograph with his eyes shut, then touching the photo with his forehead and muttering something. Pintu had promptly imitated Kamal's way of paying his respects. And, in fact, it was he who had demanded to be taken to see Kamal-mama play.

Now Pintu was fidgeting in the stands, impatiently waiting for the teams to come on to the pitch. Aruna was anxious for the game to begin as well. She still remembered the last match she had attended, which must have been when she was about the same age as Pintu. The fans had been ecstatic with Kamal's performance that day. Glancing at his watch, Bipul Ghosh turned to Amitava and asked him, 'Any idea what time it starts?'

As Amitava shook his head, a few crackers were thrown on to the pitch, exploding with a bang that almost seemed to mock the Shobhabajar team.

'There's Kamal-mama!' Pintu leapt up in excitement.

Over the last few days, Kamal had virtually been taking classes with the twelve Shobhabajar players. Using chalk marks and pebbles to represent players on the floor, he had shown them how Jatri would mount its attack and what they should do to repel the opposing team. They had sat in a circle, listening intently. Kamal had shown them intricate details using the pebbles: who led most of the Jatri attacks, where the ball was sent from, what tricks they applied to create shooting space, how they used off-the-ball running to confuse man-marking defenders and how their own defenders tended to overlap down the wings. Then he had explained each individual's role to them, repeatedly stressing the strengths and weaknesses of each of the Jatri players as well as their own tasks.

Even on the morning of the match, he had assembled them to repeat his instructions. 'I'm going to be behind the four backs, providing cover to whichever of you needs it. The defenders will just have to mark their own quarries, tackling without a moment's hesitation. They have to be challenged before they can control the ball. Especially Prasoon. Salil will follow him like a shadow. Swapan will take care of Anupam. Shambhu will play in front of the four defenders, trying to intercept every single pass so that the ball can never reach a Jatri forward. The moment he sees an attack taking shape, he must challenge it immediately.

'Ahead of Shambhu will be three midfielders. They must throw themselves at all attacks as soon as they start, fall back to help where needed, and take the ball back up again in counter-attacks. And Gopal will be stationed near the Jatri penalty box. In short, our formation will be 1-4-1-3-1.'

'But Kamal-da, I'm going to take a couple of them out,' Shambhu said in his bull-headed fashion.

Kamal looked at him sternly. 'You'll have to leave the field with the first one you take out. That can only harm Shobhabajar. Yours is the role with the biggest responsibility, Shambhu. Do you want to run away from that responsibility?'

'Says who?' Shambhu leapt up, his eyes spitting fire. Punching the wall, he said, 'Me run away? Me? My father ran away at the time of Partition. I was born on a platform in Sealdah Station, Kamal-da. My mother died of starvation, my elder brother died from a bullet during the food riots. I've had to steal, I've had to pilfer, I've had to rob. I'm going to tear them apart.'

Looking at everyone in turn, Kamal whispered, 'Shobhabajar will fight today.'

All of them stared at him in silence.

17

Then Shobhabajar began fighting.

Anupam started running at kick-off, while Prasoon sent a long ball towards the right-hand touchline. As Anupam was about to collect the ball, Swapan charged up to him like a bulldozer and felled him. Foul. Catcalls and abuse arose in the stands. Jatri's right-back launched the ball towards the penalty box from the free kick, but just as Pranbandhu jumped to head the ball, Bharat ran up from nearly fifteen yards away to pluck the ball out of thin air with a broad smile.

'Bharat! Don't do that! Back to goal!' Kamal bellowed.

Kicking the ball more than halfway up the field, Bharat said, 'Not letting anyone get their head to the ball today, Kamal-da.'

After the initial assault, Jatri surrounded the Shobhabajar penalty area with six players, with even the two wing-backs joining them. Everyone except Shobhabajar's Gopal had fallen back to the goalmouth. Kamal smelt trouble. With eighteen people jostling inside a tiny space, someone was bound to poke the ball into the goal, the goalkeeper being unsighted, as was typical in such situations. Besides, not being able to exercise clever judgement when tackling – they didn't possess the skills, after all – the Shobhabajar defenders were becoming shaky as well.

We shouldn't have become so defensive, Kamal thought swiftly. You cannot keep a skilled attack at bay with nothing but obstinate courage and stamina. You need to counter-attack – go into their half with the ball. Gopal was upfield but giving him the ball wouldn't help. He didn't have the ability to get past two stoppers single-handedly. The ball would simply come back to where it was now.

Kamal took control of the ball that had floated loose after Pranbandhu's miskick. Jatri's Abraham stood before him. One feint from the waist upwards and Abraham was history. Kamal emerged from the penalty area.

'Move up, Salil.'

Prasoon was behind Kamal, Salil chasing him. At Kamal's call, he ran upfield. As Jatri midfielder Amiyo confronted him, Kamal pushed the ball towards Salil. Four Shobhabajar players were moving up rapidly. The ball went from right to left, then back again to the right. Eventually, Anwar wrested the ball from Rudra near Jatri's corner flag.

Kamal moved up. They had managed to keep Jatri from attacking for nearly ten minutes. They would have to confine the game to the midfield and slow down the other team. Kamal began holding on to the ball, trying to slow down the pace. Rudra, Satya and Debidas took up positions in the middle of the field, Shambhu just behind them. Dispatching the ball to Shambhu, Kamal prowled the edge of the penalty box, behind the four defenders, scrutinizing the movements of the Jatri players.

The four Shobhabajar defenders were welded to the four Jatri forwards. On each of the four occasions on which the ball had been sent to Anupam, Swapan had snatched it away before Anupam could control it. When the ball came near Jatri's left corner flag, Anupam was standing, hands on hips, near the Shobhabajar right-half, close to the right-hand touchline. Swapan, who was five yards away, followed him as soon as he started walking towards the centre line. Anupam suddenly turned and retraced his steps – so did Swapan. Even the Jatri supporters in the stands started laughing when they saw what was going on. As Anupam ran towards Nemai's regular position on the left, so did Swapan. Every time he got hold of the ball, Swapan either put it out of play or kicked it away to wherever he could. Twice Anupam managed to dodge past Swapan, only to find Kamal in the way. Before he could work his way out of the situation, Swapan returned to steal the ball away.

Shambhu was slicing up the field like a madman, going after every ball sent to the Jatri forwards, charging like a bulldog towards any spot where he sensed a new attack commencing. It wasn't as though he was successful every time, but he did prevent Jatri from moving around freely. Even when they managed to make some progress through a series of wall-passes, Pranbandhu or Salil headed them off.

Prasoon then dropped back and Pranbandhu was about to move up to shadow him, but Kamal discouraged him. 'Let Prasoon do whatever he likes in the midfield, you don't need to give up your position. Stick to him again if he moves up.'

Then Jatri's wing-backs began their runs down the sides. Kamal sensed trouble. Nemai, Abraham and Anupam were running off in different directions, their shadows Balai, Pranbandhu and Swapan following them. Prasoon moved up with the ball, the two wing-backs on either side of him. Kamal kept watching, watching – which way would Prasoon pass?

Kamal took his position behind the four defenders, in the middle. Prasoon dribbled past Debidas, then evaded Shambhu's sliding tackle. Salil was moving up. Prasoon's left shoulder swivelled a little towards the goal, which meant he was going to pass to the right. Kamal turned his attention to Jatri's right wing-back as Prasoon – showing incredible flexibility – twisted his body and sent the ball to the left, where the left wing-back had moved up.

Nearly twenty-five thousand people started chanting for a goal. That deafening noise seemed to contain an incendiary message which triggered an instant explosion in Kamal's nerve centre. Twisting his torso back from left to right with the suppleness of a cheetah, he raced off to confront the player with the ball. With the goal just twelve yards away, the Jatri left-back was certain to score, but the unexpected sight of Kamal prevented him from taking the shot. In the twinkling of an eye, Kamal swiped the ball from under the left-back's feet and dispatched it to Rudra, turning the excited cries in the stands into groans of despair.

Thirty minutes gone and there had been no goal yet. Shobhabajar hadn't come anywhere near Jatri's goal all this while.

But a few seconds before the interval, Gopal suddenly picked up a stray deflection off Shambhu's feet and, unbelievably, headed towards the Jatri goal, leaving Anwar and Amiyo behind. Shyam, the goalkeeper, was charging towards him. Gopal's shot, which he virtually took with his eyes shut, eluded Shyam's outstretched hands to hit the bar and bounce back into play.

The stadium was silent in disbelief. The unimaginable – Shobhabajar scoring – had almost happened.

The spell lifted with the referee blowing the whistle for half-time. Leaving the field one by one, the Shobhabajar boys sprawled on the ground. Krishna Maiti busied himself with glasses of water and towels. None of the players spoke – they were exhausted, gasping for breath, their backs bent with fatigue.

As though he were delivering a speech, Krishna Maiti said, waving his arms, 'Time for long-passes now, stop the short-passes. Why're you staying so deep down, Satya, move up. Salil, you need to play more robustly, land a couple of kicks, Abraham is a coward.'

'Don't give them instructions now, please.' Kamal raised his arm to silence Krishna Maiti.

'It was my fault, Kamal-da,' said Salil. 'If I'd known Prasoon was going to pass the ball quite so quickly, I'd have tackled him earlier. They'd have scored if not for you.'

Pretending not to have heard, Kamal looked at the far end of the stands, trying to identify a face in the crowds. Failing to do so, he asked, 'Is Amitava here?'

'Yes, there he is. See that woman over there? He's sitting next to her. I spotted him when I went to fetch the ball.'

Kamal looked again.

Jatri's members were glowering, many of them distinctly agitated. 'What on earth is Anupam doing?' 'If they're crowding their defence, why can't you draw them out and create space?' 'Why did Prasoon have to pass instead of scoring himself?' 'Every time Shambhu tackles someone it's a foul – is the referee blind? He didn't have a problem ruling Abraham offside, did he?' 'One attack and they almost scored. All these Anwars are no good any more.'

Kamal stood up for a better view. He heard Pintu's baby voice. 'Kamal-mama, here we are.'

18

The referee blew his whistle.

'Don't forget, Shobhabajar will fight today,' Kamal reminded everyone as they took to the pitch again. Again, there was no response from anyone.

Kamal had expected Jatri to mount a furious assault, but instead they chose to play with caution, keeping the ball in the midfield. After five minutes or so, Anupam dribbled past Swapan near the corner flag and ran into Kamal as he was trying to enter the penalty box. He had no choice but to cross the ball, which Bharat easily gathered from over Abraham's head.

'What's the matter, Swapan? How did Anupam beat you to the ball?' But even as Kamal was asking him this, Anupam was moving up with the ball again.

Swapan was left behind a second time and didn't try to return for another challenge. Kamal realized that he wasn't up to it any more, and noticed that Balai and Pranbandhu had slowed down too. Salil wasn't showing any signs of fatigue, however, and Shambhu was still the emperor of the midfield, chasing every ball. Debidas and Satya had managed to advance up to the Jatri half-line a few times, playing passes between themselves.

Shambhu had just committed a foul, having kicked the Jatri right-back on his chest. The Jatri player had retaliated by grabbing Shambhu's collar with the intention of hitting him. Brickbats were being hurled at Shambhu from the stands. Rushing for the ball at the same time, Abraham, Amiyo and Shambhu all fell in a heap. But while the other two picked themselves up easily, Shambhu had to be helped off the pitch. When he returned a few minutes later, it was with a limp.

The midfield was now Jatri's realm. Shambhu groaned in agony every time he tried to run.

'I can't, Kamal-da. They've finished me. Let me take one of them out with me.'

'No. Get Ratan to replace you.'

'Let me take Prasoon out…he's playing well.'

'Let him. He has to.' A pulse started beating in Kamal's temples. 'He can't get past Kamal Guha unless he plays well.'

Shambhu was substituted by Ratan, who'd joined them from a third division club only that year. The fans started celebrating with crackers as eight Jatri players stormed in to attack, with a fatigued Shobhabajar counting the moments to conceding a goal. Then…

Like an ancient banyan tree Kamal Guha extended his branches to envelop the Shobhabajar penalty area. Sometimes he was a wild bull, sometimes a ferocious jungle cat, sometimes a venomous snake. With aggressive as well as cunning moves, he converted the penalty box into a zone of terror. One attack after another came cascading down upon them, yet Kamal repulsed them all, primarily with the help of Salil. The relentless roars in the stands had now been reduced to frustrated whimpers.

Now, Jatri, I will wreak vengeance. Kamal kept talking to himself. I've never bowed my head before you, and I'm not about to today either. All of Gulo-da's and Rathin's barbs and jibes will be thrown back at them. Prasoon's coming with the ball, let him, let him, Salil's in position, I'm behind him. Ah, the left-winger has passed the ball to Nemai, Balai's chasing him, I'm behind him.

Nemai came to a halt before Kamal. He swayed to the left, feinted to the right. Kamal was motionless, his eyes fixed on the ball. As soon as Nemai looked away momentarily, searching for someone to pass the ball to, Kamal's right foot struck like a snake to steal the ball from him.

Kamal advanced with the ball. Come on now, all of you – Gulo-da, Saroj, Rathin, Ranen Das, all of you Anupam acolytes – Kamal Guha has the ball at his feet, let's see you plunder it from him.

Kamal stopped after dodging past the right-half. Rathin stood by the sideline, his comely face distorted by despair. Kamal smiled at him. Still tormenting you, my friend. I spent years in torment too. Jatri deprived me to get you the India jersey, cheated me of the money due to me, humiliated me by benching me like any run-of-the-mill player… As soon as Kamal cut inside, two Jatri players challenged him. Accelerating suddenly, he slipped between them, the ball still glued to his feet. Did you know, Rathin – Kamal continued his silent monologue – that Jatri didn't inform me of my wife's death? They needed Kamal Guha to win the trophy, so they kept it from me…

Another Jatri player was before Kamal. He moved to his right, stopping suddenly. The goal was about thirty yards away. Stroking the ball lightly before him, he took a shot. A perfectly calibrated shot. The ball rose from the ground and soared towards the junction of the post and the crossbar. For an instant, thousands of hearts on the stands stopped beating. It was only after Shyam – with superb timing – leapt up and pushed the ball over the crossbar with the tips of his fingers that everyone could breathe again.

Corner. Shobhabajar's first one of the day, versus eight for Jatri – seven of which Bharat had plucked out of thin air. As Debidas was arranging the ball, Satya ran up to push him out of the way. Six Jatri defenders were marking the five Shobhabajar players who had come up into the opponent's goal area.

Satya took the corner kick. The ball arced smoothly through the air like a rainbow towards the goalmouth. Yet just as Gopal leapt for the ball, Shyam came in and punched it away. It fell about fifteen yards away, close to Debidas. Two Jatri players headed for him.

'Debi!'

Hearing a voice to his left, Debidas pushed the ball in that direction and swiftly moved out of the way. A figure flashed into view behind him, its left foot rising and smiting the ball which kissed the Jatri goalpost and then, to everyone's astonishment, landed inside the net. It all happened so unexpectedly that every player on the field could only stare at the assassin in total disbelief, unable to tear their eyes away.

Not a word could be heard among Jatri's members, barring a single, reedy voice that piped up. 'And who's going to eat all that mutton?'

'They scored against Jatri!' exclaimed Bipul Ghosh in complete consternation. 'Who's the scorer?' he asked, turning to Amitava.

Amitava forced the words through the lump in his throat: 'Kamal Guha,' and added bashfully, 'my father.'

Jatri invaded the Shobhabajar goal. With four minutes to go, they earned three corners and two free kicks. Balai's lips were split wide open by a sneaky punch from Abraham. But that giant, ancient banyan tree steadfastly shielded the goal behind him from every onslaught.

As soon as the final whistle was blown, Shambhu raced into the field, screaming at the top of his voice. 'I'm cured, I'm cured, Kamal-da. It doesn't hurt any more.'

Satya was the first one to wrap his arms around Kamal's legs and raise him aloft. Four shoulders materialized from nowhere to create a chair for him. The East Bengal members' enclosure was bubbling with exhilaration.

They brought Kamal out on their shoulders. Krishna Maiti was hoarse with shouting. 'Tell me, Kamal, whether or not I can tell great players from mediocre ones. I took a huge risk to play you, ignoring all the protests. Was I right or not?'

A black shroud seemed to have draped itself over Kamal's mind. He could register neither what was happening nor what people were saying. He could not feel any emotion whatsoever. Eyes glazing over with exhaustion, all he could sense were some meaningless sounds and a bunch of people bustling around him. Like a laden crane, Kamal lowered himself to the ground, burying his face in his hands as he lay down on the grass. After a long while, tears started streaming from his eyes, falling in fat drops on the grass. His heart twisting in pain, he realized that he would never again see the occupied stands from the pitch. Kamal Guha had played the last game of his life.

Getting back on his feet, Kamal walked to the centre circle, his eyes still on the ground. Looking up at the sky, he muttered, 'May I never lose my balance. May football always play with me, all my life.'

Stooping, Kamal scooped up a handful of earth, smeared it on his forehead and – as if uttering an incantation – said, 'You have given me as much as you have taken. Today I take my leave of you forever.

I have never knowingly shown you disrespect. Many new footballers will bring you glory. Please do not forget me.'

'Let's go, Kamal-da,' Bharat called from the sideline. They were waiting for him.

As he was leaving, Kamal heard an animated Krishna Maiti telling that journalist, 'I was the one who discovered Kamal, so to speak. It was me he picked up the ABCs of football from.'

Kamal smiled. Then he spotted Amitava, his heart jumping in anxiety and expectation. Advancing, he practically whispered, 'This was my last game. Did you like it?'

His voice trembling with emotion, Amitava said, 'I was proud of you, Baba.'

'Really!' An ecstatic surprise exploded on Kamal's face like fireworks. He felt as though the stands had filled up again.

'Really and truly!'

'If only you'd seen me play ten years ago.' Kamal started laughing.

Abinash's Forty-eight-and-a-half

'Is the sports editor in?' It was the receptionist ringing from downstairs.

'Speaking,' announced Chittaranjan Ghoshal from his desk on the second floor. He was under pressure right now. The advertising department had suddenly announced there was a column and a half of additional space to fill. Debabrata's dispatch from Delhi on the interstate athletics meet had not arrived yet. It was Rabi's off day. Sushanta was on two days' casual leave. He was supposed to have joined today, but there was no sign of him.

'Someone named Abinash Majumdar wants to meet you.'

'Send him upstairs,' said Chittaranjan after a few moments' thought.

Putting the phone down, he asked Dibyendu, who was sitting at the desk in front of him, 'Do you have a story? We have to fill four and a half columns in total. Can you check at the photo library for a picture or something? I'll check these old wires to see if there's something we can use.'

Unused news agency copy that had arrived on the teleprinter over the past two or three days was stored in a box file in case it could be used later. Chittaranjan took a bunch out of the box and began to read.

He was so immersed in his work that he did not notice that a man had materialized five or six feet away from his desk. Chittaranjan frowned when he finally caught sight of the stranger.

'Whom are you looking for?'

'I was hoping to meet you.'

Chittaranjan scanned him carefully. More than six feet tall, frail, three days of stubble, sunken eyes, broad shoulders across which a dirty half-sleeved light blue shirt was slung as if on a hanger, and brown trousers. The man joined his palms together in greeting. Chittaranjan nodded in response.

'There was a news item in your paper the day before yesterday, an interview with Harshit Chatterjee, in which he said he had jumped forty-eight-and-a-half feet in the triple jump trials in Bombay for the London Olympics to enter the team. He's wrong, it's a complete lie.' The man spoke calmly, with a trace of hesitation, but quite courteously.

Chittaranjan leaned back in his chair. One more controversy. He was strongly opposed to publishing interviews with ageing sportsmen. Besides seemingly suffering from loss of memory, they were naturally prone to exaggerating their own feats. Chittaranjan realized it was natural for them to want today's youngsters to know of them and their achievements. But they made the kind of claims that could not be verified through records. No one had maintained statistics or written a history. The newspapers had to trust whatever any of them claimed and publish it, and when there were protests, which was often the case, precious space on the sports page had to be wasted in publishing those too.

Without bothering to hide his irritation, Chittaranjan said, 'What can I do? He must have jumped forty-eight-and-a-half feet if he said so. How else would he have been selected? Were you there?'

'I was.'

Chittaranjan straightened in his chair. 'In what capacity?'

'As a competitor. It was Bombay's Henry Rebello who had jumped forty-eight-and-a-half feet. Tajima of Japan held the world record at the time, fifty-two-and-a-half feet, which he jumped at the Berlin Olympics.'

'So you're saying Harshit Chatterjee did not jump forty-eight-and-a-half feet?'

'No, both Harshit and I jumped forty-four-and-a-half. That's why I remember the distance. We were nowhere near Rebello.'

'I see.' Chittaranjan knew that a disagreement in human form was standing before him. A four-page letter would now emerge from his pocket, after which there would be daily reminders for it to be published.

Dibyendu came up to him with a photograph. 'Take a look at this one, Chitta-da – Edwin Moses. He notched up his 119th successive win the other day.'

'How old is the photo?'

'It's old, we ran it four years ago. But we can slip it in – no one will know the date.'

'Go ahead,' said Chittaranjan, returning the photograph to Dibyendu, and turned back to Abinash Majumdar. 'So what do we have to do? Are you going to dispute this?'

'No, I'm not. It's not particularly important. It won't serve anyone any purpose to know how far I had jumped, and even if they do get to know, it won't raise my reputation even an inch.'

'Why not? At least your children and grandchildren will be proud of the fact…'

A smile spread across Abinash Majumdar's face. Waving his right hand dismissively, he said, 'I haven't married, I don't have a family.'

'I see.' Chittaranjan was annoyed with himself for feeling flustered. 'So you're not looking for acknowledgement or anything. What is it you want then?'

'Acknowledgement for Rebello. Let the man who actually jumped forty-eight-and-a-half feet get his due. That's all I want.'

What was he saying! Chittaranjan gazed at him for a few moments. 'Is there any evidence that Rebello jumped that distance?'

'Has Harshit Chatterjee provided any evidence that he did?'

Chittaranjan was caught on the wrong foot again. Sushanta had taken the interview but he was not in the office today. Yet, he couldn't have written the piece without proof. Chittaranjan said gravely, 'The piece was written after checking the paper clippings.'

Abinash frowned, as though he couldn't believe this. 'Which paper?'

'The *Times of India.*' Lying unhesitatingly, Chittaranjan picked up the agency reports lying on his desk and resumed reading them.

But what Abinash said now was the equivalent of a thunderbolt. 'I have the *Times of India* clipping.'

'What, really?'

'Yes, though not at this moment. I can show it to you later.'

Chittaranjan breathed a sigh of relief. He'd have lost face if Abinash had pulled it out of his pocket right now.

'Bring it then,' Chittaranjan said grimly, practically throwing down a challenge.

The bearer brought some fresh copies for him. As he began reading them, Abinash hesitated and then said, 'All right then, goodbye.'

Watching over the top of his glasses as Abinash made his way out, Chittaranjan said, 'Let's assume it was Rebello who jumped that distance. Will the world come to an end if it isn't announced? What's your problem, for that matter? Who cares who it was who had jumped forty-eight-and-a-half feet thirty-eight years ago. It wasn't a world record, was it?'

'But it was a world-class performance. Rebello could have won the gold at the Olympics, he got into the final. Do you call that insignificant?'

'I'm not talking of the Olympics. Why are you speaking up on his behalf?'

'Why shouldn't I? How can the credit that belongs to one man be usurped by another?' It wasn't so much a question as injured surprise that appeared on Abinash's face. 'Imagine the desire with which an athlete starts his journey, practises, endures hardships day after day to stay disciplined. Imagine the pleasures he forsakes to progress inch by inch. And his progress signifies progress for the country, for the nation. He deserves honour and respect for this. Instead of which someone steals it from him, and you support it?' Abinash sounded agitated for the first time, raising his voice. 'Rebello will definitely not be reading your newspaper, he doesn't know Bangla, and besides, I don't know where he is now or whether he's even alive. But I'm here, and I know. It's the duty of one athlete to preserve the honour of another.'

Abinash's eyes were brimming.

Looking up Harshit Chatterjee in the telephone directory, Chittaranjan requested the operator to connect him. Harshit used to be an engineer employed by a well-known company and had started a consultancy after retirement.

'Is that Harshit-babu? This is Chittaranjan Ghoshal… Yes, hello, yes, it's well written. Yes, I'll tell him… Naturally you're getting a lot of phone calls. See how people respect talent, you achieved something all those years ago and even today… But what I wanted to say was, there's some doubt over one piece of information. You said you'd jumped forty-eight-and-a-half feet at the Bombay trials. No one in Asia besides the Japanese had jumped that distance at that time. But now we see that it was Rebello, Henry Rebello. Yes, can you speak a little louder…'

Chittaranjan listened with rapt attention. Shutting his eyes and biting his lips, he rolled out another lie as though bluffing at a card game. 'Look, someone's shown me a clipping from the *Times of India* – yes, the original. It says it was Rebello who had jumped forty-eight-and-a-half, and you and someone else named Abinash Majumdar had jumped forty-four-and-a-half.'

A slow smile appeared on Chittaranjan's face. The kind of smile that can be seen on a lawyer after he has broken the accused on the witness stand.

'You're a busy man, you could easily make a mistake…of course, even to remember something that took place all those years ago… I had heard of Rebello when I was in school. The clipping?' Throwing a sidelong glance at Dibyendu, Chittaranjan continued, 'Our Dibyendu got hold of it, Abinash gave it to him. Have you any idea who this Abinash is?'

Dibyendu was listening. He grinned, being familiar with these tactics of Chittaranjan's.

'I see. Used his sources to get to the trials. Even the running shoes were yours. The clipping says both of you jumped the same distance…mm-hmm, you had an ankle injury. Ah, I see, the forty-eight was in practice… No, there's no need to run a correction right now, no one has challenged it. If they do though… Yes, I understand you have a lot to say about this… No, dinner is impossible, as you know we work nights, we can never make it to dinner. Yes of course, some other time.'

Disconnecting the call, Chittaranjan said to himself, 'He's frightened…damned liar.'

A week passed without Abinash Majumdar showing up. Chittaranjan had forgotten the incident. One morning two young men turned up at his house with an invitation to be the chief guest at the neighbourhood rubber-ball cricket tournament final.

'You've come all the way to Shobhabajar from Ultadanga in search of a chief guest? Couldn't you find someone closer home? So many well-known players live in that area.'

Chittaranjan tried to dissuade them. But they were adamant. They wanted him and no one else. Of course, he knew only too well that it was only because he worked for a newspaper; perhaps it would lead to a few lines in the sports pages – they wouldn't have sought him out otherwise.

He went to the final. The game was played under floodlights on the road. After the prize distribution and his speech, he was escorted to a house and given a plateful of food. A few elderly gentlemen discussed sports with him. The conversation veered round to the fact that sportspersons these days made a lot of money but they couldn't match the sincerity of their predecessors in the good old days, who earned nothing, or next to nothing.

As the discussion continued, one of the people said, 'Take Abinash – such a well-known athlete once and look at him now. He has to run a repair shop for lanterns and stoves to survive.'

'Which Abinash, is it the triple jumper? Where does he live?' Chittaranjan was curious.

'Two lanes away, Jairam Datta Lane.'

He filed the name away in his memory and, next Sunday, on his way to the last rites of a close relative in Forepukur, he made a detour through Jairam Datta Lane. He didn't have the address and asked four or five teenagers hanging about on the pavement, 'A man named Abinash Majumdar, used to be an athlete thirty or forty years ago – do you know where he lives?'

It was evident from their expressions that they were hearing the name for the first time. He offered a description, 'Very thin, tall, greying hair.'

They shook their heads. They didn't know anyone like that.

'Runs a small shop for repairing lanterns and stoves.'

'There's someone who has a shop like that, I remember getting a lantern fixed there once. Go down the road to that building over there.'

The building in question was occupied by at least a dozen families, but Chittaranjan had no difficulty in locating Abinash's room. It was right opposite the wooden flight of stairs leading to the first floor.

Abinash was lying bare-chested on his bed – that is to say, a cot with a rush mat – dressed in only a lungi and reading an old almanac. When Chittaranjan cleared his throat near the door, he lowered the almanac and then shot up on the bed.

'Please come in. How did you get my address?'

'I was passing this way. No, I won't stay long, just thought I'd find out…what happened to that newspaper clipping? You accused Harshit Chatterjee of being a cheat, but where's the evidence?'

Abinash shrank back. A helpless embarrassment spread across his face.

'I did accuse him, and I searched for the clipping the moment I returned home but I have no idea where…'

Chittaranjan also swept his eyes around the room, just as Abinash did. There was no furniture under which the newspaper clipping could have disappeared. Two shirts hung on the wall, a kerosene stove stood in a corner, along with a pot, a pan, a plate and a glass on a low stool. A few tins and bottles in a niche in the wall. There might be a suitcase beneath the cot.

'I had stuck it in a notebook, and it's the entire notebook that's gone missing.' Abinash groaned, bringing his fists up to his chest. 'But I did have it. Believe me, I did.'

'That won't do. If you can't show it to me you'll be proved to be not just a liar but also a jealous man. Would I be wrong if I said you were bluffing so as to belittle Harshit Chatterjee's achievement?'

'No, no, I wasn't bluffing.'

Savouring the agonized expression on Abinash's face, Chittaranjan said, 'You spoke with such conviction. You said it's the duty of an athlete to preserve the honour of a compatriot – is it also the duty of an athlete to smear the reputation of a compatriot?'

'I have nothing to say. I have lost face, I cannot answer.'

'Get me the evidence from wherever you can – written evidence. I'll wait a week. If you can bring it to me in that time I'll run a report.'

Chittaranjan turned around and walked downstairs, throwing a backward glance as he stepped on the road. Abinash had taken a few steps down the staircase and was gaping at him. There was a bewildered look in his eyes – the kind of look that appeared on the faces of children who had been slapped without reason.

Chittaranjan rued what he had done. He shouldn't have accused Abinash this way. He had only meant to have some fun. He believed in his heart and soul that Abinash had not lied, that it was Harshit who had bluffed. But he had not yet lost his childish habit of teasing people. Chittaranjan shook his head and told himself, I have to stop this.

He'd have forgotten the whole thing had he not received a letter from Bombay twenty days later. Written in an untidy, ragged hand, it said, 'Respected sir, I apologize for being unable to provide evidence within a week, as instructed. I have visited the offices of the *Times of India* here on two occasions. They were extremely reluctant to retrieve a copy of the newspaper from thirty-eight years ago. But the librarian relented when I explained my reason. He has also agreed to make arrangements for the page to be photographed. I shall visit him again tomorrow. I pray to you not to write in the meantime that I lied to you to besmirch someone's reputation. I am hopeful that you will honour my request. My respectful greetings to you. I am, yours sincerely, Abinash Majumdar.'

At first Chittaranjan laughed loudly, and then, telling everyone in the sports department about it, read the letter out loudly to them. 'He's mad. Do you see how seriously he took the whole thing?'

An envelope arrived from Bombay a week later, containing a photostat copy of the entire report of the selection trials. Once again Chittaranjan showed it to everyone, saying, 'He's lost his head completely. Who makes such a mountain out of a molehill?' He put the photocopy away in his drawer. 'What use is this? I'm not doing a story.'

Chittaranjan was preparing to build a house in Salt Lake. The architect lived in Ultadanga. On his way back from the architect's house one Sunday evening, he decided to pay Abinash a visit. Suddenly he felt nervous as he climbed up the wooden staircase to the first floor. A woman was grinding spices in the room, while a boy of ten was busy patching his kite with rice glue. Chittaranjan discovered they had moved in as tenants here a fortnight ago.

Going back downstairs, he met a middle-aged man whom he asked about Abinash.

'Abinash gave up the room. He went to Bombay on some work. Since he had no money of his own, he pawned his shop. When he came back he couldn't pay the money back, so he sold the shop. No, I don't know where he's gone. Heaven knows why he had to go to Bombay at this age.'

The middle-aged man kept talking, but Chittaranjan didn't hear another word of what he said.

The Stories: A Publishing History

'Striker' was originally published in Bengali as 'Striker' in 1973 by Ananda Publishers, Kolkata

'Stopper' was originally published in Bengali as 'Stopper' in 1974 by Ananda Publishers, Kolkata

'The Pearl' was originally published in Bengali as 'Mukto' in *Kapil Nachchhe: Golpo, 1978–1987*

'Rehabilitation' was originally published in Bengali as 'Protyaborton' in *Nirbachito Golpo, 1959–1970*

'A Far-reaching Radiance' was originally published in Bengali as 'Bohudur Byapto Ujjolota' in *Behula'r Bhela: Golpo, 1957–1975*

'Reddy' was originally published in Bengali as 'Reddy' in *Sholoke Ponero Kora: Golpo, 1985–1993*

'The Blazer' was originally published in Bengali as 'Blazer' from *Kapil Nachchhe: Golpo, 1978–1987*

'Abinash's Forty-eight-and-a-half' was originally published in Bengali as 'Abinash-er Sharey Aath-Chollish' in *Sholoke Ponero Kora: Golpo, 1985–1993*